SIN AND BONES

PAIGE N. REGAN

Copyright © 2024 by Paige N. Regan. All rights reserved.

No portion of this book may be reproduced in any form without written permission from the publisher or author, except as permitted by U.S. copyright law.

Book Illustration by Jessica Sherburn (Ouijacine).
Dinkus Illustration by Jonas Spokas of Stardust Book Services.

Content Warnings

- Mentions of sexual assault/rape (not seen on page, past event lightly described)

- Physical, verbal, and emotional abuse

- Mention of suicide attempt/s (not seen on page)

- Suicidal ideation

- Self-harm (not seen on page)

- On-page violence and death

- Religious Abuse/Trauma

- Family member with Dementia

To the girls that crave justice in a world not built for them.

One

"Forgive me, Father, for I have sinned."

Hands clasped and sweaty, Eve confessed her sins in the cramped confessional booth, her face obscured by the thin lattice screen separating her from the priest. She murmured them once. Twice. It was never enough.

Eve Carter was going to hell, and it wasn't even her goddamned fault.

The priest's promise of forgiveness washed over her the same as water against a boulder. She felt nothing, the words moving past her as if they were meant for someone else.

A quick thank you. Some homework of Hail Mary's. Then it was over.

She left the tight box, avoiding her father's impatient gaze as she scurried to the bathroom. Benjamin had insisted on dropping his daughter off at her grandmother's personally, staying long enough to get one more good confession out of her before driving back home.

Eve peered at herself in the tiny bathroom mirror: dull, tired, ugly. The dark circles under her eyes were more prominent, her skin ashen.

Her hair had grown back a surprising amount in the past two years, at least. Eve stared at the blond locks, wishing them blue once more. She would even take the greenish color it had turned once she had rinsed all the dye out. Ben had given her three lashes for that one. It was a pretty tame punishment compared to his usual abuse, but he had also made her shave her head. The shame of that had been worse than the belt. For as many things as she missed about her home across the state, Eve did not miss her father's discipline.

Moving to rural Vermont had not been her choice. Or, in a roundabout way, maybe it had. Eve glanced down at the twin scars that stretched the length of her wrists, their pink permanence barely visible under her uniform. She tugged the blazer's sleeves down.

Eve ran her fingers through her short hair, making it presentable before grabbing her bag and walking out of the church.

Nan sat on a small wooden bench outside, lost in a conversation with Mr. Stone, their next-door neighbor. She was a spindly thing with jutting elbows and shaky knees. Her stark blue veins were hidden behind a cream sweater and skirt that were too big for her tiny frame. Eve thought she appeared lost in the bundle of clothes. A child playing dress up.

Mr. Stone, a man in his 50s with a gray beard and a penchant for wooly sweaters, fell silent as Eve emerged from the church. His smile was stretched thin. Mr. Stone was Nan's original caretaker before she'd arrived and—thankfully—still offered to take on the role during her hours at school.

Eve had only met her nan a few times before the move, although Ben talked of his mother often. She still lived in his childhood home: a two-story brick house with aging wallpaper and a kitchen that hadn't seen an update since the '70s. Eve didn't hate it, but she didn't find comfort sleeping in her father's old bedroom, either.

Ben had said the move was to help Nan—the woman was in her mid-eighties and looked it—but Eve knew the real reason. Her mother whispered about it under her breath. The old neighbors gossiped about it behind her back.

Eve was a disgrace, and the "incident" almost four months ago had been unsettling enough that no one knew what to do with her anymore.

That was fair. She didn't know what to do with herself, either.

"Where's dad?" Eve interrupted. Nan stared at her, eyes wide and blank with confusion.

"You know, I don't know." Nan peeked around, but Eve could tell her grandmother had no idea who she was looking for. Eve glanced around the street parking. Ben's truck was gone.

No goodbye, then. He truly couldn't wait to be rid of her.

"I'll be home around three." Eve reached into her bag and tossed a red scarf around her neck. The early September chill nipped at her legs, breaking through the thin nylon of her tights. It felt too early for this kind of weather.

"Where are you off to in such a hurry?"

"School."

Nan turned to Mr. Stone for confirmation before nodding. "Get there safely, Sammy."

Sammy—Aunt Samantha. Nan's daughter.

Eve frowned but caught herself, giving her grandmother a polite smile before she rushed off to school. That was another reason Eve was sent here; Nan was sick, and all her children were either too busy or too far away to take care of her.

They'd given up on their mother, just as they'd given up on Eve.

St. Peter's Roman Catholic High School was an eclectic architect's dream. The old church still stood in resistance to change, with cracking stone walls and black spires that reached up into the overcast sky like spears aimed toward heaven. Attached was a cold cement hallway that ran underground—an old bunker, Eve assumed—to an abandoned office building that had been emptied out and renovated decades ago. The girls' yellow bathrooms were ugly, but at least they weren't that sickly greenish color from her old academy.

She could still see her own blood between the mossy tile cracks.

Eve tried to focus on the chalkboard of her religion class, struggling to read Sister Heidi's cursive scrawl. She kept her eyes averted from the cross hanging directly above.

A cell phone ping went off, and all eyes turned to a boy in the back row near Eve. He slid sheepishly down in his seat.

They did not have nuns anymore, not in the way they used to. Sister Heidi was the oldest on staff and one of the few nuns they had bothered to keep on payroll. Most other teachers were outsourced.

As Sister Heidi walked between the narrow rows of desks to confiscate the phone, Eve could see hints of old discipline in the woman's face. Back in the day, she would have beaten his knuckles raw. Eve could see that she still wanted to.

Instead, Sister Heidi plucked the phone from his hands and took it back to her desk, locking it away in one of the wooden drawers.

She returned her attention to the board.

Thump-thump-thump. Someone tapped their shoe behind her, eager to leave. Uneasiness stirred inside of her as Eve gripped her pencil.

Thump-thump-thump.

She couldn't look at the cross.

Thump-thump-thump.

The smell of tobacco mixed with sickly sweet alcohol stung her nose.

Thump-thump-thump.

She glanced at the cross. The depiction of Jesus stared mournfully back at her, his face dripping with blood.

Thump-thump-thump.

The cross slapped against the bedroom wall. It hung above her as she prayed, as she begged, *thump-thump-thumping—*

The bell rang. Eve grabbed her books in a rush, nausea creeping up her throat. The fluorescent lights were too bright and disorienting. Her heart thundered in her chest. There was no danger, but she could sense it everywhere.

A hand clamped down on her shoulder.

Eve spun around with a sharp gasp. Her books clattered to the floor as she stumbled back.

The boy with the now-confiscated cell phone paused, shock written across his face. He quickly recovered, flashing her a shy smile. "Sorry, didn't mean to scare you. You're Eve, right? I'm Eric."

Eve didn't respond, wishing she could wipe away the touch of his hand on her shoulder. Eric knelt and picked up her fallen books. He was plain, with forgettable mousy brown hair and a square face.

She kept her guard up.

Eric offered her books back with a smile. Eve accepted them with trembling hands.

"Thank you," she murmured, tucking them close to her chest. Only a few more classes until she could go home.

"You just moved here, right? How are you liking St. Peter's so far?" His voice was casual, friendly even, as he followed her into the hallway. It put her even more on edge.

"Yes." Her throat was tight. Eve tried to put as much space between them as possible, but the crowded hallways offered little room. Eric continued to stare at her, and she realized she hadn't answered his question in full. "It's fine."

"Just fine?" Eric laughed, reminding her of another faint laugh in the dark. Her stomach lurched. "Yeah, I can see that. Not much to do, I guess.

But we throw some pretty fun events around here. Homecoming is in a few weeks, actually."

Eric launched into an eager explanation of their school dance traditions, and she could see the coming suggestion bubbling at his lips: *we should go together.*

"Excuse me," Eve cut him off, rushing into the first girls' bathroom she saw. She locked herself in one of the empty stalls, her breath escaping in shallow gasps as she plopped down on the toilet.

The memories came back in scattered pieces—a scent, a sound, an image—and they didn't care where she was or who she was with. Eve would remember, and then she would break apart all over again.

She stayed in the stall throughout her next class. Then her next one. Eve considered staying there for the whole day, huddled in a ball on the toilet. Once the second class let out, girls came rushing in to use the facilities and adjust their makeup. Eve wondered if there was a better place to hide. Maybe she could ditch school entirely.

The bell rang, and the bathroom cleared out once more. Eve rubbed her eyes on the cuffs of her blazer, her face red and blotchy as she stepped out of the stall.

A girl stood against the edge of one of the pink wall-mounted sinks, her silky brown hair pulled up into a high ponytail. Heat flooded Eve's cheeks as their eyes met, and she nodded curtly, prepared to make a run for it.

"Wait!"

The girl paused, one hand outstretched toward her. Eve glanced over her shoulder, her body tense and ready to bolt. The girl hesitated before stepping forward.

Eve flinched, and the girl frowned, halting in place. She stared at Eve with sympathy and something else Eve couldn't quite make out.

Then the girl smiled.

"Want to have lunch with me?"

Two

Hailey Boyle: she was a senior, too, and Eve was quickly informed that they had a few classes together. Eve felt bad that she hadn't noticed her before, but in all fairness, she didn't pay attention to most of her classmates. Hailey *also* informed her that she had seen Eve go into the bathroom two periods ago and decided to wait for her. Eve was mortified. She had worked so hard to stay quiet and unnoticed, but her efforts had been wasted.

"So, lunch?" Hailey pushed with a hopeful grin. The girl hadn't stopped talking since Eve left her stall.

Eve scrubbed at her puffy eyes in the mirror. "I think I'll pass."

Hailey frowned. "How come?"

I don't know you, and I don't want *to know you,* Eve thought. But that wasn't a nice thing to say, especially after Hailey confessed to waiting for her. If they were caught skipping class, Eve wouldn't be the only one in trouble. *Not that I even asked her to stay.*

"I'm not hungry," Eve lied, only for her stomach to promptly betray her with a loud growl. Hailey raised an eyebrow. So much for that excuse. "...Never mind, I guess."

"Great!" Hailey beamed and held open the bathroom door. Eve reluctantly followed her to the cafeteria.

Where Eve lacked in conversation, Hailey made up for it; the girl's mouth never stopped moving, constantly bouncing from one topic to the next without giving much room for response. Eve wondered if she should be taking notes.

With their trays full, Hailey led Eve to a round table near a window overlooking the parking lot. The cafeteria itself was small, with gray tables and metal chairs spaced out between red brick walls. Banners of their school crest hung in dark blue over the doorways, alongside a white depiction of Jesus at the Last Supper embroidered on tapestry. It appeared someone had attempted to liven up the scenery with the addition of autumn window clings, but they reminded Eve of an elementary school classroom.

As they approached the table, Eve's heart rate jumped at the sight of another student already there.

"This is Sage," Hailey said with a subtle nudge against her arm, using her tray to gesture at the girl.

Sage was tall, with sharp cheekbones and eyes so gold that they had to be contacts. Eve wondered how she managed to pull *that* one over on the nuns. Her dark hair was braided back in a half-up hairdo, the ends trailing down to her waist. Their blue school uniform didn't suit her—it couldn't match her cool composure, or the way she held herself with the confidence of a queen.

She was beautiful. She was invincible.

Eve's stomach churned as they approached.

"Actually, maybe I should—" Eve tried to excuse herself, but Sage's head jerked to the side, her gaze locking on Hailey. She waved to them, her attention slipping to her friend's companion. Eve shifted, the tray in her hands seeming tons heavier. She was ready to drop it and run.

One glance at Hailey told her that wasn't an option. Eve's legs moved forward, planting her in front of the table.

She and Sage stared at each other, waiting for the other to speak first. An awkward silence stretched between them.

Eve hadn't eaten lunch with anyone but herself in over two years. Should she be casual? Upbeat and friendly? Or should she be quiet and stoic? She'd been working hard to keep to herself, but now that she was face-to-face with other people, she had no idea what to do.

Hailey plopped down beside Sage, unaware of the tension between them. Eve reluctantly slid down in the empty chair beside her, wincing as she dropped her tray too hard on the table.

"Who's your friend, Hay?" Sage asked, watching Eve pick at her food. She certainly wasn't hungry now.

"Eve! She recently transferred here," Hailey said between mouthfuls of mac 'n' cheese.

"Oh, yeah. I thought I saw you around," Sage mused, although Eve was certain she hadn't seen Sage until now. Sage relaxed in her chair, tossing her hair over her shoulder before biting into a pear. Even the way she ate was graceful.

I wish I could be like that, Eve thought. She was all nerves instead, her heart ricocheting inside of her chest with the momentum of a jackhammer.

"Yeah." Eve took a sip of her water—something to keep her mouth preoccupied.

"Where'd you transfer from? St. Ive's?" Hailey asked.

"No, I moved from Manchester."

"Oh." Hailey frowned. Clearly, she'd been hoping for somewhere more exotic.

"Vermont isn't terrible." Sage poked Hailey with the handle of her fork. "You just don't enjoy the cold."

Hailey pouted. "No, I do not."

The conversation digressed from there, with the occasional question about Eve and Manchester tossed her way. They never got too personal, and Eve was content to indulge Hailey's interests. Sage spent most of the time watching them converse. Eve wondered if Sage was as uncomfortable sharing lunch with a stranger as she was.

"Did you get a new pet, Sage?"

Eve froze, startled by the new voice behind her. Sage rolled her eyes.

"What do you want, Liam?"

Eve had seen plenty of Roman Catholic boys in her lifetime. At a certain point they all started to look the same: clean-cut hair, the fake smile of straight teeth, and a personality as stimulating as stale white bread.

Liam was something else entirely.

His eyes were a warmer gold than Sage's. His messy hair was the shade of cayenne and sumac, spices that carried through his personality in a disregard for the school uniform—open jacket, untucked shirt. The first few buttons were undone to expose his sharp collarbone. Eve didn't see the mandatory tie anywhere. She could understand Sage getting away with the contacts to *some* extent, but there was no way Liam was allowed to have such blatant negligence with the dress code.

Unless his family was influential with the school. The thought left a tight knot in her stomach.

Liam took an empty seat between Sage and Eve and kicked his feet up on the table. Eve pulled her tray away in disgust.

"Eve, this is Sage's brother," Hailey said with the wave of her hand.

"Brother?" Eve glanced between the two.

Liam swung an arm around Sage's shoulders with a smirk. "You don't see the resemblance?"

"*Half*-brother," Sage clarified, throwing an elbow into his side. Liam snickered but pulled away.

She could see a few similarities between Sage and Liam—their sharp jaw lines, the strange color of their contacts, but what was most striking was how unnatural they felt. They were attractive, sure, but it was the kind of attraction that raised goosebumps on her arm and set off warning alarms in the back of her head.

Something wasn't right, but she couldn't name what.

Or maybe that was her own fear of being attracted to anyone ever again. It was tough to judge.

"It's nice to meet you," Eve said politely, offering him no more than a disinterested glance. Out of the corner of her eye, she caught a glimpse of confusion flit across his face.

"Can't say I share the sentiment," Liam said.

Jerk, she thought. Liam scanned the cafeteria with a bored expression. His eyes flicked from one table to another, never lasting on any one for long. Eve elected to ignore him. She had to get through the next thirty minutes, and then she could return to her days of obscurity.

"You're quiet," Hailey said, and it took Eve a moment to realize she was addressing her. Liam's brows rose, as though he'd forgotten her presence entirely.

"I don't have much to say," Eve confessed. In truth, she hadn't been listening to a word they said.

"We were talking about homecoming," Hailey said with a bright smile. Eve could tell Hailey was trying extra hard to make sure she was included. "Are you going? I was going to skip it this year, but if you're going, we can go together."

"To homecoming?" Eve tested out the words. Her conversation with Eric popped back into her mind. "It's not my thing."

"Why not?" Liam asked. He leaned on his elbow against the table, his body inclined toward her. Eve inched her chair away from him—something that did not go unnoticed based on his frown. "I thought everyone favored dancing."

"I wouldn't know."

"You've never tried?" The glimmer in his eyes sent chills down her spine.

"I'm not interested in finding out."

Liam sighed. "Are you that opposed to having fun?"

"What's that supposed to mean?" Eve asked before she could catch herself. She was not usually confrontational, but something about Liam irked her. He appeared unreasonably frustrated with her, and Eve couldn't fathom why.

"I think it's rather obvious."

"Liam," Hailey whispered in warning. He ignored her.

"You've been here for a week or two now, yes? You show up and ignore everyone, then someone tries to offer you some fun, and you behave as though you're too good for it," Liam continued without restraint. "You won't even look at me when I talk to you."

"Liam, that's enough," Hailey said. Sage watched the three of them, almost entertained by their fight.

"I would if there was something worth looking at," Eve snapped. Anger bubbled inside of her like a hot living entity of its own.

He did not meet her gaze kindly. "You think people don't talk about the way you avoid them? The judgment is written all over your face. You give away a lot more about yourself than you think."

The bell rang. Eve stood up at once and dumped her tray into the nearest trash can without a word.

Eve heard Hailey scold him as she walked away. "Why would you say that?"

She didn't stick around to hear his answer.

Eve was grateful that she didn't share any more classes with Hailey and her friends for the rest of the day. She wasn't sure she could face them again after that awkward encounter at lunch. She especially doubted she could hold her temper around Liam. Even the thought of having to face him again in the halls was enough to set her off.

The hardest part was that there was some truth to what he said. Eve *did* see herself apart from most of her classmates. She had lost her faith years ago; the only reason she attended Catholic school was because she was forced to.

It had been a steady progression, but each year her faith in the religion her community prided themselves in cracked bit by bit. She had questions that could not be answered. She had concerns that were brushed aside or projected back onto her with outrageous claims that Eve was doubting the good Lord's intentions. They were right, of course, but she couldn't exactly say that in her church's community.

Eve was an outcast. She knew not all the kids here were religious—if she searched hard enough, she knew she would find others similar to herself, but Eve was no longer interested in finding them. Hailey had been nice, but if Eve's encounter at lunch had taught her anything, it was that she was better off alone.

Eve resumed her classes as usual—distant, aloof, bored. The nuns preached their bigotry any chance they got, while the teachers toed the line, afraid to cross over on either side. Eve was caught in the middle, another casualty among many.

As she moved on to her last class, Eve caught sight of Hailey and Sage rushing to match her pace—well, Hailey was rushing. Sage didn't share her urgency.

"Eve!" Hailey panted once she reached her, a tired smile on her face. Eve glanced between them, and although Sage's face betrayed nothing, Hailey's said everything. "I wanted to apologize."

"You have nothing to apologize for," Eve said. Sage nodded in agreement. "That's what *I* told her."

"I'm not apologizing for Liam. You caught him in a bad mood," Hailey explained. She and Sage followed Eve down the hall. Eve wished they wouldn't. "He's usually not like that."

"He's pushy," Eve said flatly.

"He's stubborn," Hailey corrected. "I'll talk to him about that. What he said to you—that wasn't okay. I'm really sorry."

"It's fine." Eve wanted the conversation to be over. She had one more class to get through and then she could finally get out of here.

She turned to enter her English class, but Hailey caught her sleeve, eyes wide and pleading. Eve froze at the sudden touch, her earlier nausea piling up again. Hailey quickly let go, her voice laced with guilt. "You're going to eat with us again tomorrow, aren't you?"

Eve wanted to turn her down. She wanted to tell her, *no, not in a million years, never again*. She wanted to end their acquaintanceship and to part ways as strangers.

She had no idea what compelled her to say, "Okay."

Hailey beamed, relief visibly washing over her face. The only surprise Sage showed was the slight rise of her eyebrows.

"Great! I'll see you tomorrow, then."

Hailey rushed down the hall toward her next class, and Sage chuckled, following behind.

As soon as the two girls were out of sight, Eve felt the sinking regret of her choice.

Three

"It's Sharon."

Nan held out the phone to her granddaughter, the curled cord stretched thin from years of use. Eve didn't know why her grandmother kept a landline anymore, much less a corded one.

"Hey, Mom," Eve said. She grabbed the phone's base and dragged it into the dining room as far as the wire could reach. Her homework was spread out across the table's surface, although not much progress had been made. "How are you?"

"Getting by," Sharon said in a sing-song voice. "I was calling to check on Nan and thought I would see if you were around." Translation: *I want to make sure you're not going out and getting into trouble.*

"Here I am." An awkward silence stretched between them. Eve held back a sigh.

Things were always uncomfortable with her mother; Sharon tended to micromanage things, and when she didn't have control over a situation, it made her antsy. Eve was often the source of her mother's anxiety.

"How is school going? Are your grades good?" Sharon pushed.

"They're fine." Eve left it at that. She didn't have the energy to go into the details of her life at St. Peter's. What was she going to say? She had a breakdown in the bathroom? She couldn't focus in class and wondered if each lesson was pointless? It would only freak her mom out more.

"*Just* fine?"

Eve bit her tongue. Her mother had a way of turning innocent questions into a hunt for information. Anything Eve said would be scrutinized and judged and twisted into something else to suit her mother's narrative. Eve could tell her that she'd won a scholarship, and her mother would believe that Eve had danced with the devil himself to get it.

It didn't used to be that way. Before the incident at prom, her mother would sit and talk to her about anything. They didn't need safe topics or small talk—conversation came naturally.

But everything changed, and now her mother was guarded, constantly observing her daughter and shaming her for things that didn't exist.

When Eve didn't answer, Sharon clicked her tongue and continued, "What about friends? Have you made any yet?"

Eve thought of her interaction with Sage and Hailey at lunch. Eating with them had been... Eve couldn't say it was a *nice* change of pace. Sage and Hailey were okay, but Liam had completely ruined the experience. Eve doubted that eating with them at lunch again would solve anything, and they would eventually lose interest in her as everyone else had. That was fine by her.

"No."

There was a brief pause on the line. Eve could picture her mother biting down on her lip, the little crease between her eyebrows pinching together with disapproval. Even if Eve *had* told her she made friends, Sharon would find a way to disapprove. Were they good people to be with? Were they going to distract her and drag her down another path toward sin? But if they weren't there, Eve wasn't getting any social interaction, and she might hurt herself again. It was a lose-lose situation in her mother's eyes.

"You know, your father still has some friends that live around there. I bet they all have families now," Sharon said casually, but Eve could sense the pressure in her voice. "I can ask him if any of them have children around your age."

"I don't know." The idea of her parents setting her up on a playdate was mortifying. She wasn't a kid anymore.

"I'll talk to your father about it. In fact, I'm pretty sure Stan has some daughters your age. You remember Stan, don't you? Fourth of July?" Eve had no idea who her mother was talking about. "You should try to meet them," Sharon pressed. "They're from a nice family. I'm sure you could get along with them."

A nice family. Code for, *we approve of them. They'll push whatever agenda we want you to hear.*

"I'll think about it," Eve said without any intention of doing so. She was tired of being told what to do. She was just...tired.

"Promise me you will."

"Mom—"

"Why do you have to be difficult?" Sharon snapped. There it was. Eve leaned back in her chair, already zoning out as her mother scolded her. "I ask you to do one thing, and you can't even promise me that. How hard is it to go up to someone and say hello?"

"I don't know them. It would be awkward."

"That's what an introduction is for, Evelyn." She could hear her mother huffing on the other line. "Have you even thought about what you're going to do after graduation? It's only a few months away, you know."

"I know," Eve said, her voice monotonic. Graduation was more than a few months away—it was almost an entire year off at this point—but she didn't want to argue. She didn't want to carry on this conversation either. She hadn't planned to make it to her senior year, let alone graduation. What the hell was she supposed to do now?

"You need to think about your future," Sharon said seriously. Eve struggled to ignore the condescending tone. "Your father and I have been talking.

It's time to start looking at colleges, unless you want to join the family business—"

Eve groaned, cutting her mother off. The "family business" wasn't a business at all; it was another multi level marketing scam. Her mother had been bouncing between pyramid schemes for as long as Eve could remember, selling everything from overpriced candles to skincare that made her face itch.

"Didn't dad tell you to stop doing those?" Eve asked. She didn't often agree with her father, but even Ben thought the MLMs were a waste of time and money—both of which their family had little to spare.

"He's coming around to it," Sharon quipped. Another code for, *he doesn't know about it.* Or, *I kicked up such a fuss that he doesn't think it's worth arguing about.* Eve had seen it happen both ways.

"Okay." Eve let the conversation lapse. She was exhausted. She shut the textbook in front of her, completely drained. She would get back to it. Maybe. "I should get going—I need to make dinner."

"That's fine. I'll call you back on your cell," Sharon said. Eve grimaced. Either her mother didn't get the hint, or there was more she wanted to talk about. Eve wasn't interested in dealing with either scenario.

"It's kind of hard to talk on the phone while I'm cooking."

"Oh. Alright then." A pang of guilt stabbed at Eve's chest as she heard her mother's disappointment on the other line. "I'll call you another time, then. Keep me updated on the graduation plans."

"Okay, Mom. Love you, bye." Eve waited for her mother to respond similarly before dropping the phone back into its cradle. She folded over on the table, head on her arms, and sighed.

When she entered the cafeteria the next day, Eve's gaze immediately fell on Hailey's table. Hailey and her friends were already there, fully immersed in the conversation between them. Would they even notice if she didn't show up? Maybe Hailey had already forgotten she invited her to eat with them.

She stared across the cafeteria with her tray in hand, awkward and unsure. Maybe she could run off to an empty classroom and eat there. It would be less pathetic to eat alone if no one could see her.

Liam caught Eve's eye, as if daring her to approach. If she walked off now, would he tell Hailey or pretend he never saw her?

Not wanting to hurt Hailey's feelings—and admittedly annoyed by the challenge in Liam's eyes—Eve walked over.

"Hey," she said, her voice barely loud enough to be picked up over the noisy crowd. Hailey's face lit up with excitement; she must have doubted Eve would keep her word. Liam smirked, which only unnerved her, but Sage smiled, and it was enough to ease some of her anxiety.

"Eve! Come sit," Hailey said.

Eve frowned at the circle of chairs. Hailey sat beside Sage, leaving the last empty chair between herself and Liam. Eve hesitated to take it. Liam raised an eyebrow at her, and Eve sat down, keeping some distance between them.

After a moment's silence, Hailey said, "I love your necklace! It's cute."

"Oh." Eve touched the silver cross dangling from her neck subconsciously. "Thanks."

"Where did you get it?"

"It was a birthday gift." It was the last gift she got from her nan before her memory started to deteriorate: a simple cross with her initials carved into the front. Eve wore it so often that she hardly noticed it anymore.

"It's so pretty." Hailey sighed with a smile. "I got this." She pulled out a small leather booklet attached to a string from her shirt. "It has my favorite verse in it."

"If you two are done, I was in the middle of a story," Liam interjected with a scowl. Sage rolled her eyes.

"No one wants to hear your theories about troll economies, Liam."

Liam glared at her, but Sage had already moved onto a new conversation. "When's your next game?"

"Next Saturday," Hailey said between bites. "I'm totally freaking out. We're up against Sacred Heart Academy—their basketball team is *insane*."

"You'll be fine. Wear your good luck charm."

When Liam realized he wasn't going to get his sister's attention by glowering at her, he turned his attention to Eve. She sat beside Liam in silence, trying to ignore the intensity of his stare as she nibbled at her food. Liam irritably tapped his fingers against the table, but she couldn't decide if it was directed at his sister or her. Eve certainly didn't do anything to earn his ire—she didn't think so, at least.

"You haven't touched your food," she pointed out.

"Not hungry."

"You should eat it anyway. Someone worked hard to make it," Eve said, taking a hurried bite of food. She was one to talk; most days she could barely get herself to eat. The hypocrisy of it gnawed at her.

Liam rolled his eyes. "I'll keep that in mind."

"Why even get it if you're not going to eat?"

"You're awfully concerned about my eating habits," Liam said. A mischievous smile lit up his face. "Perhaps I'd be more inclined to eat if someone were to feed it to me."

Eve grimaced. "I would rather die."

"That's a smidge dramatic, don't you think?" Liam shrugged, making a point of pushing the tray as far away from himself as possible. He reached back and scratched his neck.

She turned away and let out a deep breath. She didn't want to be petty and pick a fight; she knew he was trying to get a rise out of her. This was probably better than any of the nasty remarks he made yesterday, anyway.

Eve chewed her food in silence. One lunch—that was all she had to get through.

She caught Liam smirking out of the corner of her eye.

"What?" she asked, sharper than intended.

"Somebody is sensitive," Liam crooned. He rested his cheek in his palm, propping himself up on his elbow over the table. "You aren't going to run off crying again, are you?"

It was a slap to the face. Had he seen her break down before lunch yesterday? Or was he referring to how irritated she'd been after their argument? Her stomach twisted at the thought of the former.

"Of course not," she said tightly. Her throat felt constrained by an invisible lump.

Liam raised an eyebrow. "Are you sure about that?"

"Do you have a problem with me?" Eve asked abruptly. Liam observed her, as though he was debating that very question himself.

"I haven't decided yet," he said. Eve couldn't tell if he was being honest or making fun of her. "Though it seems you have a problem with *me*."

"Maybe I do." Liam stared at her, waiting for an explanation she didn't want to give. She turned away, refusing to give him the satisfaction. His fingers drummed against the table, betraying his annoyance.

"And why is that?" Liam attempted to regard her with a casual, cocky grin, but she could tell it was forced. So, he didn't like being ignored. That was something Eve was happy to do.

Eve kept her mouth shut and ate her food. Sage and Hailey were still wrapped up in their own conversation, oblivious to the silent war raging on the other side of the table. She couldn't resist sparing a few glances in Liam's direction. She was secretly pleased to find him glowering.

"You won't tell me?" he pushed after a few minutes of silence. It was the most peace Eve had found all week. She was sad to see it go. "Very well, I'll guess. There's the obvious—you're jealous of me."

Eve snorted. The last thing on her mind was *jealousy*. God, the arrogance of this boy made her want to laugh.

Liam kept listing the reasons off on his fingers. "You could also have a stick up your ass a mile high—that would cause some brain damage." He rubbed his chin as a new devious thought came to him. "Or maybe you have a terrible crush on me and you're afraid to say so."

Eve stiffened. Of all the ridiculous suggestions, that had to be the worst of them. The idea that she could be attracted to *him*—this arrogant, self-righteous prick that probably never faced real suffering in his life—nauseated her.

No, she had been foolish once. She would never make the same mistake again.

Liam caught the sudden tension in her body and misinterpreted the gesture, his grin wide and mocking. He scooted his chair closer, intruding into Eve's personal space. She leaned as far away from him as she could.

"That's it, isn't it?" Liam mused. "I can't blame you; I have been told I'm unbelievably handsome. It was only a matter of time before you fell for my charms."

Eve blanched. He was close, too close. "You're delusional."

"I've been called worse." Liam searched her face before his smile faltered. There was a prior intensity to his gaze that now dimmed. "You look disgusted."

"I wonder why," Eve snapped. "Get the hell away from me."

Liam was utterly baffled. "Aren't you interested in me?"

Interested? She was barely restraining herself from shoving him off his chair. He hovered over her with curiosity, close enough that she caught the scent of fresh rain that clung to him.

"If you don't get out of my personal space right now, I'll dump this milk on your head," Eve threatened, squeezing the carton in her hand. Liam pulled back but did not turn away. The way he stared at her was akin to a puzzle box he couldn't break open. It was as if her existence confused him.

The bell rang and Eve took that cue to leave as fast as she could. Three more classes to get through and she could go home. Having lunch with Hailey had been a mistake. Boundaries did not seem to exist for Liam, or if they did, he had no qualms about disrespecting them. Eve didn't trust him enough to stick around.

She was barely a few paces away from her next classroom when she saw Sage and Hailey down the hall. Eve ducked her head and walked faster. Hopefully, they would ignore her, and they could pretend their whole meeting had never happened in the first place. God, why did Hailey have to wait for her in the bathroom yesterday?

Hailey and Sage stopped directly in front of Eve, blocking her path. Eve tripped over herself in an attempt to not slam into either of them. She opened her mouth to apologize—she never did say goodbye to either of them after lunch ended—but Hailey interrupted.

"Are you okay?" She flinched as Hailey's hand fell on her shoulder. It slipped off just as easily, and Hailey clutched her own hand as though afraid to make the same offense twice.

"Yeah, I'm fine," Eve lied. "I need to get to class."

Eve tried to step around them, but Hailey jumped into her path once more.

"You ran off without saying anything. I didn't know what happened," she blurted out. "I'm sorry if Liam said anything to upset you. I'll talk to him about it."

"It's okay. Really," Eve insisted. Her smile was forced. "I do need to get to class, though."

"You're going to have lunch with us again tomorrow, right?"

"I don't think that's the best idea," Eve confessed. It would probably be better if they never spoke to each other again.

Hailey winced as though she'd been slapped. Sage didn't appear to mind one way or the other what Eve did, but seeing at her friend's fallen expression, something changed.

"What would it take for you to join us tomorrow?" Sage asked.

For Liam not to be there, Eve thought without hesitation. But she couldn't kick him out of a group she didn't belong in, especially since he was related to Sage.

"You don't have to do anything—" she started. Sage held up a hand to silence her.

"I didn't say I would," Sage clarified. "Just tell me what would get you to have lunch with us again. I'll see what I can do."

Eve hesitated. Then quietly said, "I'm not comfortable around Liam."

"You don't want to see him at lunch?"

"I..." Eve wanted to insist that it was fine, that they didn't need to compromise anything in their lives for her sake. But everything in Sage's eyes told her an argument would not be tolerated. She cast her gaze downward and nodded instead.

"Alright. I'll make sure he isn't around at lunch," Sage said. "As long as you show up."

Eve gaped at her. "But he's your brother."

Sage waved off the remark with her hand. "Liam is enough to deal with at home. I don't mind getting a break from him." She peered down at Hailey. "What about you?"

Hailey nodded enthusiastically. "We can last one period without Liam."

"Good. We'll see you tomorrow." Sage pointed a finger at Eve. The invitation felt more like a threat.

Eve nodded, bidding the girls a quick goodbye before rushing to her next class.

When Eve dragged her feet to lunch the next day, Liam was nowhere to be found.

Four

Liam and Sage were odd. Not just in their strangely beautiful appearance—which was no less a fact than the sky being blue—but in how they conducted themselves.

They only showed up to school when they wanted to. Sage arrived more often than Liam, but she tended to go missing between classes or disappear for days at a time. They never turned in homework, never participated in discussions, and were outright absent during tests and quizzes. Not to mention their persistent absence during Mass, which Eve knew counted toward their grade.

Then there were their clothes: no way on God's green earth would the nuns excuse Liam's gold ear piercings or either of their bright amber contacts. Eve had gotten suspended at her old school for less, and she had seen more than one girl get pulled aside at St. Peter's for the length of their skirt or an extra set of earrings. Yet, Liam and Sage walked around in practically whatever they wanted, barely adhering to the school's dress code. Eve wondered why they bothered with the uniform at all, if they were going to ignore most of the rules, anyway.

But the weirdest part was that no one said anything. Not the nuns, not the teachers—no one in charge even noticed that they were missing most of the time. The students had caught on—one had even attempted to skip school as Liam had done and received detention for it—but even they shared a weird nonchalance about it for the most part.

Eve tried to bring up their strange behavior on several occasions—sometimes to Hailey, to other students, and even to Sage herself—but she was always brushed off or given vague answers. *It's fine,* they would say. It didn't matter what nun or teacher she asked, their answers were always the same.

The strangest interaction she had was with the office staff; the secretary had no idea who Eve was talking about.

"You know, *Liam,*" Eve said incredulously. He was kind of hard not to notice. "Red hair, piercings, looks like he's either going to commit a cult sacrifice or become one."

The school secretary, Jill—a middle-aged woman with thick rectangle glasses—shook her head, aghast. "We would never allow piercings in the school."

Jill's reasoning wasn't solid, but the interaction left Eve perplexed. Was that seriously what she took away from that?

Especially as she sat beside Liam during three of her classes that day.

Unlike Sage, who shared all of her classes exclusively with Hailey, Liam wandered between classrooms as he pleased, never sticking to one consistent schedule. Some days he was in gym, others he was in English, occasionally history and science. She never saw him in her religion studies, but she couldn't blame him for skipping that. She would skip, too, if she could.

English class dragged on, and Eve found it harder and harder to pay attention to the intricacies of Shakespeare's works when all she wanted to do was go home.

It was especially hard with Liam doing everything in his power to make this class a living hell.

This was not the first class he interrupted for her today. In fact, Liam had been in nearly every class with her this week, and Eve suspected his sole purpose was to drive her patience into the ground.

Liam sat at a desk beside her now, humming to himself as he fussed with his hair. He had been admiring himself in an intricate, golden compact mirror for at least thirty minutes. This would not normally bother Eve, except for the fact that he pestered her with enough questions that even the sound of his voice became an irritant.

"What do you think of this?" he asked, turning his chin this way and that to show off what minuscule change he'd made to his appearance. Eve did not dignify him with a response. She had barely passed her last English quiz and couldn't afford to miss this lecture.

"Perhaps it's too short," Liam mused. He flicked his hand, and out of the corner of her eye, Eve caught a sudden onslaught of red locks waving down past his shoulders. Liam stared at his reflection, readjusting his new long hair. Eve faltered, her pen dropping onto the surface of her notebook.

How did he do that? She wouldn't dare ask—expressing interest in Liam's behavior would only invite trouble. Still, she was baffled.

"What do you think?" He turned to her with a smirk, twirling one of his long strands of red hair around a slender finger. "Are you beside yourself with want and desire?"

Eve's lip curled in disgust. She shook her head and tried to pay attention to the lecture. Mr. Ceating was passionately scribbling something on the blackboard, but Eve missed what his rant had stemmed from.

Liam scowled. With the flick of his hand, his hair returned to normal.

For a few brief, blissful moments, Liam left her alone.

Then her pen suddenly veered off course, leaving a large, inky smear across her notes. Confused, Eve flipped the page and tried to write again—only for the pen to move on its own, yanking her hand with it.

"Stop it," she whispered between clenched teeth. His brow arched, but he didn't move from his seat.

"What are you talking about?"

"You *know* what." Eve's pen pressed against her smeared page, leaving a pool of ink in a small indent. She didn't know how he was doing it—she didn't see his hands move—but Eve was certain Liam was behind it. "Stop it. I'm trying to learn."

Liam's lips twitched. He glanced down at her notebook. "I can think of something far more entertaining than that."

"Not interested." The words came out instant and bitter cold. Liam leaned back in his chair, kicking his feet up on the desk.

"You can't possibly be enjoying this," he said, gesturing toward the blackboard. "I've seen moss with more charisma."

Eve's head pounded. Frustrated, she slapped her notebook shut. There wasn't any point in taking notes if she couldn't concentrate. She'd managed to keep a passing grade in the class so far—maybe another failed quiz wouldn't be the end of the world.

"That wasn't so hard, was it?" Suddenly, Liam was sitting in the empty chair in front of her and leaning on top of her desk, forcing his face into her line of sight. She tensed and tried to stare past him, but it was difficult with Liam invading her personal space. "I'll show you how to have some real fun."

"Go. Away," she ground out.

Liam sighed in disappointment but leaned back a little. He was observing her, and Eve dreaded what annoying plan he was concocting next. "You know, you need a nickname."

"What?" That wasn't where she was expecting him to go with this. A million horrible, terrible, inappropriate nicknames came to mind. The last thing she wanted was to hear what he really thought of her in the form of some weird pet name. Worse than that, what if it *stuck?* A vile taste rose in the back of her throat.

Liam pursed his lips in thought. Then, "I'm going to call you Evie."

"Don't call me that," Eve snapped too quickly, more determined to stop him from calling her *anything* than upset by the nickname itself.

That was a mistake. Liam grinned, relishing her annoyance.

"I could make it worse. Much, *much* worse," Liam teased, and she was sure he could. She was honestly surprised he hadn't already. Eve had expected something horrible, but his choice was rather lame by comparison. She was almost disappointed.

Liam took Eve's silence as quiet acceptance and grinned wider. "Evie it is then."

"I never agreed to that."

"Didn't have to, Evie."

Eve took a deep breath to calm herself and glanced at the analog clock above the blackboard. Only fifteen minutes left. She had to make it through the next fifteen minutes, and she could grab her stuff and go home.

Something nudged her elbow out of place, disrupting her tense pose. Eve caught herself, nearly smacking her face on the notebook's cover.

"Knock it off!" Eve snapped. She earned a few glances from fellow classmates and the brief attention of Mr. Ceating, but soon the lecture continued, and Eve glared back at Liam. Lowering her voice, she hissed, "Just leave me alone."

"Where's the fun in that, Evie?"

"*Don't* call me that."

"Why not, Evie?" Her elbow slipped out from under her again. This time, Eve was prepared and adjusted herself accordingly.

"Because I said so."

"That's not a good reason, Evie." Another nudge.

"Do. Not. Touch. Me." There was no humor in her voice: only the cold, quiet hatred that stirred inside of her. Eve was used to being passive. She was used to taking the high road, the backseat, and everything else her parents and priests shoved on her to keep her sweet, docile, and subservient. Stay quiet and out of the way and nothing bad will happen, right?

But bad things happened to her all the time. And she was sick of letting them get away with it.

She was so *fucking* sick of it.

Liam smirked, thrilled by the sudden challenge. They stared each other down, daring the other to make the first move.

Her elbow was shoved out from under her, and Eve nearly smacked her face against the desk.

She grabbed her pen and threw it at his face.

Liam ducked. The pen flew forward, right into the back of Mr. Ceating's bald head.

Shit.

Eve sunk down in her chair as all eyes turned on her. Liam was, inexplicably, gone. Her only guess was that he saw what was about to happen and decided to sneak out before he could be implicated.

"Miss Carter," Mr. Ceating said. Eve flinched at the acidity in his tone. "Is my lecture so boring that you think throwing things is an acceptable response?"

"No, sir," Eve mumbled. Her face burned in shame. She wanted to sink into the floor and disappear into the boiler room underneath; living with the mice there would be better than this kind of attention.

"Then why did you throw it?"

Eve opened her mouth, fully prepared to blame Liam, but who was going to believe her? He wasn't there now, and she couldn't explain how he'd left the classroom so quickly without anyone noticing. She glanced at her classmates, hoping one of them could interject and explain what happened, but none of them had even paid attention to her.

Eve was alone.

Unable to provide an excuse, Eve clung to silence. Mr. Ceating's gaze narrowed.

"You'll see me after class, Miss Carter."

School was long over by the time Eve escaped Mr. Ceating's office with little more than an after-school detention. Eve supposed she should feel lucky; if it had been almost anyone else in the school, she would have gotten a suspension and a call home. Mr. Ceating was relatively understanding though, and he was more worried about what caused the outburst than being attacked by a rogue pen. There wasn't much she could say either way, considering Liam had suddenly disappeared from the classroom, so Mr. Ceating had no choice but to at least dole out a punishment.

The late afternoon sun beat against the side of St. Peter's as Eve trudged down the concrete steps. She was surprised to find Hailey and Sage lingering at the bottom of the stairs. Hailey beamed up at her and waved.

"What are you two still doing here?" Eve asked as the other two rose to their feet and began their trek home.

"We were waiting for you," Hailey said. "What took you so long?"

Eve flushed, ashamed. She didn't use to care much about the delinquencies she earned in school, but confessing them to Sage and Hailey was more embarrassing than even her parents knowing. "I was in detention."

"What did you do to earn detention?" Sage grinned, amused. "Are you creating trouble?"

"You can ask Liam," Eve said sourly.

"Ah." Sage nodded, immediately understanding. Hailey chuckled nervously at her side, shaking her head.

"He's the worst sometimes. I swear, I don't know how you put up with it, Sage," Hailey whined, but it came out more playful than genuine.

Eve had to bite back her annoyance. Hailey was used to Liam's antics, and Eve was sure he rarely—if ever—used them on her. Eve couldn't blame Hailey for being an outside observer and finding humor in his behavior. Maybe if she had been born in another life, Eve would have found him humorous, too.

"He acts like he can do whatever he wants," she said. "And people let him get away with it. I haven't seen anyone tell him off—or even come close to it."

"Imagine having to live with him," Sage said under her breath.

"I don't think he's trying to do any harm," Hailey said, but even Eve caught the skeptical glance Sage tossed in her direction. "Liam's just, you know, special."

Eve scoffed. *Special*. Privileged was more apt. Just because he was handsome didn't mean he should be allowed to get away with harassing her for shits and giggles every day.

"Do you guys want to come over to my house this weekend?" Hailey asked, eager to change the subject. "It's supposed to be warm out; we can hang out on the patio."

Eve hesitated. Her acquaintanceship with Hailey and Sage had lasted as far as the corner of Walnut Street and Third Avenue where they would all inevitably part on their way home. She hadn't even *seen* Hailey's house, much less visited anyone else in almost three years. What if she did something weird by mistake? Eve was already pretty awkward and quiet at school, and at least *there* she had some conversation starters to fall back on. Hailey's house would be a whole new environment.

"I'm not sure that's a good idea," Eve decided. Then, when Hailey was about to argue, "I have to take care of my nan."

Curiosity flickered across the girls' faces. That's right—Eve had never mentioned her living situation to them. Would they find it weird that she lived with her grandmother? Eve bit down on her lip.

"Is your nan sick?" Hailey's question took Eve by surprise. She found herself answering before she could think better of it.

"Sort of; I think she has dementia. She hasn't been diagnosed yet, though." Nan refused to see a doctor for it, and Eve didn't think her parents took it seriously. But what was she supposed to do? Drag her grandma there by herself?

Hailey's cheery demeanor dampened, and the mood grew solemn. "I'm so sorry. My grandpa died from Alzheimer's a few years ago. I know how much it sucks." She took Eve's hand in her own and squeezed hard. Eve tried not to flinch at the contact. "I'm here if you need anything, okay?"

"Thanks." Eve pulled her hand back and hid both inside of the pockets of her cardigan as she shuffled forward awkwardly. Hailey was kind, maybe too kind for her own good. Eve couldn't tell if she was being fake or not, but she felt guilty for even considering the idea.

You can never be too careful.

Eve cleared her throat. "I'll see if my neighbor is able to hang out with her on Saturday. Maybe I can stop by for a few hours."

Hailey grinned. "I'll text you the address, okay?"

Eve nodded, mentally convincing herself not to back out now. *Everything is going to be fine.*

Five

Hailey's house was close to the center of town, so upon request, Eve stopped at the gas station to grab drinks and snacks. She didn't know anyone's preferences, and Hailey was no help with her indecisive texts—*Just get whatever sounds good!*—so Eve went with a wide variety in the hope that everyone would find something they enjoyed.

With the snacks paid for, Eve walked a few blocks down until she found Hailey's address. The house had clearly been renovated over the summer with its new baby blue siding and a fresh white trim. An American Flag stuck out from the porch roof, the stripes rippling against the light autumn breeze. The yard was half-hidden behind a wall of neatly trimmed shrubbery, and an inlaid stone path led up to the porch. They'd already started decorating for the season—pumpkins lined the porch steps and a scarecrow with a childlike face smiled at her from beside the front door. It leered at her with its painted grin and bulging blue eyes. Eve grimaced, thoroughly creeped out.

What did Hailey's parents do to afford a place like this? Eve knew land was always cheaper in smaller towns, but even this was excessively nice, considering they also had to pay to put their daughter through a private school.

Hailey greeted Eve with a beaming smile and ushered her in. It didn't take long for Eve to figure it out: framed medical articles and a wall display of awards greeted her in the front hallway. Her father was a surgeon—no wonder they could afford such a nice house. Eve thought of her own parents' tiny apartment with a wave of embarrassment. The thin walls were barely big enough to contain the three of them, let alone company.

Eve was grateful for her room at Nan's.

Hailey scooped the gas station bag from Eve's arms and led her through the house to the kitchen. She was talking, but Eve struggled to pay attention. She had never been in a house this large before. The pastel paint was crisp and vibrant, without any chips or scuffs, and the second-floor hallway had a balcony beside the stairs to overlook the dining room. The carpet was plush under her feet, each step softer than clouds as she passed the wide, white-trimmed windows that filled each room with warm sunlight.

The most exciting of all was the fridge—when Hailey pushed a cup underneath one of the levers, *ice cubes* tumbled out.

Eve stared at the appliance in wonder. *So, this is what being rich is like.*

"—outside?" Eve caught the end of Hailey's sentence as she set up a tray with glass cups. She arranged the soda bottles artfully in the middle.

"Sorry, what was that?" Eve asked.

Hailey smiled and gently nudged the finished drink tray toward her. "Could you bring this outside? We're going to hang out on the patio."

"Oh, sure." Eve picked up the tray awkwardly in her arms, smiling gratefully at Hailey as she ran over to hold the back door open for her.

Sage was already there, enjoying the unusually sunny afternoon from a worn out plastic patio chair. Eve was unused to seeing the girls outside of the confines of St. Peter's, but Sage was completely at ease in her tight black jeans and matching leather jacket. Eve supposed she had never thought of what they would wear on their days off, but she couldn't picture Sage wearing anything else.

A sense of dread overcame Eve as she noticed Liam leaning back in his chair. He precariously balanced himself on the plastic hind legs as his feet worked against the table's ledge to keep him upright. Eve was dangerously tempted to push him over.

Liam wore all black, although he was dressed in a pair of jeans and a plain cotton T-shirt. Wasn't he cold? Eve found herself bundling up in her turtleneck and shawl. Her long skirt swishing against her ankles as she set the tray of drinks down on the table and took a seat beside Sage.

Sage was quick to catch on, rolling her eyes as Liam nearly fell backward in his chair. "We didn't invite him. He followed me here."

"Great," Eve droned. Liam's grin stretched wide, mocking her.

Hailey came out then, the snacks Eve had purchased laid out on a Thanksgiving platter in her arms. Somehow, she had made junk food aesthetically pleasing. Eve was impressed.

An awkward beat passed as Hailey settled down.

"You know what I recently found out? Apparently, pork intestines are a snack in the south," Hailey said, steering toward a safer topic. It worked, because Liam and Sage were suddenly fascinated by Hailey's findings.

"Where did you hear that?" Sage asked with a laugh.

"One of my dad's patients."

"Yeah, they're called chitlins," Eve said, earning a round of confused stares.

"So, you eat them raw?" Liam asked.

"They can't consume *raw meat*, Liam," Sage said.

"Isn't that what sushi is? That fish stuff Hailey brought last time?"

"That's different," Hailey interjected.

"They're deep-fried," Eve explained.

Liam stared at her as though she were stupid. "The fish?"

Eve's smile twitched. "No, the pork intestines."

The conversation took off from there, diving from one subject to the next. At some point Hailey called in a food order, although food was the last thing on Eve's mind. Any time she had something to say, Liam would counter her, no matter how dumb his response may be. Eve couldn't tell if he was doing it to annoy her or if he was genuinely stupid.

"Not quite." Eve found herself in the process of explaining differences between Vermont and Georgia, where her Uncle Bob lived. She'd only visited him there on a few occasions, but apparently that was farther south than any of her companions had traveled. "So, it's pop up here, but they all call it Coke in Georgia no matter the company. Some say soda, but usually it's Coke."

"What is the point of calling it something else? Pick a name and stick with it," Liam said. He ran a frustrated hand through his hair.

"It's a regional thing," Eve said for what was the hundredth time this afternoon. "Like how you call billfolds *wallets* in Vermont."

"*I* don't call it that."

"Then what do you call it?"

"I don't call it anything."

Her blood pressure rose. He was just being difficult. He had to be.

Liam tilted back in his chair, close to tipping over.

She couldn't resist. Eve stretched her leg out under the table and nudged Liam's chair out from under him.

Liam's jaw dropped, the perfect look of shock flitting across his face before he fell backward, toppling out of his chair and onto the soft grass. Eve bit back a satisfied smirk.

Sage hid no such thing, her laughter loud enough to startle a flock of birds out of their nearby tree. Hailey tried to contain her laughter as she rushed to check on Liam, but she too was thrown into giggling hysterics. Liam climbed to his feet, his face red and his clothes smeared with grass and dirt. He glowered at Eve, picking up on what had happened.

"Are you okay, Liam?" Hailey asked between bursts of giggles. She reached out to help him, but Liam brushed her off.

"I'm fine," he snapped. He wiped his hands over his shirt in an attempt to remove the grass stains before marching into the house. The laughter subsided, a tense silence filling its place.

"Should we check on him?" Hailey wondered. Eve grimaced. She wasn't particularly interested in apologizing.

"He'll be fine," Sage said. "He's just going to pout for a bit."

Her words eased some of Eve's guilt. Sage would know him better than anyone, so if she said he was fine, Eve was ready to believe that. Hailey was less inclined but nodded, rejoining the girls at the table.

A few minutes passed, but Liam still hadn't returned. That infamous Catholic guilt crept up on Eve. Although Hailey and Sage kept themselves preoccupied with mouthfuls of snacks and conversation, Eve found herself glancing at the kitchen door. Maybe kicking his chair out had been a step too far; he was annoying, sure, but he didn't deserve to be kicked around.

No, he's always trying to pick on me. It's fine, Eve thought. If she hadn't done it, gravity would have gotten the job done, eventually. Eve simply expedited the process.

But he still wasn't back. Eve's regret quickly turned to frustration. Was he deliberately taking a long time to punish her? He had no right to make her suffer, especially after the crap he put her through this week. Eve's fists balled under the table. No, she wouldn't allow guilt to ebb at her. Not over this.

Hailey's phone buzzed on the table. She glanced down, swiping across the screen. "Oh, the food's here."

"I'll get it," Eve volunteered. Neither girl objected as Eve rose from her chair and headed inside. She needed a moment to calm down.

Eve kept an eye open for Liam as she wandered through the house. She didn't know if she would apologize or not when she saw him. She didn't *want* to, but the good little Catholic girl in her told her it was the right thing to do. Eve hated that part of herself. If she could, she'd yank her out and strangle her. Then she would never feel guilt again.

The doorbell rang twice. The deliverer was getting impatient.

"Coming!" she called. The doorbell rang again. She threw the door open, an apology on her lips, "Sorry, I—"

Her words cut off. Nothing came out.

Eve could only stare as her assaulter greeted her on the other side of the door.

Six

Eve was fourteen when she developed her first crush. It was different from her infatuation with cartoon princesses and the attractive depictions of Jesus that graced their apartment. This boy was *real*, with gelled brown hair and a clean, shaved face. His deep brown eyes and baby face made him appear younger than he was: a senior ready to graduate, whereas Eve had only begun her high school career.

His name was Colton Davis, and he was perfect.

Colton didn't date much according to the other girls at school, although he was the apple of the academy's eye: smart, funny, and attractive. He was even planning to go to seminary after graduation. There couldn't be a more respectable combination.

In an academy filled with girls far richer and from more respectable families than Eve's, she didn't stand a chance.

She had all but given up on her crush until the spring of her freshman year.

Art class was among Eve's favorites: the smell of fresh paint, the colorful canvases that hung around the classroom. Her family was too poor to afford any of the nice supplies at home—let alone fit it in their tiny apartment—but the academy had a wide variety of materials. There were some that Eve had never heard of before. And she was allowed to use it all.

Eve shared this class with two of Colton's closest friends: Nick Palenti and Logan Richards. Despite Colton's admirable reputation, Nick and Logan were less admirable. Nick was a class clown, always searching for the next prank to pull, no matter how unfortunate the outcome may be for his victim. Logan, on the other hand, was a known flirt and rarely stayed in once place for too long. Eve didn't understand how Colton fit into their friendship, but she often saw the boys spending their free time together in the courtyard, laughing and fooling around. *Boys will be boys,* her father always said.

Eve had never spoken to them before, so it came as a surprise when Nick approached her after art class.

"Colton wants you to meet him in the courtyard," he sniffed, congested with spring allergies. Eve thought it was another one of his pranks, but sure enough, Colton waited for her in the courtyard, a small bundle of roses in his hands. This was his proposal to prom.

The following month and a half passed in a blur. Eve managed to snag a cute dress from the thrift store and a pair of shoes to match. Her friends helped with her hair and makeup, primping and prepping her to fit with the *Midsummer Night's Dream* theme.

The dance was held on school grounds, so it didn't bother Eve in the slightest when Colton asked her to meet him there. The hall was filled with student-made decorations of giant floral props, a carpet of turf stretching from the entrance to the dance floor. Couples meandered in and waltzed across the floor, always at arm's length.

Eve was taken aback by the whimsical lights and beautiful dresses her classmates wore. Prom was typically reserved for juniors and seniors; being there was almost a glimpse into her future. She smiled, making her way to one of the empty tables.

"There you are."

Nick approached her from behind, laying one of his heavy hands on her shoulder. His breath smelled sour and strangely sweet at the same time, as if he'd mixed too many drinks with a bag of cotton candy.

"Are you *drunk?*" Eve asked, aghast. Nick shook his head, his short black hair already matted to his forehead with sweat.

"Colton needs you," he said. Before Eve could object, Nick grabbed her arm and dragged her from the dance hall.

"Where is he? Is he okay?" Eve asked. Nick gripped her shoulder with uncomfortable strength, his fingers pressing down into her skin unnecessarily hard as he led her back to the dormitories. Eve tried to subtly relinquish herself from his grasp, but he only held onto her tighter.

Uneasiness stirred inside of her as Nick led her into the boys' dormitory. Girls were not allowed here, even for visitation. But Nick was rushing, and if Colton was sick—or worse, hurt—she wanted to help.

The dormitory was empty, save for the freshman and sophomores on the lower floors. They didn't register Eve as Nick led her up the stairwell.

They came to a halt on the fourth floor. It was completely abandoned—all the seniors had gone to the prom. Nick gestured toward one of the doors, his large body blocking her from running past him. His behavior unnerved her, but there was nowhere else to go.

And Eve wanted to help.

So, she opened the bedroom door.

Nick Palenti had not changed much in two-and-a-half years. His body was still as large and muscular as Eve remembered, perhaps even more so, and his skin had burned with the sun's exposure. A fuzz of cropped black hair sprouted from his head, most of it hidden under a worn baseball cap.

Eve stared. She could not hear the rapid thump of her heartbeat in her chest, nor the annoyed grumblings of Nick as he tried to pass off the delivery. She was back in Colton's dorm room, her throat tightening from the strength of Nick's thick hands around her neck, squeezing, squeezing, *squeezing* until the others had to pull him off—

"What are you doing?"

Liam hovered from behind her, the grass stains mostly gone from his clothes. He cocked his head at her silence, but Eve couldn't bring herself to face him.

"Are you gonna take the food or not?" Nick huffed.

Eve blinked back tears and accepted the bags with trembling arms, careful not to touch his skin. From the look on his face, Nick didn't even know who she was. Nick grumbled a few more things at her before leaving. Eve watched him go. Even once his car was completely out of sight, she was frozen to the spot.

"Do you know that guy?" Liam asked. Her throat tightened. She didn't want to deal with anyone, but especially not Liam.

Eve shoved the bags into his arms. Liam cursed, nearly dropping them on the floor. "I'm going home."

"What's going on with you?" Eve could feel his eyes following her back to the front door. "Evie—"

Liam grabbed her arm, whirling her toward him. There was too much happening in her mind to keep herself composed. Whatever Liam saw on her face, it was enough for him to let her go.

She kept her eyes on him as she stumbled out the front door and down the porch steps. Then she was down the street, running as fast as her legs would carry her.

Until there was no Colton, no Logan, no Nick, and no Liam.

Seven

Eve did not show up to school on Monday.

She didn't show up on Tuesday.

Or Wednesday.

Or Thursday.

Or Friday.

She didn't notice. She didn't care.

In her mind, Eve was back at the academy: two-and-a-half years younger and falling apart each day.

Nick may have led her up to Colton's bedroom, but he was not the only one there. Colton had been waiting on the bed, Logan smoking a cigarette on the floor. Whatever they were joking about ended when Eve arrived. They had something else to laugh about now.

Once they were done, Colton kicked her out of the room. Her new dress was ripped and hanging off her shoulders like a shiny rag. The makeup her friends had applied was smeared, her long hair tangled and knotted. She didn't know what happened to her underwear.

The walk back to her dormitory was long and silent. She did not speak to her roommate when she returned.

She did not speak to anyone .

On a hot June afternoon, a few weeks after prom, Eve made the mistake of telling her mother what happened. Sharon wanted to know why her daughter had failed every test and assignment in the past three weeks. Why the end of her freshman year had taken such a downward spiral.

Eve wanted her mother to understand.

"I didn't raise you to be a whore!"

The words cut deeper than the inevitable betrayal as her mother conveyed the information to her father. It was worse than her father's temper when he berated her for her behavior over dinner. Worse than the shame of being caught in a pool of her own blood in the academy's ugly green bathroom with her father's pocket knife still clutched in her fist.

It was worse because, somehow, this was Eve's fault. It didn't matter that three boys had planned this out and held her down. It didn't matter that Eve had begged, that she cried, that Nick had threatened to slice her goddamn *throat* if she didn't shut up.

And almost killed her when she wouldn't.

Eve had worn a dress that reached above her knees. That was all her parents could focus on. To them, to everyone she knew, Eve had been asking for it.

Eve, seventeen years old and in her father's childhood bedroom, pulled the covers over her head and cried.

The sky was still dark when Eve heard a faint tapping at her window. She assumed it was a tree branch, but when the tapping persisted, she climbed out of her bed to peer through the glass.

Sage stood two stories down, a handful of pebbles in her palm. Her hand lifted to toss another but, upon seeing Eve's face, stopped. She gestured for Eve to meet her outside.

The old analog cat clock read 2:13 a.m. when Eve passed it on the stairs, its large cartoon eyes flitting back and forth with each ticking second. She couldn't imagine a creepier clock, but somehow Nan found it charming enough to place it at the top of the stairs where it could always watch her.

Eve avoided its stare as she hurried downstairs and cracked the front door open. Nan was a light sleeper; she would be furious if she caught Eve up so late. Nan might have dementia, but she still had a routine to follow.

"Hey." Sage stood on the porch in a pair of black combat boots and her leather jacket. Eve blinked heavily, unconvinced that this wasn't a stress dream.

"Hey," Eve said. She glanced back up the stairs, checking for Nan, before she carefully stepped onto the front porch. At Sage's odd look, she added, "Nan's asleep."

"Right." Sage followed Eve to the creaky porch swing. It was only once she was sitting down that Eve noticed the manila folder in her arms. Sage passed it over, Eve's name scrawled in black ink at the top. "Homework. Hailey was going to deliver it to you, but I offered to do it."

"Oh. Thanks." Eve stared at the folder. She had no intention of doing any of it. "You're here late."

Sage blinked, as though the thought had just occurred to her. What kind of life did she lead, that visiting in the middle of a Sunday night was normal? What was she doing up at this hour in the first place?

"Hailey's been worried about you," Sage said, changing the subject. Eve sighed. She wasn't surprised. Eve didn't even say goodbye to her before she left, and she'd ignored all of her texts this week.

I probably hurt her, Eve thought, troubled. She would have to apologize when she saw her again.

"Sorry," Eve said.

"You can make it up to me by coming to school tomorrow," Sage replied. Eve was taken by surprise, but nodded. She would have to go back tomorrow anyway unless she wanted her parents to find out she'd been skipping. Eve had already managed to intercept a few calls to Nan, but she was sure the next call would be to her mother. The only reason she knew they hadn't called yet was because neither of her parents had shown up on her porch, threatening to send her overseas.

The girls sat in silence, the night breeze cool against their skin. Eve ran a hand through her greasy hair, suddenly aware of how unkempt it was. She hadn't showered all week. These were the same pajamas she put on when she got home from Hailey's, and they probably smelled like it, too. She scooted a little further away from Sage, self-conscious.

Sage never smelled bad—she had a distinctly pleasant scent to her that Eve could only reason to herself as nighttime and dreams. Maybe some jasmine. She couldn't think of any other way to describe it.

"Why'd you skip?" Sage asked, staring out at the clear, starry sky. Eve bit her lip. She had been hoping Sage wouldn't ask.

"I was sick."

Sage didn't fight her on it, but she did size her up, sensing the lie. Eve smiled weakly in return.

Sage's eyes moved down Eve's arm and caught on something. Eve followed her gaze, blanching when she realized her scars were exposed. She flipped her wrists over quickly and pressed them against her thighs. Silence stretched between them as Eve waited for Sage to ask the inevitable.

She didn't. Sage pretended to focus on the folder instead, and Eve nearly breathed a sigh of relief.

The swing's chains creaked as Sage stood up and stretched. Eve followed suit, holding the manila folder close to her chest. Maybe she *would* get this stuff done tonight. She wasn't tired anymore, and any distraction was a welcome one.

"See you tomorrow," Sage said. It wasn't a question. Eve better be there, or else.

"See you."

The aging floorboards groaned under Sage's boots as she thudded down the stairs and walked back toward the street. Nan lived far enough from the center of town that there was no sidewalk on the streets and even fewer houses. If she squinted, Eve could make out the church and its cemetery a few blocks away. The surrounding forest was menacing in the dark, the treetops stretching up against the blue-black sky like claws.

Eve called after her, "You didn't tell me why you're here so late."

Sage kept walking.

Eight

The return to school was awkward. Eve weaved in and out of her first set of classes for the day, keeping her head low and conversations short. By now, everyone seemed to have gotten the hint that Eve preferred to be alone, but there were still a few fresh faces that asked where she'd been. Even Eric regarded her with some sympathy, regaling in his own flu stories when she gave him the quick "I was sick" excuse. He didn't mind at all that she'd run out on him during their first conversation together. Eve didn't quite know what to make of that.

As Eve made her way to the cafeteria, she saw Hailey pushing toward her from the end of the hall. Eve tensed as Hailey threw her arms around her.

"There you are! I was so worried. Liam said you ran off from my house, and then you weren't answering my calls or my texts—I didn't know what to do!" Hailey's words exhaled from her lips in one long gush. She let go and Eve relaxed, grateful for the space between them. "I was going to stop at your house, but Sage promised she would check up on you for me."

Eve sheepishly played with the short ends of her hair. "Sorry. I was sick."

"How are you feeling now?" Hailey's eyes were wide with worry, as if Eve was still on the cusp of breaking down. Eve did her best to smile comfortingly.

"Better."

Hailey smiled and left the conversation there. Eve was grateful to move on to another topic and didn't have to fake her interest when Hailey caught her up on everything that had happened during the past week. There wasn't much she missed outside of a few funny classroom anecdotes and a pile of homework she still had to finish filling out for class. The bulk of their conversation consisted of Hailey's win during a basketball game on Saturday.

"The after party was even better," Hailey said as they traveled through the lunch line. Eve's stomach growled. She hadn't eaten much during her week away. Even the cafeteria food was appetizing. "We went back to Sage's house, and she and Liam invited some friends over."

"Anyone we know?" Eve had more trouble keeping her interest in the conversation with her newfound appetite.

Hailey shook her head. "No, they're not from around here."

"Visiting from out of town?"

"Sort of."

What was that supposed to mean? Eve waited for her to elaborate, but Hailey paid for her food and walked back to their usual table with nothing more to say on the subject. Eve sat beside her and ate, trying hard not to shovel all the tray's contents into her mouth at once. How long had it been since she ate a real meal? She'd been too depressed to eat much of anything she made for Nan this week, but now her appetite came back in full force, rioting against her for sustenance.

After a few minutes, Eve glanced at the remaining empty chairs. "Did Sage skip today?"

"Yeah," Hailey said sullenly. "I guess she's busy."

"Oh." Eve nodded, taking another bite of her food. She thought of how insistent Sage was about her attendance last night, yet she wasn't even here to make sure it happened. Eve almost wished she'd skipped again.

As they ate, Eve could sense Hailey's gaze on her, waiting as if an explosion was about to go off. A blush crept up her neck. She hated being observed, no different from an animal behind a cage. Eve tried to keep her tone light as she asked, "What's up?"

"Nothing." It was obviously something. Eve waited. "I was just thinking about how we met."

The heat intensified on her face.

"What about it?" Eve asked carefully. She wasn't sure she wanted to hear the answer.

Hailey hesitated, running her finger in a figure eight over the table's smooth surface. Her voice lowered as she said, "I don't know what you're going through, but you can talk to me about it if you need to. I promise I won't tell anyone. You always look so sad."

It was as though a bucket of ice water had been dropped on her. Eve stared, her body rigid as anxiety coursed through her veins. She struggled to keep her voice calm. "What do you mean?"

Eve knew her breakdown in the bathroom had been a slip up, but she thought she was doing a pretty good job of keeping herself in check. How much had Hailey guessed? What did she know? The idea of Hailey—of *anyone*—finding out what nightmares kept her awake at night made her sick to her stomach.

Hailey took her time answering, chewing slowly on a piece of celery as she thought. Eve clenched her fists on her lap, nails digging into her palms as her heart thundered in her chest.

"I know how it feels, you know? Like everything is falling apart and you have nowhere to go." Hailey stared across the cafeteria with a faraway look in her eyes. "Sage and Liam helped me get out of that. Liam especially."

"Liam?" Was she hearing her right? Eve had trouble imagining Liam doing anything relatively helpful.

"I know you guys got off on the wrong foot, but Liam isn't as bad as you think he is. He asked about you this week while you were gone."

"Why, so he can find a way to bother me at home, too?" Eve muttered. The only reason he'd ask after her was because of his own boredom. Poor Liam without a toy to play with. She was grateful he didn't show up at school today; he was the last thing she wanted to deal with, especially after how she'd left Hailey's house. He would never let her hear the end of it.

Hailey's eyebrows pinned together, her fingers coming together to form a steeple on the table. She peered up at Eve with a doubtful expression. "I know he can be a jerk sometimes, but Liam can help you with whatever's bothering you if you ask."

Eve balked. Liam was not going to help *her*.

"I think I'll pass." The words came out harsher than she intended, but Eve couldn't bring herself to apologize. Liam *helping* her? Ridiculous. She wanted to laugh at the absurdity.

But Hailey was not deterred. "You don't know him like the rest of us do, Eve. You should think it over."

"There isn't much to think over." There were a lot of dark things Eve would do to avoid telling Liam what her problems were. No doubt he would find a way to twist her words around and blame her for the incident. Worse, Liam could find ways to use it against her, bringing it up whenever an argument went too far. She wasn't about to risk that. "He's not going to help me—not that I'd even want his help in the first place."

"You won't know until you ask him." Eve was surprised by the conviction in Hailey's voice. She was certain. But how could she be when she didn't even know what the problem was? It was easy to offer help, but it was harder to commit to it.

"Even if I *did* ask, there's nothing he can do about it," Eve said with a defeated sigh. She stabbed her fork into the piece of cake on her tray and swallowed hard.

"Isn't there?"

There was a mischievous gleam in her eyes, the kind Eve had only seen on Sage or Liam. It was even more unnerving on Hailey. *She's been spending too much time with those two.*

"If you have an idea, be my guest," Eve said with a tinge of sarcasm.

Hailey's lips pursed, cautious, but her eyes held enough excitement that Eve thought she might burst. "Do you believe in miracles?"

Eve didn't hesitate. "No."

Hailey pouted. "That's not very open-minded of you."

"I didn't say I was an open-minded person," Eve joked with a wry smile. Hailey's expression didn't change, and Eve sighed. "Alright. What were you going to say?"

"You're going to laugh at me," Hailey accused.

"I'm not going to laugh at you"—Eve paused—"Probably."

Hailey pouted doubtfully. Curiosity pricked at the back of Eve's mind. Hailey glanced about the room before she leaned forward and whispered, "Liam is blessed."

Eve waited for the punchline. Or *was* that the punchline? Eve didn't think it was funny. Were all of Hailey's jokes this bad?

"You've lost me."

Hailey frowned. Eve stared at her. Did she expect Eve to take her at face value? Maybe any other Catholic student would have at least shown some interest or curiosity at her claim—but Eve wasn't Catholic, and she had met Liam several times now. There was nothing divine about him, of that much she was certain.

"He's blessed," Hailey repeated, as if that made it make any more sense. "Liam can create miracles. It's—it's magic. But obviously not magic cause, you know, that would be a sin. But you tell him what you want, and Liam will take care of it for you."

"And he does it out of the generosity of his heart?" Eve scoffed. This whole thing reeked of bullshit. "That doesn't sound like Liam."

Hailey bit down on her lip. "There is something he asks for in return. Usually it's not that bad, though."

Of course. You could never get something for nothing.

"That sounds a lot more like making a deal with a demon than a blessing, Hailey," Eve pointed out.

Hailey shook her head, stubborn. "I would never make a deal with the devil."

No, of course, Hailey would never make a deal with a demon. She was too good a Catholic for that. Even though that's exactly what ran through Eve's mind.

"I'll think about it," Eve promised without any real intention of doing so. The whole situation was absurd. Hailey couldn't be this naive, right? Hailey didn't come across as the kind of girl to even consider lying, which only left Liam and Sage.

Eve had come to rely on Sage as a sort of friend, although Eve still knew that there was some kind of wall between them. It was something she wasn't quite comfortable admitting aloud yet.

But then there was Liam: arrogant, cruel-tongued Liam. She could easily see him constructing false promises and making it appear as though he accomplished them in order to maintain some kind of hierarchy over his classmates. It explained why people were so willing to go along with whatever he said.

This was exactly the kind of thing he would do.

Anger simmered beneath her veins. What right did he have to lie and manipulate his way through life? Did he truly think there would be no consequences for him?

There weren't any for Colton.

Anger gave way to sadness, and Eve slumped back in her chair.

Eve *wanted* it to be true. Deep down—way, *way* deep down—and against all of her better judgment, Eve wanted Liam to be blessed. She didn't want to think of how tempting a magical solution could be, but she couldn't help herself. Tell Liam that she wanted her abusers rotting away, never to hurt another girl again, and it could happen? How wonderful would that be?

Even better, what if they ceased to exist at all?

There is something he asks for in return. She didn't want to know what this request would cost her. Men were selfish; they always wanted more than what they gave. Liam could end up asking her for more than she could ever afford. Worse, he could want her to do something impossible in return.

The image of her abusers locked away in a dirty cell lingered in her mind. Would it be worth it?

It's not real, she thought, catching herself in a moment of embarrassment. She'd been so caught up in the fantasy of *what-if*s that she forgot it was simply that: a fantasy. People were not blessed, whether it was by God or by their own arrogance.

People were people, and they suffered and trudged on the same, Liam included.

NINE

Two weeks before prom, fifteen-year-old Eve was a wreck.

She sat on the floor of the art room, her long hair pulled back into a ponytail while she hunched over a blank canvas. Well, not entirely blank—there were small traces of pencil where her design would go, and several more eraser streaks in between. Tiny bottles of acrylic paint remained untouched beside her, waiting to be poured onto her palette.

It wasn't supposed to be that big of a deal; it was just a small piece of a bigger collaboration between the different art classes to show off how their skills had improved throughout the year. But Eve had agonized over it, from the fine details in her sketch to the brand of paint she wanted to use. Her father had suggested hanging up whatever she put together in their meager living room. It *had* to be perfect.

Eve sighed and drew another line before erasing it again. The end of the year collaboration always had a theme and this year's was *Hope*. It was pretty basic, but considering they had to base their paintings on something from the Bible, Eve had plenty to choose from. She decided to go with her favorite verse, *The Canticle of Mary*. It was told from Mother Mary's point of view as she praised God for blessing her, a lowly handmaid, of all people. It was a hopeful reminder to Eve that, even in her poorest moments, she could still be blessed and loved by the Lord.

"You're *still* working on that thing?"

Nick Palenti watched her from the doorway, his massive body brushing against the chipped frame. He crossed his arms, mockery written plain on his face. Nick was still in his football uniform, his shiny skin sweaty from practice.

Eve shifted her weight away from him, gripping the pencil in her hand. Something about the way he watched her around campus unnerved her. She was rarely the subject of his interest, but when she caught him staring, it was as if a spike of ice drove through her. Every alarm in her head screamed at her to run.

But he was Colton's friend. Maybe she was being paranoid.

"It's due next week," Eve said after a beat of silence. "There's not a lot of time left."

"But on a Saturday?" Nick curled his lip in disgust.

"It's the best time to work." Eve glanced out the window. Morning had passed by in a blur, leaving the afternoon sun to stretch out over the art room in warm rectangle patches. The stained-glass projects hanging from the ceiling reflected on the walls in a spinning arc of color. She enjoyed her Saturdays in the art room, preferring the peaceful solitude over the noisy classroom chatter. She could listen to whatever music she wanted, use as much art supplies as she desired, and she wouldn't be interrupted in the middle of her project.

She narrowed her gaze at Nick. He'd moved closer to her side, his body blocking out the sunlight against her back as he hovered over her to get a better look.

"What is *that* supposed to be?" He pointed vaguely at the canvas.

"It's *The Canticle of Mary*," Eve explained. Nick scoffed behind her. Her pencil hovered over the sketch, but she couldn't dedicate herself to making another mark. Nick was too close, his shadow hanging over her like a cloak. She cleared her throat and tried to keep her voice light as she asked, "Did you decide what to base yours on?"

"Yeah." Silence.

"What did you pick?"

"Psalm 137." She could hear the grin in his voice.

It took Eve a moment to register what he said. "The one with the babies?"

"And the rocks." Nick chuckled. Eve paled. She had only read it a couple of times, but Psalm 137 was meant to be a cry for justice and revenge after exile. The verse suggested violent acts, such as bashing of infants' heads against stone in atonement. Ultimately it ended in trusting God to take care of them, but the imagery disturbed her.

Nick wasn't the type of student to do much critical thinking, though.

"I don't think that's what they meant by hopeful," Eve mumbled, half-hoping he wouldn't hear her.

"Isn't art about perspective or some shit?" He leaned over her further. Eve's nail scraped against the pencil in her hand. "You're the art girl. You should know this."

"Hm," Eve hummed in response. Her throat was suddenly dry. Everything was too warm, too close. Was it getting stuffy in here? "You know what, I think I'm going to take a break for the day."

"Good. Then you can come to the game tonight," Nick said easily. He clamped a hand down on her thin shoulder. "We're up against St. John's."

"Yeah? I'll think about it," she lied with a forced smile. Nick opened his mouth to object. "I have to clean up here first."

"Right, right." He let go and stepped back toward the entrance, much to Eve's relief. Even the suggestion of tidying was to be a repellent to him. Before she could collect herself, his gaze stopped her cold. "I'll know where to find you if you don't show up."

Eve nodded, her body rigid. She watched Nick leave, his dark eyes trailing over her as he made his exit.

It was only once he was gone that Eve packed up her supplies and hurried to the safety of her dormitory instead.

It was a chilly Wednesday morning when Eve walked the long, familiar path to school. There was no promise Liam would be there today—there was no promise Liam would be at school *any* day—but that didn't deter her.

Eve couldn't get the idea of the blessing out of her head. It lingered in her thoughts, a parasite worming its way into the deepest crevice of her mind. She wished Hailey had never mentioned it to her, never suggested that there was hope for some arcane justice in this world.

Because now she did hope, and she knew it was all going to blow up in her face.

Eve found Liam lingering outside of the school's side entry door with a small burlap bag in his palm. As she got closer, Liam plucked a berry from the bag and popped it into his mouth.

"Do you plan to go in?" She asked. Liam shrugged.

"Maybe. Haven't decided," he replied between bites. Liam was as concerned with the school's warning bell as he was with the juice dripping from the corner of his mouth. "You were gone for a while."

"So were you. Find someone else to torture while I was away?"

"Alas, no one is nearly as entertaining." Liam smirked. "I take it you're not here for banter, so what is it you want? There are no chairs for you to kick out from under me here. Are you going to pour milk on me instead?"

Tempting. "No."

Liam raised an eyebrow and waited for her to continue. Eve jumped straight to the point.

"I hear that you're blessed, supposedly," she said, working to keep her tone casual. If her accusation surprised Liam, he didn't show it.

"What a wild rumor. Where did you hear it?" Liam popped a few more berries into his mouth, the juice rolling in a trickle down his chin. "Supposedly."

"Hailey told me."

"Ah." Another bite. She waited for him to continue, but Liam merely stared at her, offering neither confirmation nor contradiction. "Well?"

"*Well*, I was wondering..." She felt stupid for saying it now. For even thinking it could be true. Hailey must have been toying with her, or she was so brainwashed that she believed whatever Liam told her. Eve waited for Liam to laugh at her and prove her right.

He didn't; he kept watching with those curious amber eyes, his lips stained red from fruit.

Eve cleared her throat.

"Is it true?"

"Is what true?" Liam drawled. He placed another berry on his tongue.

Eve scoffed. Was he seriously going to make her say it aloud? The implication was embarrassing enough.

Liam stared at her.

It appeared he was.

"Are you *blessed?*" It sounded even more ridiculous hearing it aloud. Eve almost wanted to change her mind and leave all of this behind. It was so stupid, stupid, stupid—

Liam did not laugh. He didn't even smile, although one of his eyebrows rose high as he observed her reaction. Eve's expression faltered. He was serious, but was it an act or genuine? She couldn't tell.

"Do *you* think I'm blessed?" he asked. *No*, Eve thought. *Yes*, Eve hoped. She crossed her arms tightly over her chest in denial.

"I think you're a spectacular liar."

Liam grinned, finishing off the sack of berries in his hand. "You're pretty skeptical for a Catholic. I thought your whole thing was blind faith?"

She normally would have laughed, but the accusation bothered her more coming from him than it did anyone else.

"I'm not Catholic," Eve said. They were words long pent up, tied back by the rigid expectations of her family, but it was freeing to finally say it. It was small—not being part of a religion shouldn't be anything *but* small—but to her family, her community, her *church*, it was the biggest sin one could commit.

Liam watched her with a strange mixture of fascination and surprise. She could see the questions burning in his eyes, and his mouth moved to sound out several words without them ever passing through his lips.

"But you go to a Catholic school," he finally said.

"Not by choice."

"Hm." Eve could practically see him tucking that piece of information away in some internal file in his memory. She wondered how much information he kept on everyone and if it was all stored in his mind or written down somewhere later. It bothered her. How much did he think he knew about her already? How much *did* he know? She waited for him to prod her for more, but Liam stuffed the burlap bag back into his pocket and said, "What is it you want from me, Evie? You wouldn't bring up the rumor unless you wanted something."

"I don't want anything," she said too quickly. Liam cocked an eyebrow. He could see right through her, and she hated it. "You can't prove you can do what I want, even if I said it."

"Then say it. What do you want?"

Eve hesitated. *Revenge.* The word curled around her tongue, sweet enough to make her teeth ache. She didn't want it, she *needed* it. Every instinct told her to scream it to the heavens, to demand justice against the men who took everything from her.

But saying it would give into the belief that Liam *was* powerful and that there was even a chance of him magically pulling through. Her pride wouldn't allow it.

Silence stretched between them instead, and Liam's face fell.

"If I'm being honest, I don't know if I'm inclined to do anything for you." Liam licked the berry juice dribbling down his chin. "Even if you *did* tell me what it is."

She couldn't blame him, but it still stung to hear. Her one chance at justice, and he was dangling it in front of her: a carrot on a stick. *I guess that makes me the stubborn mule.*

Eve bore a new kind of exhaustion as she glared at Liam. She knew this was his way of getting her to tell him what it was she wanted. Honestly, there was no way it would even happen if she didn't. But the idea of even having to explain what she wanted, let alone *why* she wanted it, was more mortifying than asking if he had magic powers.

Which he definitely didn't.

"I don't think you *can* do anything for me," Eve said airily. Then, "But if you could, I would need to see proof."

"You want something for nothing? How human of you." Liam grinned, and she could see the stain of red on his teeth like blood. She shuddered. "I can't prove anything without an actual task, you know." He licked his juice-covered fingers. "And something in return."

"I don't have any money," Eve said honestly. All of her money came from a weekly allowance her parents sent, and it wasn't much.

To her relief—and suspicion—Liam shook his head. "I don't want money."

"Then what do you want?"

"Something you can't give me," he muttered with a dry smile. "I suppose I can make do with something else in the meantime, though…"

Liam tapped his chin in thought. Eve tried to ignore the sinking emotion that settled in her stomach. She could think of quite a few things men wanted, and several more she wasn't willing to give. But with the thoughts of her abusers actually paying for what they did... she wasn't sure what she would tell him.

"I want you to answer a question."

Eve eyed him warily. "What kind of question?"

"I haven't decided yet." That didn't bring her any comfort. Eve crossed her arms, pulling her navy-blue cardigan tighter around her body as if it could shield her. "But you must answer truthfully. It won't be a fair deal if you're lying."

Eve didn't know how to respond. He could ask any number of things—and there was a lot that Eve didn't want to tell him. A question could mean anything, but it was also incredibly small in exchange for the task she had in mind. This was obviously a farce.

She was going to call him out on it.

"Fine. I'll answer your question," she said, and Liam opened his mouth at once to speak. She held up a hand. "*If* you can prove you're capable of handling my real request."

"What is your real request?" Liam pushed. She shook her head.

"Prove to me you can handle something else first. I want you to do something magical."

Liam rolled his eyes. "Shall I play a card trick, then?"

"You know what I mean," Eve huffed, but Liam wagged his finger at her, and she was rather partial to the idea of tearing it off.

"You need to be *specific* with these things," he scolded her, similar to a parent trying to teach an insolent child a new form of manners. "I'm being generous with you because it's your first time, you know. Others won't be as kind." His eyes narrowed. "How do you want me to prove that what I say is true?"

Eve bit the inside of her cheek and thought hard. She hadn't come prepared with anything in mind. There was only a general desire to see him prove—or more likely disprove—that he had any sort of blessing. But fine, if he wanted specifics, she would give it to him.

"I want..." Eve hesitated, unsure. Then with more conviction, "I want you to steal the tabernacle during Mass."

It was an impossible task—one she was sure Liam would fail. There was no way any normal person—much less a person blessed by *God*—could get away with this, not in front of an entire church of people. The tabernacle at her church was an ornate box made of bronze that was kept locked at the back of the stage. It held the little wafers—the Eucharist—that the priest reserved for the end of Mass. It was always present, always within view.

There was no way a sermon could occur without someone noticing him taking it. If he couldn't do this much, there was no way Liam could properly find and punish her rapists. She smiled triumphantly, positive she'd found something to prove him a liar once and for all. If Liam promised to do this and failed, she could easily expose him for the fake he was.

"That'll be easy," he assured her. Eve's gaze narrowed.

"For someone 'blessed', you don't seem to have any issues stealing from a church."

"And?" He waited, but Eve bit her lip. It was suspicious, but arguing wasn't going to get her anywhere—not here, not now.

"Nothing."

"Is that your entire request, then?" There was an intensity in Liam's eyes that planted the seeds of doubt in her mind, but it was too late to back down now. She couldn't think of anything better.

"It is."

Something sparkled in Liam's eyes. "Alright. It's a deal."

His words, while light and almost playful, cemented in her mind. They carried a weight—a promise—she was afraid to see him keep. She tried not to show disappointment as she thrust her hand out toward him.

"Fine." His hand gripped hers and they shook on it. His palm was warm. Firm. Something tingled between their skin, a spark that made Eve pull her hand back at once.

Liam didn't notice, and Eve had to wonder if she signed a deal with the devil.

Ten

Eve's heart raced as she followed Nan into their usual pew near the front. She had hoped to sit near the back so she could make sure Liam was there, but Eve was reluctant to leave Nan's side. Today had been one of Nan's worse days, and Eve hoped that the rigid structure of Mass would help improve her grandmother's memory.

There was no sign of Liam as Eve took her seat, but she could make out the tabernacle on the chancel. It remained untouched and daunting.

The church was crowded, as Eve expected. Sunday sermons were always packed to the brim with families and neighbors that otherwise were too busy during the week to attend. There was no way he could get away with something as obvious as taking the tabernacle without someone spotting him.

Blessed or not, at least she had the pleasure of knowing he had to suffer through Mass.

Eve glanced around the church again, her patience thinning. Where was he? Mass was going to start any minute. If he thought he could bail out now—

"Could they make these aisles any thinner?" Liam's annoyed voice cut through the murmur of churchgoers. He slipped into the seat beside her, ignored by the family he had pushed through to get there. Eve checked her phone: 9:58. He was cutting it close.

"I thought you weren't going to show," Eve said, her gaze narrowing. He wasn't dressed for church at all; it was a small miracle unto itself that he was allowed through the front doors. She waited for someone to say something, for glares to be cast in his direction, but nothing. Not even Nan acknowledged his presence.

"And miss your lovely face first thing in the morning? I wouldn't dream of it." Eve rolled her eyes and scooted a few inches away to make room for him on the pew. "Besides, we made a deal, didn't we?"

"You must really want to ask that question," Eve muttered, suppressing a yawn. It was too early for nice clothes and preaching. She'd barely had the energy to pull on her sweater and skirt this morning before heading out the door.

"I am a terribly curious creature by nature," Liam said. "So, what is a tabernacle?"

"Seriously?" She gestured toward the front of the church. "It's that bronze box up there."

Liam raised his brow. "That's all?"

"Yes."

"Easy." Eve wanted to hit him. Instead, she turned back toward the chancel in time for the music to swell and Mass to begin.

Eve didn't pay attention to the priest's preaching on a normal Sunday morning, but today was a new level of disconnect. Father could have reenacted the entirety of Jesus' crucifixion naked, and she still wouldn't have noticed. Her focus was reserved solely for the tabernacle and where it would—or would not—go.

Liam shifted at her side, ignoring all decorum and expectation of the church. Maybe he wasn't Catholic either; it would explain a lot. Eve was kneeling again, one of many times expected in Mass, but Liam didn't move. He didn't even try to stand.

Disappointment weighed down heavily in her chest. She knew he was lying to her, but to have it confirmed was disheartening. It was as though a light had been snuffed out inside of her. She shouldn't have hoped Liam was the answer to all of her problems, but she couldn't help herself. If there was an apple dangling in front of a starving man, wouldn't he try to take it?

She stared at the tabernacle on the chancel and waited for... nothing. It was there, a box of bronze glinting underneath the poor church lighting, mocking her with its presence. She could almost hear God laughing down at her.

Then it was gone.

A loud crash followed by a soft, angry curse went ignored among the church attendees. Eve swiveled toward the sound—perhaps the only one who had heard it—and turned toward the display of candles lit for the dead, but she saw nothing. The candle display clattered slightly and a few of the flames disappeared, as if someone had stumbled into it, but the pathway was clear.

The sermon carried on—no one else had noticed.

Eve glanced back at the seat beside her: empty. When had he walked off? How hadn't she heard him? The choir was loud, but not loud enough to cover the sound of creaking pews or echoing footsteps. And yet, Liam was—impossibly—gone, and so was the tabernacle.

He'd done it. Liam was... blessed.

No, not blessed. Someone blessed by God—or whatever deity was out there—wouldn't be allowed to steal from a *church*. Liam was something else. Something darker. But Eve had no idea what and, in that moment, she didn't care.

Liam could enact justice on her rapists. She could trust him to do that much. She would have to. Her heart thundered in her chest, a mixture of anxiety and excitement.

For the first time in what was a very long time, Eve smiled. Genuinely smiled.

The sermon carried on until it was time to open the tabernacle and eat the body of Christ. Confused whispers carried across the church from the altar boys and, eventually, the priest. Father turned toward the crowd after a few moments of searching, his cheeks flushed pink with indignation.

"It would appear," he said calmly, his voice heavy with disappointment. "That our tabernacle has been misplaced. While the acolytes are tending to this matter, I will give the opportunity for anyone to come directly to me on anything they might have seen."

No one moved. Confused murmurs rose from the crowd instead, and it was only with Father's raised hands that they quieted down.

"I see." Father hung his head. "If no one is willing to come forth, then instead, I would like us all to reflect on Exodus 20:15..."

Mass ended a while later, after a long sermon on the sins of theft and deceit. As Eve escorted Nan out the giant wooden doors and back into the chilly autumn air, an elderly figure in a gaudy pink floral dress caught her eye.

Mrs. Kensinger waved as she approached, and Eve struggled not to groan. She gripped her grandmother's arm and tried to usher her away, to pretend not to see the old gossip, but the damage had been done.

"Cecylia!" Mrs. Kensinger's high-pitched trill pierced Eve's ears. Nan perked up in recognition.

"Babs," Nan said. Eve felt a spike of jealousy over Nan remembering Mrs. Kensinger's name and not hers, but knew she shouldn't. It wasn't Nan's fault. Still, it stung all the same. "How are you, dear?"

"Oh, I'm fine. What a sermon, though; I can't believe they couldn't find the tabernacle. You know this never would have happened when Father Paul was around," Mrs. Kensinger said with a laugh. "How are you, dear?

Getting along with your granddaughter alright?" She made no effort to hide that she was pretending Eve wasn't there.

Nan stared at her for a moment before a false smile clicked into place, her eyes betraying her confusion. "We're getting along fine."

"I'm sure. Dorothy was telling me over there"—Mrs. Kensinger pointed to Dorothy, a stout woman with a pretty smile and dark curls—"that her grandson came out as *gay*. Can you believe it? And she doesn't even mind! Now, I'm not sure about you, but *I* think—"

"Now, now, there's nothing wrong with that," Nan interrupted.

Eve's pride in her grandmother grew, but she remained silent at her side. Would Nan still feel the same way if she knew Eve wasn't exactly straight, either?

Mrs. Kensinger's expression faltered, but she picked herself up quickly.

"Oh, I don't know about *that*." Mrs. Kensinger's laugh was too high and jarring for Eve's ears. "But it's *who* he's involved with that will surprise you."

Eve tried to tune the older women out as Mrs. Kensinger broke into another story, but it was hard to ignore the unnerving smile the old woman gave her. She knew Mrs. Kensinger was wondering the same thing she did about every newcomer in town: what was Eve's story? What was wrong with her, and who could she tell about it? Eve could tell she was being dissected by Mrs. Kensinger's wide, watchful eyes. She was a frog under a scalpel, ready to be torn open so Mrs. Kensinger could see every little thing that was wrong, wrong, *wrong* with her.

Eve looked away and pretended to be interested in the gloomy weather. Anything to avoid Mrs. Kensinger's quizzical eyes.

She caught a glimpse of Liam lingering in the cemetery, his long bony fingers *tap-tap-tapping* away on one of the headstones. He watched her, waiting.

"I'll be right back," Eve said. Nan didn't acknowledge her, but Mrs. Kensinger smiled and waved Eve away, as if her staying any longer was an intrusion. Whatever Eve was hiding, the old woman would not discover it today, and so her interest was gone. Eve was determined to drag her grandmother as far away from the old woman as she could as soon as she got back.

Eve followed Liam through the cemetery—it was surprisingly large, considering the small church attached to it—until they were out of sight from the nosy townsfolk. Liam produced the bronze box from inside of a tree stump; it was larger up close.

"This belongs to you," Liam tossed the tabernacle at her. Eve stumbled to catch it, cursing under her breath when one of the sharp spires sliced her thumb. It was heavier than she imagined and even more awkward to hold.

"You couldn't have set it down?" Eve hissed, sucking on her thumb.

"I thought you had better aim." Liam scrutinized her, his golden eyes alight with greed. "Now, my question."

Eve's heart sank. That's right—he did get to ask her something, and she had to respond truthfully. In her brief moment of elation, she'd nearly forgotten about her end of her bargain.

"What do you want to know?" Eve asked, still struggling to hold the tabernacle. She opted to set it on the ground instead; it wasn't as if she needed the thing. She merely wanted to see if he could do it.

"Did I do something to warrant your hatred?"

Eve crossed her arms over her chest. "Do you need a list?"

"You said you would answer honestly," Liam reminded her. Eve sighed.

"I don't hate you," she grumbled. Telling him as much was closer to pulling teeth. "But you piss me off."

"What about me?"

"Your face. Your attitude. Your..." She gestured vaguely at him. "You."

Liam had the nerve to *grin*. "Go on."

"You never face any consequences," Eve huffed. "*That* pisses me off the most. So no, I don't hate you—I just want to punt you into a lake sometimes. Satisfied?"

"Hardly," Liam said. He stretched his limbs out long and wide, somehow appearing even more nimble and annoyingly pretty. "Since I've passed your little test, what is it you *really* want?"

Eve swallowed hard. This was it.

"I want you to find some men for me."

Liam blinked, surprise flitting across his face before he laughed outright. His smile was amused but cruel. Eve could already see the way Liam would make fun of her to Sage and Hailey behind her back. "That's it? You want a boyfriend?"

Eve shook her head in disgust. "No. I want—There are three of them—"

"Hot."

Her eye twitched. Liam was insufferable. How was she supposed to work with someone that didn't take her seriously? She was ready to call the whole thing off.

Eve clenched and unclenched her fists at her sides. No. She'd come too far, suffered too much, to change her mind now. This was her only chance for revenge, for justice. She needed it more than she needed air.

"I want you to make them *disappear*," she said slowly, hoping he picked up on her intent. This whole conversation moved sideways and nothing she said was coming across how she wanted it to. "I never want to see them again. I want them gone, permanently."

If she wasn't going to hell already, this deal certainly sealed her fate. You didn't send out a hit on somebody without making peace with the devil.

She could hear her heartbeat in her ears in the silence that followed. Liam's expression fell, suddenly serious.

"You want them gone?" he asked in disbelief.

"Gone."

"What are their names?"

Speaking them aloud was almost a curse, an ill omen. But there was a job to do. "Colton Davis, Logan Richards, and Nick Palenti."

Liam nodded, his expression unreadable. If he was disturbed by her request, he didn't show it. Eve couldn't tell if that was a good sign or not. "Does this have anything to do with the man that showed up at Hailey's door?"

Eve's chest tightened. "I already answered your question."

A tense silence sat between them before Liam finally gave in. "Alright. I'll remove them."

"They don't all live here," Eve warned. She had searched their names online during her depressive episode. The closest one was Nick, who lived a town over. Colton had moved to Massachusetts but visited Logan in her hometown frequently. "You'll have to—"

"Distance doesn't matter," Liam cut her off. "I'll have it done."

Eve waited for the elation to come, the relief, but it was dulled by his terse response. He wasn't happy about it, but could she blame him? She was asking him to murder three men. That was hardly something for Liam to cheer about.

And yet, as his confirmation settled in, Eve's body relaxed. It was as if a weight had been lifted free from her shoulders, the burden of sharing the same air as her rapists suddenly lighter. She felt taller. Freer. There was hope—*real* hope—that Eve might live past seventeen after all.

But only if he could make it happen.

"Perfect," she breathed. Her hands shook. She was so close to justice she could almost taste it. Was it wrong to dream of their deaths if they had killed her already?

Eve drew her attention back to the church. It was barely visible between the trees and headstones, but she could make out the large white cross sticking up from the highest point of the building. It assured anyone passing by that this was a holy place.

Was. Until Eve stole the tabernacle and requested murder in its backyard. She grimly wondered what Nan and Hailey would think of that.

"Aren't you going to ask me what I want in return?"

Eve froze. Of course—a deal required two sides. Liam leaned against one of the trees, one red brow raised and his arms crossed.

"What do you want?" she asked cautiously. Eve was on a thin tightrope, too close to teetering off the edge.

She didn't know Liam well enough to guess what would come out of his mouth. His question had been a small price to pay for a ten-thousand-dollar tabernacle, but it was not something she expected from him. He didn't have a good sense of value, which could work in her favor.

Stealing was different from killing, though. It was hard not to see the weight in that.

Liam observed her with one hand pressed over his mouth in thought, but Eve could see in his eyes that he had already decided what he wanted. It was hard to breathe.

He pushed off from the tree and walked toward her, stopping only a few paces away. Eve was used to keeping her distance, so it was easy to forget how much taller he was, his body closer to a willowy tree than human. He had to bend down to face her properly. Eve squared her shoulders and tried to ignore the anxious beat of her heart and the shake of her knees.

"I want your name."

Eve blinked. "What?"

"Your name—your True Name, the full thing. I want it." Liam pressed a hand against his hip and waited.

Eve contemplated if he was dropped on his head as a child. Surely he couldn't want her name, right? What could he even do with it? It wasn't as if he was asking for a social security card or credit card number.

"Um, Eve Carter?" Even she sounded uncertain saying it. "Or, uh, Evelyn Marie Carter, I guess."

Liam regarded her suspiciously. "You *guess?*"

"That's my name," Eve said, annoyed. "I can show you my birth certificate if you don't believe me."

Liam briefly considered it but shook his head, tossing the idea aside. "No, that'll be fine. *Evelyn Marie Carter.*"

The way he said her name sent a strange shock through her body. At the same time, her body grew rigid and a sudden pull tugged at her, forcing her to pay attention. It was as though a string had attached itself to her brain, and wherever it went, so would she. Eve didn't know what to make of it.

Liam nodded to himself, satisfied. "Good. That's all I needed."

Her focus on him wavered. Eve hadn't realized she'd been holding her breath until her chest grew tight and painful and she released it all in one shaky exhale. Eve turned away, hating herself for her reaction. It brought on phantom memories that made her want to puke. She hoped Liam didn't notice, but the quirk of his lips told her otherwise.

Liam flashed her a devilish smile as they both turned to leave. "I'll see you at school, Evie."

She hated the smug grin on his face, as if he was the real winner here instead of her. Idiot. If he wanted to think her name was a fair trade for death, then so be it. This was the easiest trade she'd ever made in her life.

If he could pull it off.

She paused, calling over her shoulder, "Have you ever killed anyone before?"

Liam's steps slowed. "Yes."

A chill ran down her spine. But this was what she wanted.

"Alright."

Eve turned to leave but stopped when she saw the tabernacle resting on the ground. An adventurous spider was quickly making it its home. She brushed the arachnid off and picked up the bronze box. Damn, this thing was a pain in the ass to hold.

She could feel the weight of someone—Liam? God?—watching her struggle to carry it out of the forest, but they offered no help or insight on how to transport this thing. What was she even going to do with it? She didn't have the key, so it's not like she could clean out the wine and wafers to sell it. Eve was pretty sure there were some serious moral implications involved in that, anyway.

Maybe she should leave it in the forest and let the bugs and birds and whatever other wildlife lived out there have their way with it. There was no reason for the church to have a ten-thousand-dollar box anyway, not when they still had the audacity to collect tithe each week. The idea of returning it bothered her even more than selling it.

Eve left the tabernacle in the woods and returned for it later with the help of a rusty old wagon left in Nan's basement. She shoved it in a corner of her closet, and pretended it had never existed in the first place.

Eleven

The days passed slowly. Each task was as productive as swimming through cement, and time made every conceivable attempt to keep her there, trapped in an insufferable state of purgatory.

Eve tapped her pencil against the cover of her notebook, the sound and movement bringing her comfort. She knew she had to be patient, but how could she when Liam was committing murder on her behalf? She wished she had insisted on getting updates. Was she supposed to trust him to get the job done?

Yes. But that didn't make it any easier.

"You trying to drill a hole?" Hailey teased from the desk beside her. Since they'd started hanging out, Hailey and Sage made an effort to sit beside Eve in every class they had together.

Eve paused her tapping, but the jitters only moved to her feet instead, and her right shoe *clack-clack-clacked* against the hard limestone floor. Neither of them knew about the deal she made with Liam. She wasn't sure how either of them could stand to be around her if they *did* know. When Hailey suggested Eve seek help from Liam, she doubted that murdering ex-rapists was on the bubbly girl's mind.

"If I am, it isn't working," Eve joked back, trying to lighten her own mood. She had to stop thinking about it. What if Liam did succeed and someone correlated the murders back to her weird behavior?

Now she was being paranoid. She had been careful to search Colton's and Logan's profiles up on a private browser, and her only recent connection to Nick was when he delivered food. He hadn't even recognized her. What connection could they make? That they attended the same school? The church had done a good enough job covering up everything the boys had done to her that Eve doubted anyone would find much there. Even if they did, it would require members of her school and religious community to acknowledge what happened to her in the first place.

"You've been tense lately," Sage noted from Hailey's other side, her cheek pressed against her folded arms on the desk. She was ready to take a nap. "Is something going on?"

Eve's mouth went dry. She shook her head, immediately turning her attention to the group project sheet on Hailey's desk. It was nearly filled out, no thanks to Eve. "How were you able to work through that already?"

Hailey frowned at the sheet. "Mostly guessing."

"That sounds about right," Sage said with a snort. Dangerously close to falling asleep, Sage sat up and stretched. Their teacher, Mr. Hollis, made rounds through the room, peering at each group's progress before resuming his spot at his desk, a pile of homework still requiring grading at his side.

Eve turned her attention toward the rain-streaked window, the overcast sky creating a gloomy atmosphere in the science room. While Hailey had complained earlier about the weather, Eve found it soothing. Sure, the sky was gloomy, but Eve enjoyed the steady patter of rain against glass and the soft shaded clouds that reminded her of a warm blanket. It felt safe.

The bell rang, dismissing the class.

Eve stood and gathered her things. Hailey and Sage paused, their attention caught on something behind her. "What?"

"Eve, you got a minute?" Eric's familiar voice startled her. Eve whirled around, clutching her books to her chest. Eric smiled bashfully. "Sorry, didn't mean to scare you."

"You didn't," Eve replied, working to calm herself down. With a glance over her shoulder, she could see Hailey and Sage were still lingering in the room, although they'd moved away to give her some privacy. "What's up?"

"I was wondering if you were going to the dance on Saturday." Eve stared at him. "Homecoming?"

"Oh. Right." Eve shifted uncomfortably, her knuckles white from gripping her textbook. She vaguely remembered him mentioning it three weeks ago, and it was impossible to miss the bright posters that hung around the halls: *Get your tickets by September 24th!*

"No one asked you yet?" Although he said it sadly, maybe even with a little surprise, she could hear the hope clawing its way through.

No. But that didn't mean she wanted to go. In fact, she had done everything in her power to avoid going.

"No, but—" Eve started. Eric cut in.

"Then how about we go together?" he suggested. His smile carried more confidence now, but she could see it ticking away with each passing moment of silence on her part. "We could, you know, go grab dinner and then hit the dance."

Her throat was tight. She wanted to puke. Even the idea of going to another school dance sent chills down her spine, with or without an escort.

"I'm busy that night," she said, as polite of a rejection as she could think of. It wasn't a lie, anyway; Hailey had invited Eve and Sage to her house for a sleepover as a sort of rebellion against school dances. Eve was surprised Hailey suggested it, but she was more than happy to jump into any excuse to avoid homecoming.

"What are you doing?" Eric tried to phrase his question casually, but it was clear he was disappointed. "Is it something that can wait for another day?"

Eve shook her head. "Sorry. I already made plans with someone else."

"Oh." Eric looked down at his feet. This wasn't what he had expected, but Eve couldn't pity him. She barely knew the guy. "That's fine. Have fun, anyway."

Eric rushed out of the room, disappearing into the hallway without another word. Eve stood still for a moment, trying to process what had happened.

"Someone has an admirer," Sage said with a teasing smirk. Eve grimaced.

"An unwanted one," she said.

"Poor guy," Hailey sighed. Then, with more sincerity, she added, "If you did want to go to homecoming with him though, that's okay, Eve. You don't need to use the sleepover as an excuse."

"I don't want to go to homecoming with anyone, trust me," Eve said firmly. "I hate school dances. You couldn't pay me a million dollars to go to one."

"Amen to that," Hailey agreed. Eve was surprised; she thought Hailey was the kind of person that would love homecoming. Hearing her talk poorly about it threw her off.

"Why don't you want to go?" she asked.

"They're boring," Hailey said. Sage nodded in agreement beside her. "I can't relax and have fun when I have a bunch of adults staring at me and judging me for what I'm wearing, who I'm with, and how I'm moving my body."

"That's fair," Eve said absently. She hadn't considered that. Her only experience with one had been traumatizing, and even then, she had barely been exposed to the dance itself before she was dragged off. She had no idea what they were like for a normal teenage girl.

"You should go to one of Sage's parties sometime instead," Hailey said with an eager grin. "She and Liam throw the best parties. It's way better than homecoming."

Sage shot Hailey a look but shrugged. "They're alright."

"They're better than *alright*. You have *live music* there! Who else does that?"

"I don't know if I'm a party person," Eve said quietly, more to herself than to either girl. The idea of maneuvering through an unsupervised house of sweaty, drunk teenagers and loud music put her on edge. It was too easy for something to go too far, for people not to notice where she was or what was happening to her.

"It'll be fun," Hailey promised. "Trust me, Sage's parties are totally different from anything you've been to."

Eve wasn't sure what to think of that, but she didn't have the energy to argue.

By the time she dragged herself into Nan's house, Eve was completely drained. She barely had enough energy to kick her shoes off and toss her backpack on the coat hanger.

Nan sat in her usual chair in the living room, her eyes flitting to Eve in polite confusion while she put together a puzzle on the small table beside her.

"Hello," Nan said with slight uncertainty, and Eve sunk onto the couch. Her uniform was stiff and uncomfortable, but she was too exhausted to bother changing out of it. If she put her pajamas on now, she would go to sleep.

"Hi, Nan." Eve didn't have the energy to explain who she was today. Maybe that made her a bad granddaughter, but she didn't have the energy to care about that, either. All the anxiety that had built up inside of her chest throughout the morning finally caught up to her, leaving Eve in a lethargic state.

An old Western played out on the TV screen, occasionally interrupted by advertisements for joint pain medicine and other movies that would be shown throughout the week. They watched the film quietly, the chatter of the TV and the washing machine running in the basement, the only sounds that interrupted them. This was often how their evenings went: reruns, dinner, bed. Sometimes if the internet was working, Eve would spend some time watching videos online in her room, but her connection was usually too poor to stay on for long.

Glamorous actors and actresses moved across the television screen, lost in the old theatrics of their scripts. When she was little, Eve dreamed of being one of them—a dolled up icon with a transatlantic accent and pinched red lips. But those kinds of celebrities were a thing of the past. Her parents never approved of such a dream anyway, and the idea was tossed into a hopeless pile of whims to be forgotten.

"I used to have a magazine of him under my bed as a girl," Nan said suddenly, breaking their silence. Nan pointed to the youthful man on the screen, his light hair slicked back under his cowboy hat.

Eve's eyebrows shot up. "You had a crush on James Dean?"

"*Everyone* had a crush on James Dean," Nan corrected her. "Except for my mother. Oh, you should have heard her when she found that magazine. 'Cecylia, we do not ogle young men in private like some harlot!'" Nan pitched her voice higher, imitating who Eve could only guess was her great-grandmother; the woman had died long before she came around. Eve choked out a laugh. "I remember crying the day he died. My friend Suzie and I had our own little vigil." Nan chuckled at the memory and shook her head.

"I didn't know you were interested in that stuff." *Interested in bad boys like James Dean,* Eve wanted to say.

"Of course I did. Everyone is young once," Nan sighed. The scene changed and Nan's attention drifted. Eve took that as a sign their conversation was over.

Nan smiled dreamily at the television, and for a moment, Eve could see the youth her grandmother used to be. Behind the wrinkles and thin white hair was a girlish smile and starstruck eyes, blinded by her old crush. Eve could almost imagine Nan in her youth, her gaze wistful as she admired the handsome celebrities that appeared on the screen.

This was a side of her grandmother she had never seen before. Her father always talked about how strict Nan was growing up, but now Eve wondered how much of that was true. Eve couldn't imagine raising Ben, stubborn and hot headed as he was. Where did the Nan go who snuck magazines of cute boys under her mattress and held vigils for celebrities she never met? How could someone like that bring her father into the world?

Eve shook her head, shoving the thought far into the back of her mind. She didn't want to think of the role Nan had in forming the abusive man her father had become, not when the elderly woman was suffering from her own memory loss. Besides, it could have as easily been her grandfather's fault. But Papa Joseph was long dead, and any answers he carried with him were buried six feet under.

Nan didn't interrupt the film to ask about school, and even after the movie ended and Nan switched over to the news, the topic never came up. Eve was grateful for that. Maybe she was taking advantage of the situation, but Eve was happy to ignore the subject as long as she could.

Instead, Eve rummaged through the fridge and tried to think of something to prepare for dinner while Nan watched the TV. It was a miracle her grandmother even ate before Eve arrived. Nan was content to sit in one spot for the rest of her life, viewing the world through the screen of her television set.

Eve frowned at the empty shelves before settling on some pasta and tomato sauce. She would need to go grocery shopping again soon, unless she could ask Mr. Stone to pick up some things for her on his next trip. She hated bothering him, but without a car, it was practically impossible to do a full shopping trip and haul all those bags back to Nan's house by herself.

With a sigh, Eve left a reminder on the fridge to make a list and ask Mr. Stone tomorrow. She could get by on some deli sandwiches and leftover pasta until then.

Eve returned to the living room twenty minutes later with two hot bowls of pasta and some bread. Nan thanked her but didn't make much of an effort to touch her food. Eve stared at her grandmother's thin figure with a troubled frown. Had she lost more weight? Eve made a mental note to look up calorie-heavy meals to prepare. Even if Nan wouldn't eat much, Eve wanted to be sure she was getting something to sustain her.

The news chattered on with the occasional input from Nan, who would mutter her disagreements with certain politicians. Granted, the poor woman thought Reagan was still president.

Fed up with the reports, Eve reached for the remote. There had to be something better on than this.

Before she could change the channel, the picture of an all too familiar face appeared on the screen, stopping her cold. The remote slipped from her hand and thumped onto the carpet.

A well-groomed reporter frowned through the television screen as a grinning picture of Nick appeared beside him. "A search is underway for a local resident that went missing yesterday afternoon."

Twelve

Nick Palenti was dead.

Relief collided with anxiety for the rest of the evening. All night Eve found herself glancing down the stairs at the front door, expecting the police to barge in and carry her off for questioning. She laid in bed, half drunk with relief and half torn with guilt as she stared at the shadows on her ceiling, waiting for the flash of blue and red sirens.

No one came. Eve got ready for school in the morning, still partially convinced that the cop car passing by would pull over and haul her off to jail. She made it to St. Peter's without incident. She walked to her locker without a glance in her direction. It was just another day.

No, not just another day. Nick was dead, but Eve was *alive*.

An overwhelming sense of relief welled up inside of her as Eve proceeded through her classes. Never again would she fear Nick showing up at her doorstep. Or feel his hands on her throat. Or stay up at night wondering if he'd come back one day to finish the job.

For the first time since that horrible night, Eve was free.

"You're happy this morning." Eve was surprised to hear Liam whispering to her from behind. Eve didn't dare glance back—Sister Heidi's eyes were that of a hawk's—but she nodded.

"Why wouldn't I be?" Eve hoped he could hear her; she barely moved her lips in case Sister Heidi peered in her direction. "I saw what you did on the news."

"And here I came all this way to tell you. I should have stayed home," Liam mused. "You are a strange girl, you know. Not many humans would be this excited to hear about a missing person."

"So, you're not human." He had implied as much before, but there was a layer of truth to it now. She felt a rush of satisfaction in knowing she was right. "What are you, then?"

"Do you want to guess?" he offered. There was a playful hint to his voice as he placed his chair beside her, his golden eyes twinkling with mischief. Eve got the sense that Sister Heidi was somehow being influenced to divert her attention away from him—or she couldn't see him at all.

Eve bit her lip. She did want to know—she had been mulling it over in the back of her head for some time now—and if Liam was willing to tell her, it couldn't hurt.

"I can try," she said. "At first I thought you might be a vampire, but I don't know of any vampires that grant wishes or go out in the sun."

"I couldn't possibly give up garlic," he said, then shook his head. "No fangs, either."

Eve tapped her chin. "A djinn, maybe?"

"No."

"Werewolf?"

Liam had the gall to be offended. "Certainly not."

"Alien."

"I don't even know what that is."

Eve thought hard. She wasn't exposed to many mythical creatures growing up—such thoughts would send her to hell, supposedly, but it was too late for that—so she wasn't aware of most supernatural beings. If that's even what Liam was.

Sister Heidi said something that Eve didn't catch, resulting in several different answers from her classmates. She did not participate.

"You're definitely not an angel," Eve concluded dryly. Liam pressed a hand to his chest in mock offense.

"You wound me, Evie. Some people consider me nothing but angelic."

Eve scoffed under her breath. *Demonic is more like it.* But since he didn't burst into flames in church, Eve doubted that mythological creature suited him, either.

"Supposedly you have magic," she said slowly. "Or you're tricking people."

Liam was quiet for a moment. Eve thought he decided to give up on talking to her entirely, but when she glanced in his direction, she saw that Liam was deep in thought. He rested his chin on his folded hands, elbows propped up on his knees, and stared ahead.

"Can't it be both?"

Liam's suggestion surprised her. She searched his face long and hard, trying to decipher the lie. Liam looked back at her, head cocked, expression unreadable.

"I don't know," Eve decided. She turned her attention back to Sister Heidi and feigned interest. She could sense Liam's eyes on her, but she did not give him the satisfaction of peeking in his direction. She tried to think of another creature that fit with his new clue when Sister Heidi slapped a long pointer stick against her desk, gathering the class's attention. She glared back at Eve.

"Attention up *here*, Miss Carter."

"Sorry, Sister."

Eve folded her hands on the desk, but when she turned to Liam for another guess, he was gone.

Thirteen

Hailey pursed her lips and stared at the small collection of paper faces still standing upright in her *Guess Who* tray. "Would your person ask to see the manager?"

Eve considered, analyzing the bald man on her card. "Probably not."

Hailey flipped down a few more faces on her board. It wasn't technically how they were supposed to play, but there were only so many times she could ask if Hailey's card was a redhead or had facial hair.

Sage watched them play back and forth from atop Hailey's bed, uninterested in participating herself. After playing a few rounds against her, Eve had quickly come to realize that Sage was terrible at board games. Not just this one, but *every* board game they'd played together. Their sleepover had only lasted a couple of hours so far, but Sage managed to lose everything from *Clue* to *Sorry* to *Guess Who* in a matter of minutes.

"Is your person recently divorced?" Eve asked. Hailey barely held back a laugh.

"Definitely."

Eve smacked down the rest of her characters. "It's Robert."

Hailey groaned, tossing her card face up to Eve: Robert's face stared back at her. "Too easy. He's one of the only ones that's miserable."

"Some people are happy when they get divorced," Eve countered. "Robert got the losing side."

"Maybe he ended up with the kids," Hailey said. Eve snorted. Hailey lifted the tray upside-down, setting it up for a new game. Eve helped, glad to have ditched homecoming for this.

A soft knock at the door interrupted their conversation. Hailey's mother opened it wide with a disapproving frown on her face. Catherine Boyle was almost a glimpse into her daughter's future: short brown hair, styled at her shoulders, an athletic figure, and Hailey's eyes marked with early crow's feet.

That was where the resemblance stopped. Catherine was constantly hovering nearby, eyeing Eve and Sage as if they were intruders in her home. Paranoia crept in under Catherine's watchful gaze. Eve quickly learned that she couldn't even go to the bathroom without noticing Catherine's glare from down the hall.

"Door *open*, Hailey," Catherine reminded her. Eve didn't miss the accusatory look she gave Sage and then Eve, as if they had been responsible for the closed door in the first place. Eve didn't understand the rule, but there was a lot she didn't understand about Catherine's behavior.

Hailey sighed dramatically. "*Yes*, Mom."

Catherine didn't rise to her bait. "Dinner will be ready soon. Come eat at the table with us, alright?"

"Okay," Hailey promised, although she wasn't pleased by the fact. Catherine nodded once and left. Hailey followed quietly after her, peering out into the hall to make sure she was gone before settling back down on the carpet floor. "She's been so weird lately. She never had a problem with me keeping my door closed before."

"Weird. When did it start?" Eve asked idly as she helped Hailey clean up their game. Hailey wasn't interested in playing anymore.

"This summer," Sage answered for her. She played with the black silk of her pajamas in irritation.

"Did something happen?" Sage didn't answer, but Hailey shrugged, at a loss.

"Not that I can think of," Hailey said. "She just started getting weird when I had friends over. Door open, dinner with the family, a bunch of other stupid stuff. It's like she thinks we're going to throw a satanic ritual when she's not around."

Sage smirked. "It would finally give her a reason to be worried."

"We're not sacrificing anything, Sage."

"At least consider it."

Hailey scowled and tossed a balled-up sock at Sage's head. It bounced off her shoulder, rolling under the sticker-covered nightstand.

A few minutes later, Catherine appeared back in the doorway. Before she could open her mouth, Hailey was on her feet. "We're *coming*."

Eve was used to awkward family dinners, but the tension at the table was palpable. Eve kept her mouth shut, afraid that if she tried to speak up, she would choke. She spared a glance at Sage, who ate her meal in unconcerned silence. If she was as uncomfortable as Eve, she didn't show it.

Dr. Frederick Boyle was tall, with a square-cut jaw and a desensitized gaze that had become accustomed to the horrors of surgery. Eve watched the way he feigned smiles and engaged in small banter with his wife and daughter, working hard to disguise the emotional drain his career left on him.

"So, Hay-Day, how are those college applications going?" Fred asked with a scoop of his spoon into his mashed potatoes. He brought it up to his mouth but didn't eat it, waiting for her answer.

Hailey grimaced. "They're okay."

"Where have you applied so far?" Catherine pushed. "You're still looking at nursing school, right?" The *you'd better be* was heavily implied.

Hailey pushed the food around on her plate. "I haven't put in applications *yet*. I'm still deciding on what schools I want to go to."

"I thought we planned all that out during the summer," Fred said. "There was Villanova, Mount Saint Joseph, Duquesne as a backup—"

"I haven't decided yet." Hailey bit down on her lip hard, trying to rein in her irritation. Eve understood the feeling well, but the sight was new to her; she'd never seen Hailey *upset*.

Nan had avoided the topic of college, but Eve still received plenty of calls from her mother asking what she planned to do. It was kind of hard to decide on a future you didn't think was going to exist in the first place.

Plus, there are application fees, Eve thought, remembering the numbers she came across when her mother had pressured her to research universities. They were certainly prices the Boyles could handle, but to Eve, even one application wasn't worth it.

Catherine and Fred shared a look, the kind Eve was most familiar with.

"You need to get on that," Fred said, and while his voice was light, Eve could detect his worry. "You'll run out of time before you know it. October is right around the corner."

"I know."

"You need to get your grades up, too," Catherine scolded.

"I *know*." Hailey stabbed her fork violently into a piece of broccoli and chewed hard.

"Oh, 'you know', do you? Then tell me why your applications aren't in yet." Hailey glanced away. "Perhaps if you spent less time goofing off and focused more on your studies, you wouldn't hear us talk about it."

Hailey didn't respond. Fred placed a hand over his wife's and gave it a squeeze, offering an apologetic smile to their guests. "Maybe now isn't the best time for this conversation."

Eve offered a thin-lipped smile in return. She wasn't hungry, but she put her fork to her mouth and went through the motions, too anxious to pay attention to the flavor.

She hoped Fred's interference would put an end to the awkward conversation, but Catherine wasn't having it. "We agreed to talk about it this weekend."

"The weekend isn't over."

"Can we talk about this *later*?" Hailey asked, refusing to take her eyes off her dinner plate. Eve recognized the subtle movement, the way she shielded the rising blush on her neck and face with her hair.

Catherine opened her mouth to speak, but Fred squeezed her hand again.

"We want what's best for you, Hay-Day," Fred said gently, but there was an undertone to it, a warning.

"You know I'm going to apply for sports scholarships," Hailey insisted. "Okay, my grades aren't great, but you know I'm one of the best on the team. It's not that big a deal."

"It is if you want to get into a good school," Catherine said, her temper rising. "Why don't you invite some more of those smart boys in your class around? I hear Mrs. Cable's son got into Harvard—"

Eve listened to their little spat in uncomfortable silence, at a loss for what to say. The scene was too familiar, as if Eve were the one being scolded instead.

She glanced at Sage, who was glaring at Catherine and Fred with nothing short of hatred. It was bold—bolder than Eve was.

"There's no guarantee you'll get one of those scholarships," Fred was saying gently. Eve had missed part of their conversation.

"Exactly," Catherine agreed. "They're going to be giving those out to the *real* athletes, so it's important to have a backup plan."

"She *is* a real athlete," Sage snapped at the same time Hailey said, "I *am* a real athlete." Hailey's gaze narrowed at her mother, whose face and neck were red with anger. Fred coughed uncomfortably into a napkin.

"Well," he said, "To be fair Hailey, it's an all-*girls* team—"

"What does that have to do with it?" Hailey pushed. From her seat, Eve could see Sage squeezing Hailey's hand under the table.

"Nothing, we—" Fred started, but Catherine interrupted, smacking her hands down on the table.

"Do what you want, Hailey," she snapped. "Don't let us stop you. When have our opinions ever mattered, anyway?" Catherine grabbed her plate and carried it to the kitchen. A series of loud clanks and splashing water followed.

Hailey pulled her hand away from Sage's and pushed her plate toward the center of the table. Her face was beet-red, reaching up to the tips of her ears.

"I need to go to the bathroom." She didn't wait to be excused, tossing her napkin down on her plate before walking briskly up the stairs.

Fred stared at the half-full plates and bowls of lukewarm food on the table. Shaking his head, he collected the dishes and walked into the kitchen without a word.

When it was clear he wasn't coming back, Sage stood and gestured for Eve to follow her upstairs.

"Do they always fight over dinner?" Eve whispered once they were back in the relative safety of Hailey's room. Everything about Sage's posture was tense. No matter how much she tried to position herself comfortably on Hailey's green beanbag, there was no getting rid of the harsh scowl on her face.

"Every time I'm here." Sage glared at a family photo on Hailey's dresser: Hailey, her parents, and a boy that must be her older brother. They all shared the same dark brown hair and pearly smiles.

"What happened?" Eve wondered.

"They don't want Hailey to have girl friends," Sage explained bitterly. "Or *girl*friends."

"I didn't know you two were dating." Although Eve had heavily suspected it. Sage didn't practice the art of subtly around Hailey.

Sage's lips curled into a sneer, but there was something sad about the way she admired Hailey's printed selfies around the room. Eve's heart cracked a little when Sage said, "We're not."

The door swung open. Sage shut up, keeping her arms crossed over her chest while she pretended to be interested in the sunset-colored nail polish bottles scattered on the floor.

Hailey slammed the door shut behind her and clicked the lock in place.

She plopped on the floor and said, "If they have a problem with it, they can remove the door themselves."

Fourteen

October crept in with the slow turn of amber leaves and a quiet rustling like whispers carried in the brisk autumn breeze. Eve watched the steady rise of jack-o'-lanterns on front porches arrive with indifference, her anticipation quelled by her own budding impatience.

Any anxiety she'd suffered over someone potentially discovering her connection to Nick eased as the days passed, and Eve was eager for Liam to make his next move. Nick may be gone, but there were still two more on her list. Eve tried to remind herself that these things took time. Liam not showing up to school was a *good* sign.

That still didn't make her any less anxious for some news.

Eve bit down on the soft wood of her pencil, distracted. She had spent the past couple of weeks trying to figure out what he was, because *blessed* was far from the truth. But each answer she came up with didn't sit right with her.

Did it matter what he was if he was upholding his end of the deal?

She set her pencil down and turned to Hailey and Sage instead, welcoming the easy diversion. The girls were huddled over Hailey's desk, completely ignoring the science movie playing on the ancient projector behind them. Most of the class were in similar situations, talking among themselves while the documentary droned on. Their teacher was fast asleep at his desk, the occasional snore slipping out and overpowering the volume of the film.

"Just because he asked doesn't mean you have to say yes," Sage snapped, her voice barely above a whisper. Wait, what were they talking about? Eve tuned back into the conversation.

Hailey wasn't paying attention to the frustration on Sage's face; she was staring ahead, pretending to care about the documentary. "I know."

"Sorry, what are we talking about?" Eve whispered. She instantly regretted interrupting now that she realized how tense the atmosphere was. Maybe she should have pretended to focus on something else.

"Eric asked me out," Hailey said absently. She glanced toward Eve shyly. "I know you turned him down, but I didn't want to say anything, just in case."

"No, no. That's fine," Eve reassured her, stunned. She was relieved to have Eric off her back; he hadn't spoken to her since she turned him down *again*, but a small part of her had feared that he would try to pressure her into a date if she didn't keep her guard up.

Sage obviously disagreed. She stared at Hailey in a mixture of irritation and disbelief. "But you don't even *like* him."

Hailey shrugged. She still wouldn't meet Sage's gaze. "I never thought about it."

"You're going to consider it now because he asked?" Sage's words were filled with venom. "If you had any interest in him, you would have said something before he put the idea in your head."

"You don't know that." Hailey was irritated, an emotion that Eve rarely heard from her. It was a jarring contrast to Hailey's usual bubbly personality.

"I know a lot more than you think."

Eve wondered if she should step in, but she had no idea what to say. She didn't know what happened between Sage and Hailey before she moved here. Or if anything happened at all. But the history was there, hinted at with longing glances and offhand comments, and Eve was an outsider.

"Why are you upset about it? I thought you would be happy for me," Hailey said, hurt. "I haven't had a boyfriend in over a year."

"What about this would make me *happy* for you?"

Hailey flinched, finally turning to Sage with her wide, puppy dog eyes. Sage pulled back, instant regret flickering on her face.

They lapsed into silence, Hailey pretending to watch the documentary while Sage picked at a sticker on the side of the desk. After a few minutes, Hailey stood up and walked off.

"Where are you going?" Sage asked, softer now.

"Bathroom," Hailey said. She didn't turn back as she stepped out of the room, shutting the door quietly behind her.

Sage stared after her, lips pulled into a tight frown. She sighed and ripped a piece of the sticker off the desk.

"Should we go after her?" Eve suggested.

"No. She wants to be alone." Sage ripped another piece off. "She hates when I follow after her. Hypocrite."

Eve bit down on her lip. There was a lot she wanted to ask, but how much of this information was she entitled to? Were they close enough that she could ask what happened, or would that be overstepping her boundaries?

"Does Hailey know that you like her?" Eve asked timidly. Sage's fingers halted on the sticker, leaving an eyeball ripped in half over a yellow smiley-face. Eve's heart hammered in her chest as the silence stretched between them.

"She's supposed to," Sage finally said. She tore the eye clean off. "She did before."

"What do you mean?"

Sage glared at the black and yellow sticker; all that was left was a hollow smile, its eyes plucked and torn into tiny scraps on the desktop.

"I'm going to check on Hailey," Sage said. The chair shrieked loudly against the tile floor as she stood up, startling their teacher awake. Sage didn't bother explaining to him where she was going as she left the room.

Fifteen

The announcement that Logan Richards was a missing person came a few days later with Liam sitting on the ledge of her bedroom window at 6:43 a.m. The early morning mist rolled in behind him, highlighted by the sunrise.

"Two down," he said as Eve stood stock-still in the doorway. She was still in the process of buttoning the bottom of her collared shirt. "The last one isn't convenient to get to, but I'll manage."

"Jesus *Christ*," she cursed, slamming the door shut behind her. "What the hell are you doing here? How did you know where I *live?*"

"It's a small town." That didn't explain how he had managed to climb to her second-story bedroom; there weren't any rails to grab onto or trees to climb. The wall was perfectly flat.

"That doesn't explain why you're in my *room*," she hissed. Nan didn't have many neighbors, but what if someone had seen him break in? What would they think—who would they tell? The implications were enough to make her head spin.

"I thought you'd want to know how things were progressing."

"Not like this!" Eve shoved him against the open window in an attempt to push him out. "Get out! For God's sake, don't go crawling into my bedroom! It's creepy!"

"Is it?" Liam appeared genuinely puzzled by her outrage. He held his hands out to either side of her window frame, preventing her from defenestrating him.

"*Yes!*"

"Odd. I'll keep that in mind." Liam easily sidestepped her and cocked his head, his gaze trailing over the various additions to her room. Her father's childhood bedroom still held a few marks from his youth: muted blue walls, flattened beige carpet, a few baseball trophies left on wooden shelves to collect dust.

Eve's additions were minuscule. A few books and a pile of dirty clothes were the only indication that she lived there at all.

Liam lifted the cover to one of her discarded sketchbooks on the desk, but Eve slapped his hand away before he could get a good look.

"Get. *Out.*" She pointed to the door, then regretted it. What would be worse for her neighbors to see—him being tossed out her second-story window or casually walking out the front door? God, it was too early for this.

A second alarm went off on her clock in her bedroom: the final warning before it was too late to leave. Eve stumbled over a pile of dirty laundry to shut it off before Nan woke up.

"I need to finish getting ready," she said, jabbing a finger into his chest. "By the time I come back up here, you'd better be gone—and don't let anyone see you leave. Got it?"

"You're certainly bossy for someone that is relying on my help," Liam said with a raised brow. Then, "Very well. You won't even know I was here."

Eve gritted her teeth but hurried downstairs to pack her lunch. She didn't trust him to keep his word, but by the time she arrived back to her bedroom, Liam was gone. She peered out of her bedroom window.

How the hell did he get up here? She wondered, then pushed the thought aside. Maybe she was better off not knowing.

Liam wasn't at school.

Eve was relieved as much as she was annoyed. A part of her had been hoping to confront him about his unwarranted visit to her room. She wanted to know exactly how he managed to get up there and ensure that he never had the opportunity to do it again. Without him there, though, she was stuck speculating.

A part of her was tempted to tell Sage and Hailey what happened. She'd love to see them chew him out. But aside from Liam potentially revealing the reason behind his visit, her friends were preoccupied with their own problems.

Hailey and Sage had barely spoken without bickering since their confrontation in the science room. The tension had only grown as Hailey's date with Eric loomed closer. Hailey had accepted Eric's invitation to dinner and a movie at the behest of her parents, although she didn't appear particularly excited about the date herself.

Sage seemed oblivious to Hailey's own feelings on the matter. She was solely focused on the fact that Hailey and Eric had a confirmed date. That was enough to convince herself that Hailey was excited for it, too.

Eve sat between the girls in her homeroom, practically a physical buffer between them. They had been at a tense stalemate for ten minutes, each one barely glancing in the other's direction. Every time Hailey tried to bring up a topic, Sage found a way to bring it back to Eric, and the conversation ended there. It was exhausting.

She glanced back at the analog clock hanging at the front of the room. Normally, they would have been sent to their classes by now, but the seniors were held back for assigned meetings with their counselors. The school wanted to make sure they were all on track to graduate and assist with any college questions the students might have. Eve had forgotten all about it until this morning, but now she wished she'd stayed home.

A few more students were called out of the room. Eve watched them go until she heard, *"Eve Carter, please report to the office."*

Eve's chair scraped loudly against the floor as she trudged out of the classroom. She didn't know what was worse, sitting in that awkward silence or having to talk to a counselor about her future.

Definitely the counselor, she decided.

Jill, the secretary, greeted Eve with a nod as she stepped into the office and gestured toward a narrow hallway. "Third door on the right. Mr. Chaplin will be waiting for you."

Eve had never met Mr. Chaplin before, but his office was the last thing she expected; *Funko Pops* intermingled with books and certificates on his bookshelves. Pictures of family vacations hung alongside crayon drawings dedicated to their father. There was a small print of The Last Supper on the far wall, but it was insignificant compared to the memorabilia.

Mr. Chaplin smiled at her from behind his desk. His hair was a thick mixture of gray and brown, and a tiny pair of rectangular reading glasses sat on the bridge of his nose. He was dressed casually in a polo shirt and slacks, not any different from most of her teachers.

"Eve? Please have a seat." Eve reluctantly sat down in one of the opposite chairs. "I don't believe I've had you in previous years; you're a transfer, I take it." Mr. Chaplin flipped open a folder on his desk and reviewed some printed notes. "I see you've been struggling to adjust to the curriculum. Are you having trouble understanding the work?"

"No," she said. When she did the work, it wasn't hard to understand; the problem was having the energy to do it.

Mr. Chaplin nodded. "And how are things at home?"

"They're okay." What was she supposed to tell him, that her family had given up on her and the person she lived with couldn't remember who she was? Eve wasn't about to spill her guts to anyone about that, especially not a stranger.

Her counselor nodded again, but remained unconvinced. His eyes scanned over the sheets in the folder, catching on a few highlighted points. "I see. If there *is* anything troubling you, though, you can talk to me about it. I'm here to help." A beat passed as Mr. Chaplin waited for her response. "But for now, let's see where you are for graduation."

Mr. Chaplin reviewed her classes and grades, pulling out one of the sheets for Eve to read. It wasn't promising.

"We're still early on in the year so we can try to turn these around, but universities are going determine eligibility from last year's grades," he said. "The application essays and SAT scores are going to be your biggest priority here." Mr. Chaplin paused. "That is, of course, if that's your intended goal. Are you interested in going to college, Eve?"

"Um," Eve hesitated. She'd never been asked what *she* thought of the whole thing. It had always been an expectation, but being asked directly left her uncertain. "I don't know."

"That's understandable; it's a big decision," Mr. Chaplin said. There was something soft and understanding about his voice that put Eve at ease. "There are a lot of options available to you: trade school, community college, university, study abroad programs and the sort. You can also choose to take a gap year if you need more time to think about it, or—if none of these appeal to you—you don't have to go at all." Eve stared at him blankly. "The focus of this meeting is to make sure you graduate and are on track for whatever it is you want to do afterward. So, what do you want to do?"

"I, um," Eve scrambled for something to say. She had no idea. Painting had always been a beloved hobby of hers, but there was no way her parents would support that. Eve wasn't sure she had the energy to make a career out of it, anyway. She wasn't sure she had the energy to do *anything* after graduation.

Mr. Chaplin watched her patiently, his hands folded on his desk. Eve gave a helpless shrug. "That's alright. It's hard to know what you want to do at this age. Have you visited any colleges yet?"

"No," she answered. She'd come to understand that was something reserved for wealthy families.

"We're having a field trip to St. John's University in two weeks," Mr. Chaplin explained. "It's late in the semester, but they have rolling enrollment, so it's a great option for students who aren't sure if they want to apply yet. If you haven't checked out at any colleges yet, I recommend giving it a try."

Mr. Chaplin reached into his desk and passed her a field trip form. Eve stared down at the paper uncertainly. Going on the field trip was a surefire way to get her mother to stop badgering her about her future—but it could also unleash a relentless onslaught of expectations.

"I'll think about it," Eve promised, folding the paper in half. That seemed to appease her counselor.

"One more thing before you go." Mr. Chaplin pulled out another sheet of paper and passed it over. *VOLUNTEER HOURS* was printed in bold at the top, and a few pamphlets were stapled in the corner. "One hundred and fifty hours of volunteer work is required to graduate. I've attached some local brochures for you, but if none of these interest you, there are plenty more online."

Eve grimaced. She was already volunteering all her time to take care of Nan; where was she going to find the time to do this, too?

"Let me know if there's anything else you need, alright? My door is always open." Mr. Chaplin gave her a warm smile, but Eve took that as her cue to leave. She nodded, clutching the papers in her hands as she shuffled out of the office.

Eve walked back to her homeroom in a daze. She had never expected to live this long—and now her future had come crashing down on her all at once. Volunteer hours, college applications, gap years. Where was she going? What was she supposed to do?

Eve peered into the classroom, surprised to find Hailey alone at her desk. Sage was nowhere in sight. Eve sat down beside her, taking notice of the exhaustion on Hailey's face. Apparently, she wasn't the only one completely drained by her meeting.

"Hey." Eve nudged her gently. She smiled uncertainly; this, at least, was a decent distraction. Hailey smiled back, the gesture not quite reaching her eyes. "Where'd Sage go?"

"She wasn't here when I got back." Hailey worried at her lip, tearing the skin between her teeth. Eve wondered if Sage took the opportunity to skip school. Sage rarely left Hailey's side, but this week the distance between them was practically a chasm.

"Have you and Sage ever fought before?" Eve asked before she could think better of it.

Hailey shook her head. "Not that I can remember." Realization flashed in her eyes as a memory hit her. "Oh, maybe once this summer. I can't remember what we were fighting about, though."

She seemed troubled by this. Her teeth continued to scrape against her lip, ripping away dried skin.

"You're going to tear your lip off if you keep doing that," Eve chided, using the words her own mother said when Eve made her anxiety visible. Already a spot of blood had pooled at the corner of Hailey's mouth.

"Sorry." Hailey stuck her lip out, but it soon found its way back under her teeth once more.

Eve wondered how much Hailey actually knew about Sage's attraction to her. Eve had thought it was obvious, but knowing Hailey—the girl was dense when it came to subtlety. Sage's words in the science room came back to her: *She should. She did before.*

What had she meant by that? Did Hailey forget that Sage confessed to her? Or was she pretending the confession never happened in the first place?

It was entirely possible that Hailey wasn't attracted to girls, but that wasn't an excuse to pretend Sage's feelings for her didn't exist. Unless Hailey had rejected her already and Sage was still clinging to the hope that something would happen between them. That was equally possible.

Eve wanted to be surprised by the idea of Hailey condemning Sage for her sexuality, but she'd been around the church enough that it wasn't entirely off base. Hailey was, after all, from a religious family, and Eve had heard enough whispers around town to know that girls like Eve and Sage were not openly welcome there. Would Hailey react the same way if she knew Eve was bisexual?

"Do you know why Sage is upset?" Eve asked around the lump in her throat.

"I have no idea," Hailey said, pulling Eve back to the present. "Maybe Eric pissed her off? Do you think he said something to her?"

I don't think she'd be happy about anyone you went out with, Eve thought, but that wouldn't be useful to the conversation. And if Hailey didn't know what Sage felt for her, it wasn't Eve's place to make that known.

"Probably not, but you could ask him."

"Yeah," Hailey said absently. "Oh, you don't need to wait for me to walk home today; I have basketball practice, then Eric's picking me up later."

"Okay, I'll let Sage know," Eve promised, although she wasn't sure she'd see Sage at all. Eve paused. "So, how did the meeting go?"

Hailey took out her phone and frowned. "Oh, you know. I'm applying to nursing schools."

Eve hesitated. "Is that what you want to do?"

"No," Hailey said. She didn't look up from her phone. "But we don't always get to do what we want to."

Sixteen

The Painted Hound was a local staple of town, caught between the corners of Seventeenth Street and Fourth Avenue. It was established in the eighties and had changed little since, with depictions of puppies and dogs happily covered in bright splotches of paint. The food was mediocre, but the desserts were always colorful and fun. The owner had attempted to make it into a chain decades ago, but after several failed attempts, this was the only establishment that remained.

That was what *Google* said, anyway. Eve scrolled through her phone from inside of the restaurant as she waited for Sage to show up, flipping through pictures and reviews of various dishes. When Sage asked her to hang out tonight, the last place Eve expected her to pick was *The Painted Hound*.

Eve shoved her phone in her pocket and peered out the window. Sage was running late. If it wasn't for the fact that she knew Sage was already having a hard time, Eve would have left. She shouldn't be eating out anyway. She hardly had the money for it. But when Sage invited her on their way home, Eve had been so shocked that she agreed without even thinking about it.

Eve watched a figure clad in black push through the rain toward the front door. She stood, quick to hold open the door as Sage ducked into the lobby. The hostess greeted them with a practiced smile before leading them to their table.

It was crowded; families and dates alike had decided to celebrate their weekend with some local cuisine and vibrant cocktails. Eve frowned at a particularly involved couple nearby whose hands were more on each other than the food in front of them. She couldn't imagine taking a date where the mascot was a rainbow dog, but to each their own.

"Your server will be right with you," the hostess promised before returning to her station. Eve flipped through the menu and was immediately greeted by Halloween-themed appetizers and desserts on a laminated insert. She flipped past it, searching for the cheapest option.

"What do you think you're going to get?" she asked.

"Mmhmm," Sage hummed, distracted. Eve caught her wrinkling her nose at the menu, her distaste growing more with each page.

Eve reviewed the menu once more before the server arrived for their drink orders, but another face from across the room caught Eve's attention before she could decipher what she wanted.

Hailey had outdone herself tonight; her makeup was soft and subtle, and she wore a yellow halter dress that Eve was certain she'd never seen before. Instead of her usual ponytail, Hailey's hair was curled and draped over her shoulders, styled with a headband to complement her dress.

Eric sat across from her, his outfit pretty average in comparison with his T-shirt and jeans. At least he brushed his hair.

But why were they here? Weren't they supposed to be on a date?

No, better yet, why were *Eve and Sage* here?

Still staring at Hailey, Eve asked, "Sage, what are we doing here?"

"Getting food." Sage's eyes scanned the menu.

"Do you see who else is here?"

Sage glanced up, her lips twitching into a wry smile as she spotted Hailey and Eric a few tables away. She wasn't even surprised. "Oh, would you look at that."

"You did this on purpose, didn't you?" Eve lowered her voice, suddenly afraid that even with the significant space between them, Hailey would overhear. "Did you ask me out to *spy* on them?"

"Hmm," Sage hummed noncommittally, and although she pretended to browse the menu, there was only one thing in this restaurant she was drawn toward.

"Sage."

"What's wrong with this place? There's hardly anything edible here."

"*Sage.*"

"*This* is where he decided to take her?"

Eve pushed out her chair. "I'm leaving."

"Calm down, Eve." Sage set her menu down with a *slap* against the table. She waited until Eve was seated before continuing, "Yes, it is the same restaurant that Hailey is on her date. There are barely any places to eat around here. I'm not going to go hungry because her ugly wart of a date can't afford to take her out of town."

"Why drag me into this?" Eve groaned. She placed a hand beside her face, blocking off Hailey and Eric from view. As if that would disguise her.

"I didn't want to go alone."

"I don't want to spy on her."

"And I don't want to hear you complain, but here we are." Eve glowered at her. "Relax. I will handle the meal, so just think of it as a pleasant evening among friends."

Eve opened her mouth to object, but the waitress stopped by to check up on them. Eve waited patiently for her to leave, still undecided on her own order, before speaking again.

"I never agreed to this."

"No, I distinctly remember you promising to come to dinner with me if I found someone to watch your grandmother," Sage said with a raised brow. "And I did that, didn't I?"

"Yes," Eve admitted begrudgingly.

"A deal's a deal." Sage cleared her throat and sat up taller. "It's not as if this will be torture, although this menu is starting to convince me otherwise."

Eve kept eyes on Hailey and Eric, doing her best to obscure her face from their view in case either of them noticed. She didn't need Hailey to see them, and she *especially* didn't need Eric to see *her*. What if he thought she was jealous? Maybe that was his plan in asking Hailey out all along. But seeing how he dressed for their date, jealousy was the last thing on her mind.

Eve was about done with the whole operation. It was silly trying to hide herself in the middle of a restaurant. She was irritated at Sage, too; she thought that they had honestly grown close enough that she wanted to hang out one-on-one. Instead, Eve had been reduced to a lackey in Sage's relentless pursuit of Hailey's heart.

"I'll be right back," Sage said, suddenly standing. Eve's eyes widened.

"You're not going over there?"

She shook her head. "Bathroom."

Eve relaxed, relieved as Sage walked in the opposite direction. Not without glancing back at Hailey—never without glancing at Hailey.

God, this was a mess. They hadn't even ordered their food yet, and Eve was certain the waitress was starting to suspect they didn't intend to eat at all. She stared at the menu hard, determined to make a decision.

"Don't you know how to read?"

Eve nearly dropped her menu. Liam stood beside her, his black clothes sticking out against the brightly painted walls.

"What are you doing here?" she demanded.

"I was searching for my sister." Liam raised a brow around the restaurant, scanning the tables. "What are *you* doing in that ridiculous getup?"

"Nothing." An embarrassed heat crawled up her neck and face. Eve had tried to dress nicely—or as nice as she could with a hand-me-down dress and cardigan—but she wasn't well versed in the art of fashion. Her style was fairly plain, but she thought she was cute.

Until Liam came along, anyway.

"It doesn't appear to be nothing," Liam said, peering over her shoulder. "The words aren't even that small. Do you need glasses?"

Hailey shifted at her table, and Eve carefully maneuvered her menu in front of her face. "Can you please get out of here? I'm busy."

"Doing what?"

"That's none of your business," Eve hissed. Hailey's gaze flickered in her direction, and Eve sunk lower behind her menu. *Please go away.*

Liam plopped down in his sister's seat and picked up her glass, swishing the cola inside until it swirled in a miniature cyclone.

"You know, you should be thanking me for all the hard work I've put in for you," Liam said, taking a sip. He grimaced. "It isn't easy to simply make men disappear. Not to mention all the tracking I had to do..."

Her heart dropped. "You can't talk about that here."

"Don't worry, no one's paying attention to us." He gestured to the other tables flippantly. "I thought that you would be interested to hear about all the strenuous work you put me through." Liam tipped back in his chair, his knee keeping him precariously lifted against the table. He saw the way Eve's eyes darted to his chair and added, "Don't think about tipping me over this time."

"Wouldn't dream of it," Eve muttered. She found herself constantly glancing around the restaurant, waiting for someone to turn around and condemn her for her crimes. Abductor. Accomplice. *Murderer.* She thought she was going to be sick, but she couldn't risk leaving Liam here alone in case Hailey saw. How would she explain herself?

Liam set the glass down on the table. "It's finished."

"Your drink?" Eve glanced at the half-full glass in confusion. Liam shook his head, annoyed.

"Your request. They're gone."

Eve stared at him, a mixture of relief and guilt raging inside of her. Gone. Her abusers, her rapists, her tormentors. Gone.

But the memories weren't. They were still there, lurking in the dark corners of her mind, eating away at her sanity.

Don't, she scolded herself. Now was not the time to drown in guilt. She wanted to be happy, whatever that meant.

She laughed. That laugh turned into a sob. Eve ducked her head behind the menu, struggling to regain control of her emotions. She almost couldn't believe it. If not for the seriousness on Liam's face, Eve would have called him a liar.

But these men were human; they were susceptible to whatever tragedies humans were privy to. It isn't unusual that a person goes missing in the world.

Liam watched her, and Eve could see his surprise at her reaction. He didn't understand. He didn't know. All he saw was a girl breaking down in front of him at the news of a successful killing spree.

God, he must think I'm crazy.

Eve used her napkin to dab her eyes. None of the other tables noticed or cared, and she was grateful.

"Are you ready to place your order?" The waitress appeared at her side, awkwardly taking in Eve's puffy red face. "Er, do you need a few more minutes?"

"No, we'll order," Liam said before she could object. Sage wasn't back yet, but Liam took over with ease. "We'll have, uh, these—" He pointed to an item on the menu. Eve was sure he didn't even look at it before choosing. "—And this thing."

The waitress jotted everything down. "And to drink?"

"I'll have some wine." The waitress stared at him skeptically. Liam rolled his eyes. "Fine, milk." Satisfied, the waitress reached for the menus.

"I'll keep this," Eve said. The waitress nodded and scurried off.

"It's not going to do a good job of hiding you," Liam pointed out. Her eyes narrowed.

"We didn't invite you to eat with us," Eve said, returning to her normal demeanor. Now that she was no longer on an emotional roller-coaster, embarrassment burned at the tips of her ears. The last person she wanted to see her in a vulnerable state was Liam.

"Since I have to wait for Sage to return, I should enjoy myself," he said, relaxing in his chair with ease. "What exactly did I interrupt, anyway?"

Eve kept her mouth shut but couldn't resist glancing in Hailey and Eric's direction.

Liam followed her gaze. "Are you spying on Hailey?"

"No," Eve lied. Amusement twinkled in Liam's eyes as he watched Eve sink lower behind her menu. Hailey and her date were already on their entrées, and Eve watched as Hailey laughed at something Eric said. It wasn't jealousy she felt, but pity; Sage would be devastated to see this.

Liam watched them, his expression sobering.

"Did my sister put you up to this?" Eve hesitated. That was as much as a confession. "I thought so. She never knows when to let things go." Liam sighed and finished off Sage's drink, making a face as he did so. "Very well. What are we looking out for?"

"What do you mean *we*?" Eve's brows furrowed. "You're not going to sit here and spy with us?"

"What else am I supposed to do? Sage is off somewhere, and I can't go back without her. Perhaps you'll provide some entertainment," Liam drawled in self-pity. "Existing is so *hard* when there's nothing to do. Do you know how to juggle?"

"No."

"I see." Liam sighed dramatically. "A shame."

Eve rolled her eyes. It was easier to accept his being here than to argue. "Just don't get caught; it'll be bad enough if Hailey sees me and Sage here. She'll know something is up." She was surprised Hailey hadn't caught them already.

"Are you worried for me, Evie?" Liam teased. Eve glared at him.

"You couldn't pay me enough to worry about you."

Liam chuckled but adjusted himself so that his back was facing Hailey and her beau. Eve was reluctant to accept his help, but she had to admit, it was better than being alone.

"Is there a sort of code you're using?" Liam asked. "What happens when she touches his arm? What if she kisses him?"

"There are no codes."

"Oh, you're not having *any* fun with this," Liam complained. "What good is a stakeout without codes?"

"Is this *supposed* to be fun?" Eve asked, annoyed.

"Anything can be fun. Anyone with an ounce of creativity in their body knows that," Liam said.

"Like climbing into my bedroom window?" Liam smirked. "How did you do it, by the way? I tried to climb up myself when I got home. It's impossible."

"Oh, I wish I could have seen that." He laughed. "You must have looked like a turtle on its shell trying to scramble up there."

Eve clicked her tongue in annoyance. "Don't do it again."

"Yes, yes, you have my word," he promised. "I didn't think it would be such a problem, but your kind are so peculiar about these things. It's a wonder how you have any fun."

Eve glared at him hard, her resolve wavering. He didn't seem to have any intention of invading her privacy again. The waitress returned with their meals, and Eve dropped the subject. Maybe he was telling the truth. If he wasn't and Eve found him in her room again, being tossed out a window would be a mercy compared to what she had in mind.

"No one invited you," Sage said as greeting upon seeing her brother. She sneered down at Liam with utter coldness.

"Nice to see you, too."

"You're in my seat."

"Get a new one."

They stared each other down, Sage in irritation and Liam with his smug grin. Sage grabbed the edge of Liam's chair and turned it over, dumping him out onto the floor, before promptly sitting down. Liam grumbled as he stood, cursing under his breath as he dragged another table's chair over and plopped down.

Sage finally peered down at her plate. "That's not what I wanted."

Liam waved her off, taking a bite from his own meal. "You weren't here to order."

Eve didn't bother to complain about that Liam had ordered for her; she was too hungry to care. Her interest in Hailey's date had died down, and the fact she hadn't eaten in nine hours was finally getting to her.

Sage, on the other hand, barely took a bite.

"Staring at them isn't going to change anything," Liam said. Sage scowled.

"Shut up."

Liam shrugged and resumed eating.

Hailey's meal was long finished, but she and Eric kept talking as they'd done throughout the entire meal.

Eve frowned, glancing back at Sage. She could see the jealousy ripple through her, and she was surprised that Eric remained oblivious to the glare Sage was giving to the back of his head.

"Why are you here, Liam?" Sage asked tersely as desserts were passed around. Eve poked holes in her orange mousse dome, taking small bites so it wouldn't go to waste.

"Oh." Liam swallowed hard, his mouth full of chocolate ice cream. "Father wanted to see you."

Sage's gaze hardened. "Why?"

Liam shrugged and scooped another spoonful. "I don't know. He told me to fetch you."

"You are utterly useless." Sage's fork hovered over her untouched dessert—some kind of puppy-shaped cake with colorful icing. She was upset, but Eve sensed it extended beyond Hailey's date.

"What's on your—" Eve started, but the words caught in her throat. Hailey and Eric were preparing to leave. Eric placed his jacket on her shoulders, his fingers lingering down her arms. Hailey smiled up at him, bright and shining and utterly Hailey.

Eric brushed a hand over her cheek. Hailey placed her hand over his.

He kissed her.

Sage saw everything.

"Sage," Eve tried, then stopped. What could she say? The heartbreak was clear on Sage's face. She couldn't tell if Sage was going to cry or rage at them. The thought of either filled Eve with pity. "I'm sorry."

Sage dropped her fork on the table and stood, yanking her leather jacket back on.

"Sage," Liam spoke her name in warning. He reached out for her, but his sister moved away.

"I'll see you at home," she muttered. Eve and Liam watched her go, the front door clattering in her wake.

Seventeen

Sage didn't show up to school the next day. Eve didn't expect her to, but it still worried her that she didn't.

Eve sat beside Liam in English, but all efforts to focus on the class were null. Liam cracked open nuts and tried to catch them in his mouth. For once, she didn't mind his annoying presence; anything to keep her distracted from thoughts of the disaster that was last night's spy fiasco.

Hailey never did find out about her and Sage being there, but that didn't lessen Eve's guilt.

She was relieved when class ended, and they filed out into the hall. Liam lingered at her side, his mood strangely morose.

"Why did you come to school?" she asked once students had spread out in the hall.

"Sage is being difficult," Liam said, annoyed. "It's wise to avoid her today."

Eve didn't know what he meant—the Sage she knew was usually calm and collected—but she took his word for it. If Sage needed a day of grieving for her crush, she could give that to her.

"But that doesn't explain why *you* decided to come to school," Eve pointed out. Liam opened his mouth to answer. "And don't tell me it's because you're bored—there's got to be better things to do around here than listen to lectures all day."

"You would be surprised." Liam inspected his nails, digging out the dirt underneath. "No, rather, I came in regard to your end of the deal."

"My end?" Her brows rose.

"Don't try to get out of it," Liam warned. "I'm not in the mood today."

"But I've already given you my name," she said, lost. There was nothing more they'd agreed to, nothing more he could want from her.

Liam *tsk'd* and wagged his finger at her condescendingly. She bit back the urge to slap it away. "You're so naive. *Evelyn Marie Carter.*"

Eve's body tensed. She froze in place, an electric shock running through her as she hung onto Liam's every word.

"Answer me truthfully," Liam continued. "Are you compelled to obey my command?"

Eve answered before her mind could register what he was saying. Her mouth moved on its own, the words flying from her lips, "I do."

"Ah, it works." He grinned. "I wanted to be sure."

Eve's hands shook. She stared at her trembling palms as a sickening feeling settled in her gut. Her body had moved on its own.

"What was that?"

"A test. I have a task for you; an important one," Liam said. "You are to find me *cloth the shade of twilight, a bird as soft as butter, hair as liquid as ink, and a name as fleeting as the sun.*"

His words cemented into her mind. The weight of them pooled in her body, a command that she could not physically resist.

Something had gone horribly, horribly wrong.

"What did you do to me?" she demanded. The task thrummed against the back of her head, an engine that wouldn't quiet.

"I needed to make sure you wouldn't be negligent in your handling of this task," Liam explained. "It was a drastic measure, but my options are limited—"

"*What did you do to me?*"

He almost appeared sorry for her. *Almost.* "A name is never *just* a name, Evie. Look at your God, your rulers, your friends; you say a name, and someone comes to mind. They respond to it. They're *attached* to it."

"And your point is?"

"Names have power, and you've given me yours."

"You're lying," she said automatically.

"If only I could," Liam sighed. "Truth is an unfortunate part of the territory. I cannot lie even if I wanted to."

Eve swallowed hard. The memory of him saying her name—her True Name, as he'd called it—in the cemetery came back to her.

She had done this. *She* had done this. Evelyn Marie Carter had given her name—all her power, everything—to Liam.

Eve's knees locked in place. The chaos of the school hallway sounded distant and faraway.

She was going to be sick. Or maybe she was going to faint. Eve was vaguely aware of her body shaking as the news settled in.

"What does that mean for me?" she demanded, numb and aching. A part of her already knew.

"It means that when I say your name, *Evelyn Marie Carter*—" Her body tensed and leaned forward against her will. "—then you will do whatever I command. That is the power of a name, Evie."

Whatever Liam wanted. Eve shuddered to think of what kind of cruel, sadistic ideas Liam had in mind for commands. She would prefer killing her rapists herself over obeying whatever sick orders Liam was bound to give.

But she didn't have a choice.

"Why?" The word came out as a plea.

"I told you: I can't afford any setbacks." Even as he said it, a stubborn frown pulled at his lips. "A life for a life; it's only fair, don't you think? You wanted their lives, and you'll give me yours."

"I didn't agree to that. I—" Tears choked her. What had she done? She was trying to get rid of men's control over her, to finally free herself for the first time in years—maybe even her life.

And she had given it all away.

"I didn't know what I was doing," she managed. The words came out small. Weak. Exactly how she felt. Any confidence she'd been building these past few months vanished, throwing her back into that little dark hole she'd only begun to crawl out of.

"A deal's a deal," Liam said, echoing Sage's words from last night. "I'm not in the mood for bargains."

Eve thought she would fall. She thought the sadness would come for her again, pull her under its spell of razors and vomit and blood on a bathroom floor.

Anger came instead—hot and burning and furious, willing to tear him apart with her bare hands. He'd tricked her. He'd *tricked* her.

Of all the things Liam could have asked for, why her name? Why *her*? Surely, he didn't think she possessed any kind of special skills that would be useful to him. She wasn't magic, she wasn't special. She was just Eve.

And he'd taken that, too.

Liam's head reeled back before she realized what she'd done. Her hand stung where she'd hit him, his cheek blooming a bright red. He rubbed his jaw, eyes wide in shock. Good. He didn't get to be smug, not about this.

"I'm not your *plaything*. Do you understand?" Her voice was surprisingly calm, considering the raging inferno occurring inside of her body. There was a deadliness to her quiet. "You can't order me around for the sake of your amusement."

Her fist shook and she wanted to hit him again. Liam grasped her wrist and forced it down. "This is a precaution. I don't intend to abuse my power over you."

"You already have." Eve snatched her arm away.

Liam fumbled for a response, but there was nothing he could say to dissuade Eve from her pain. She pushed through the hall, desperate to get away from him as fast as possible.

Eve didn't care what Liam wanted to use her True Name for. He took her free will, and that was already too much.

Eighteen

Eve hadn't intended to go on the tour of St. John's University. She had crumpled up and tossed the slip into the trash as soon as she got home. But once Hailey mentioned how excited she was for the trip, Eve was inclined to join her. A part of her hoped to keep the trip from Sharon—Eve had convinced Nan to sign the slip in her stead—but an email had gone out, and Eve's mother was ecstatic.

"They have rolling enrollment, so you haven't missed any deadlines yet," Sharon had gushed over the phone. "You could start the application process when you get home!"

Eve grimaced. She *could,* but did she want to?

"Caty isn't going to college," Eve said. She didn't know how true it was; Eve had only glimpsed at her ex-friend's social media once or twice. From Eve's understanding, Caty was more focused on popping out babies at eighteen than furthering her education. Eve didn't care either way, but the idea of someone her age settling down—with kids, no less—made her uncomfortable.

"Caty got married. She has a family, she doesn't need college," Sharon insisted, as if it were obvious. Eve expected the response. Her family only had four options when it came to postgraduate plans: go to college, work for the church, fight for your country, or get married and start a family. She knew even college was a part of her mother's thinly veiled plan for Eve to find a husband as the other daughters in her parish had. Eve would be held to the same expectations of her mother and her grandmother and all the women before them.

"I don't want to waste money," Eve argued, although she knew her mother wouldn't hear it. Money would be found one way or another. Scholarships, part-time jobs, student loans, her mother had talked through them all. Sharon was oblivious to the fact that times had drastically changed, and that it took a lot more than a summer job's worth of savings to pay for school.

You could always take a gap year, Eve thought, Mr. Chaplin's words coming back to her. She squashed the thought as soon as it occurred; her parents would never allow it.

"Why the long face?" Hailey interrupted, pulling Eve back to the present. They waited in a hallway outside of the auditorium, a dozen students bundled in coats and scarves as Mr. Ceating watched for the bus outside. "This is exciting! We never get to skip class. I'd seriously do anything to get out of European history. You have no idea how hard it is trying to remember all those dates. My dad is going to kill me if I fail that class."

Hailey was a ball of talkative energy at Eve's side, jumping from one topic to the next, so there was little room for silence. Eve guessed it was Hailey's way of distracting herself from Sage's continued absence. Sage had been MIA for almost two weeks now. Eve didn't know if they spent any time together outside of school, but she thought the subject was too sensitive to ask.

Something tugged on Eve's sleeve. She glanced over her shoulder and her stomach plummeted.

Liam stood in line behind them, appearing out of thin air as if he'd been there the whole time. There was a little green frog perched on the shoulder of his black coat. If she didn't know better, Eve would have thought the frog was observing her.

I hope you give him warts, she thought bitterly, shifting her glare from the frog to Liam.

"What are you doing here?" she demanded. This trip was already going to be miserable enough with the added pressure of knowing Sharon would be calling her after school to talk about plans to apply. Having Liam there brought on a whole new set of complications.

He shrugged. His snarky grin didn't meet his eyes. "I have nothing better to do."

Eve clenched her teeth. He had kept his distance since she slapped him in the hallway, but here there was no escape. No way to forget that with the breath of her name, Liam could have her jump off a cliff if he wanted.

God, sometimes she hoped he would.

"They're not going to let you on without a signed permission slip," Eve said, jerking herself away from those dangerous fantasies. She was trying, but sometimes they would come back as serpents in the water, slithering their way through her most mundane thoughts until they'd integrated themselves into her daily routine.

"A what?"

"Never mind." Let him find out for himself.

"Where did you get the frog?" Hailey asked, reaching out to pet the creature's head. It inclined itself toward her touch, something Eve had never seen a frog do. "It's cute."

"Not *that* cute. He can be real annoying," Liam said. As if offended, the frog let out a croak and hopped off. One of the other students, noticing the creature, opened the door to let it out, and the frog disappeared into a set of bushes.

"That wasn't your pet, was it?" Hailey asked, worried. "Shouldn't we go get it?"

"He'll be fine."

Hailey pursed her lips, unconvinced. Turning to Eve, she asked, "Where have you applied, Eve? My reach school is University of Notre Dame."

"I thought your dad wanted you to apply to Villanova." Eve steered away from Hailey's question, eager to be out of the spotlight.

"Yeah, but Notre Dame has a great girls' basketball team." Hailey grinned. "Plus, you know, they have a nursing program, too."

"Won't that be hard to balance?" Eve asked. She didn't know much about how colleges handled their different programs, but she knew nursing and basketball were both time-intensive fields. Would Hailey be able to handle it?

"Yeah," Hailey admitted as a bus stopped outside of the school; it was time to go. The small senior class shuffled out into the autumn afternoon. Hailey took a moment to adjust her windblown hair, frustrated with the thin strands that kept managing to cling to the inside of her mouth. "But at least I'll still be able to play basketball."

"I think it's all a waste of time," Liam scoffed as they boarded the bus. Mr. Ceating didn't acknowledge him—Eve couldn't decide if Liam was lucky or if he was invisible to the others again. Eve had started to pick up on the way he was magically ignored and acknowledged at his own whim.

"I think you're a waste of time," a voice said from behind.

Their attention snapped to Sage, who walked up beside Hailey as if nothing had changed. Hailey searched her face, timidly hopeful.

"Hey," Hailey said gently. "I was worried about you. You haven't been at school for a while."

"There were some things I had to take care of at home," Sage answered easily as they walked down the thin bus aisle.

As she moved to sit, there was another tug on her sleeve, followed by Liam's voice whispering in her ear, "Sit with me in the back."

Eve's jaw clenched. He hadn't used her True Name, but if she rejected him, would he try? The memory of his quest thumped dully in the back of her mind like a drum. She wondered how long it would sit there demanding her effort.

"Eve?" Hailey called from behind her. Eve had stopped in the middle of the aisle.

Eve decided to test him. She ignored Liam's request and took the first empty seat she found, pointedly putting her backpack beside her as a message: *Do not sit near me.*

She met his scowl head on, daring him to command her. He claimed his actions weren't malicious? Let him prove it.

Liam's brows pinched in frustration—then he moved on, sweeping to the back of the bus alone. The tension in Eve's shoulders eased. There was a sliver of satisfaction as Hailey and Sage slipped into their seat in front of her and others passed by her seat without interest.

Eve inserted her earbuds and preoccupied herself with music for the duration of their bus ride.

St. John's University's campus stretched out across grassy fields covered in an array of vibrant autumn leaves. Eve could make out a few buildings in the distance—the nearest town.

Eve meandered through the tour behind Sage and Hailey, more interested in their conversation than the tour guide. In the span of their short bus ride, they were back to their normal close-knit friendship. She made a mental note to ask Hailey what they talked about on the bus when she had a chance.

She tuned back into the tour guide, instantly regretting it. He was talking about the same thing she'd heard on repeat recently: the future. Opportunity. Jobs, careers, clubs, decisions of eternity being made at eighteen. Eve crossed her arms over her twisting gut, wishing the tour would end already.

"Don't throw up on me," Liam said beside her. He showed no interest in the tour, either. Eve had watched him discreetly trip the guide on multiple occasions, flustering the poor intern as he tried to keep his composure throughout the tour. Well, she didn't *see* him do it, but from the growing smirk on Liam's lips, and the frequency of the young man's falls, Eve had her suspicions.

"I'm not going to throw up."

Liam raised his brow skeptically and put exaggerated effort into stepping away from her. Eve rolled her eyes and bit back a remark. He was pretending everything had gone back to normal, but Eve wasn't going to indulge him. As long as he could command her to do his bidding, Eve had no intention of being nice.

"This is our art department," the tour guide said, gesturing at the corridors around them. Hallways stretched on to various classrooms separated by medium, but a few finished pieces were displayed in the common area, showing off the more talented students' pieces.

The tour moved on to another room, but Eve lingered behind, drawn to the display of oil-painted canvases. A small piece of her heart tugged at her, a longing for something she'd buried deep inside of her. She missed art. She missed creating, imagining, thinking. Picking up a paintbrush felt clumsy to her now, her strokes never quite right and the paint duller than she wanted. Why couldn't she do anything right?

Eve turned to find Liam watching her, his expression unreadable. She thought he'd left with the others.

"Do you enjoy staring at these?" he asked, averting his attention back to the paintings.

"Obviously. Everyone likes art," Eve replied hotly.

"Not everyone." Liam reached up and stroked the canvas' dried paint with his fingers.

"Don't touch that." Eve slapped his wrist. Liam regarded her for a moment before shoving his hands deeply into his pockets. She glanced down the hall where the others had left. She needed to return before they noticed she was missing.

"Do you paint?" he asked before she could excuse herself.

"Why do you care?" she snapped.

"I'm curious."

Eve wanted to tell him to screw off, that he didn't deserve to know this part of her. Not after he took everything. But the answer lingered on her tongue, longing for acknowledgment. She hadn't had the motivation to paint in years, but the yearning for a brush in her hand tugged at her like a phantom limb.

"No." Then she clarified, "Not anymore."

Liam's brow furrowed. "Why not?"

"None of your business," she said.

"It's only a question."

Eve ignored him and walked in the direction of the tour group. They were probably already gone from the building, but she was determined to get as far away from Liam as possible.

Liam's footsteps echoed behind. He scrutinized her, trying to pick apart the loose threads that made up her tangled personality. He could command the information from her at any time, if he wanted to—but he didn't.

She was gone for longer than she realized; students were already piling back into the bus upon her return. Eve hurried after them, slipping into the small crowd.

"Where have you been?" Hailey whispered as they boarded.

"Bathroom," she lied. She watched the other kids step onto the bus. Liam walked past her, briefly meeting her gaze. He vanished just as quickly, as if he'd never been there from the start.

Nineteen

"Crap."

Eve stared at her bleeding thumb before running it under water in the sink. A pile of half-peeled potatoes sat on the counter while the scent of stuffing wafted from the stovetop. There wasn't time to make homemade stuffing before everyone arrived—boxed would have to do.

"Are you alright, Sammy?" Nan appeared at her side, peering down at the wound. Eve nodded and forced a smile.

"I'm fine, Nan," Eve reassured her. "Go relax; everyone will be here soon."

But Nan ignored her, moving to scrub another surface of the kitchen. That was what she'd done all day: scrub and clean while she waited for guests to arrive. Eve was sure the counters would be the shiniest they'd been in decades by the end of the night.

Bandaging herself up, Eve returned to the potatoes and glanced at her phone. Thirty minutes. Her heart leaped into her throat; that wasn't a lot of time.

It'd been months since she saw her parents—even longer since she saw her extended family. She was sick with worry. They were friendly enough, sure, but Eve preferred her private, isolated life with Nan. Eve would need to be careful—her parents were known to twist her words into knives that came back to stab her.

She wished Hailey were here. Hailey was an expert at easing awkward situations. But even if Hailey *wasn't* currently on a short mission trip to Costa Rica, Eve knew her friend would be spending the holiday with her own family instead.

Eve was, unfortunately, on her own.

She finished putting the mashed potatoes and stuffing into fancy chinaware when a heavy knock on the door startled her.

It was time.

Eve swung open the door, struggling to keep her heart rate down as her father's gaze met hers.

"Dad," she choked out with a forced smile.

Benjamin Carter was a hulking mass of a man, with broad shoulders and a beer gut that hadn't gone away since college. He wore his Sunday best—khakis and a polo that stretched thin around his waist, a compliment to Sharon's ankle-length pink dress that was more suited to Easter than Thanksgiving. Eve had seen her wear the same gown for at least three holidays every year.

"How's my little peach doing?" Ben pulled his daughter into a tight bear hug, squeezing the breath from her lungs. Eve reluctantly returned his gesture, too afraid to reject him. He let her go, keeping one strong hand on her shoulder. "Let me get a good look at ya, kid. Hair's growin' back. That's nice. Sharon, come see your girl."

Sharon smiled at her daughter, but it was not the kind of motherly affection Eve had grown up with. This smile held worry, and Eve couldn't help noticing the extra wrinkles on her mother's face and the poorly concealed dark circles under her eyes. She glanced at her daughter's wrists, but the skin was fully covered by a long-sleeved plum dress. If she was searching for any evidence of recent self-harm, she wouldn't find it.

"You're all grown up," Sharon said softly. She reached out to pet Eve's hair, frowning as her fingers slipped through the short strands. Her mother had loved Eve's long hair more than she did. "You're eating? Going to church?"

"Yes." Eve didn't dare glance at her father, but she could sense his hard gaze on her, hunting for even the hint of a lie. "I take Nan every Sunday. We have a pew near the front."

"That's good." Ben gave her shoulder a squeeze of approval. "Where is your nan?"

"In the bathroom," Eve said, pointing upstairs. Her shoulders sagged in relief when Ben removed his hand and tromped up the stairs, shaking the house in the process.

Sharon hovered in front of Eve, her eyes flickering over her daughter as if trying to memorize every detail of her appearance. There was disapproval in her mother's gaze when she noticed imperfections—lint stuck to Eve's dress, a stray hair, a rip in her stockings. Eve's body grew tense under her scrutiny, her tongue ready to lash out in defense.

"Your dress is short." There it was. "You must have outgrown it. You should donate it after it's washed."

"This is how it's always been on me," Eve said.

"That can't be right. I don't remember it looking like that." Sharon frowned at Eve's legs, her skin covered by a thin stretch of black nylon. She had more to say, but Sharon bit her lip and raised her gaze. "How are Stan's kids?"

"What?" The abrupt change in conversation threw her off, and it took Eve a moment to realize who her mother was talking about. "Oh. Um, they're okay, I guess."

"You guess? Aren't you spending time with them?" There was an accusation to her tone—the implication of *I thought I told you to do this. Why are you disobeying me?* clear in her voice.

"Not really," Eve admitted. She looked away, silently wishing Sharon would drop the subject. She was lucky enough that Hailey had forced herself and Sage into her life. The thought of trying to reach out to her parents' friends' kids made her internally cringe.

A knock at the door saved her from further accusation. The rest of the family was here, and a proper Thanksgiving was going to happen whether she wanted it to or not.

Eve rushed to the door, and the cold swept in as her Uncle Bob, his wife, Amy, and their two daughters shuffled inside. There was a new face among them, a sobbing bundle that clung to his mother's shoulder as he wailed at the top of his lungs.

"Meet Jimmy," Uncle Bob said after a round of hugs and hellos. He passed the baby to Eve without question, although Eve had no idea what to do with the screaming infant. "You mind watching him for a minute? Amy needs a break."

"Um, I don't—" But they were already gone, mingling with Sharon while Ben escorted his mother down the stairs. More hugs and welcomes went around, but whatever conversation ensued, Eve couldn't hear it over the crying of little Jimmy.

Her two younger cousins, Iris and Jane—Eve had trouble remembering which was which—stared up at their brother with distaste. They couldn't be past the second grade, but already they were tired of the youngest member of the family.

Me too, Eve thought, her ears ringing.

"He does that all the time," One of them complained, her arms crossed over a sparkling champagne dress. "It's so annoying."

"Will you play with us, Eve?" the other whined and clung to her arm, nearly dislodging the baby to the ground. "Let's play! Let's play, let's play, let's play!"

"Hold on—" Eve struggled to readjust Jimmy in her arms. He only wailed louder, his tiny hands fisting and stretching back out in the air. "Let me see—just—Mom?"

Eve turned helplessly to her mother, keeping Jimmy at arms' length to pass onto another adult. None of them heard her; they were all lost in their recollections of moments that were long gone.

"Mom?" Eve nudged Sharon's shoulder lightly. The baby still screamed, his face bright red and full of snot and tears. Gross. "Can you just...?"

She tried to offer Jimmy to her mother, but Sharon waved her off in annoyance. "Eve, get that screaming baby out of my ear. We're trying to have a conversation."

"Ah, Eve's got the baby?" Ben grinned down at her. "Look at her, like a little mom." Her skin crawled as her father laughed.

"I'm not—" But they weren't listening; she was as good as invisible to them.

"Where are all the toys?" The girls were back, clinging and pulling at Eve's dress with their sticky hands. She tried to push them off, but the task was next to impossible with the baby trying to launch himself out of her arms. "I wanna play! I wanna play!"

"Just a minute." Eve gritted her teeth. She didn't hate children—she didn't think she did, anyway—but it was hard not to hold some resentment when she was assigned to be the babysitter at every family function.

The doorbell rang, and everything stilled, with the exception of a sobbing Jimmy. The adults ceased their conversation, heads whipping in confusion to the front door. Everyone was already here.

Finally—thankfully—Sharon took Jimmy from Eve's arms and attempted to soothe him.

"Are you expecting a friend?" Ben asked and although his voice was kind, his eyes weren't. This was family time; you did not interrupt family time.

"No," Eve said with a shake of her head. The doorbell chimed again.

"Go get it."

Eve stepped into the entryway and opened the door. Several heads peered out in her direction, craning their necks to see who had interrupted their wholesome dinner.

It was a good thing she wasn't holding Jimmy—she would have dropped him.

Liam grinned at her from the other side of the door.

Twenty

Eve was going to kill him.

Grabbing him by the collar of his shirt, Eve yanked Liam onto the porch—out of eyesight from her parents—and slammed the door shut behind her.

Liam barely wore more than she did: tight black trousers and a loose white shirt with an open V. A black cloak hung around his shoulders, its thick material the only source of warmth in his attire.

"What the *hell* are you doing here?" she hissed. "Go away."

She tried to push Liam toward the stairs, but he wouldn't budge. He touched his chest in mock offense, and his brow quirked incredulously. "Is that any way to treat a guest?"

"You're not invited." Panic seized her. If her father knew that a boy had come to her doorstep and intruded on their family reunion, he would murder her on the spot. "You need to leave. Right now."

"And miss out on meeting your family? Hailey told me they were coming in this week," Liam said with a mischievous grin. "She asked that I check up on you, so I'm only fulfilling my duty to her."

Eve blanched. Was he going to use her True Name in front of her family? What would he make her do? Sick, twisted thoughts played out in her mind, each one worse than the last. Eve was going to be ill.

"You saw me, so now you can go." She pushed her hands against his shoulder again. Liam took a step away from the door but quickly grabbed onto the banister before she could fling him down the stairs. "I swear to God, Liam, if you don't get out of here, I'll strangle you myself and bury you in the backyard."

"Why the rush?" Liam tsk'd. "You worry too much, Evie."

"And you don't take anything seriously!" She was at her wit's end. Moisture stung her eyes, but she blinked it away. "Please, Liam. You don't understand. Whatever crap you have planned for me needs to wait. If my dad catches you out here—"

The door swung open. "What's the holdup, peach?"

Eve froze. The light from the entryway cast a distinct golden rectangle over the porch that highlighted Liam's face, obscured only by Ben's figure in the doorway. Eve kept her back to him, flinching once at the sound of his voice. She didn't dare look at Liam or her father. Her mind was too busy searching for an answer, a response, *something* she could say to tame Ben's temper.

"Uncle!" Liam said suddenly, gently pushing Eve to the side. "There you are. Eve mentioned you would be here."

Eve stumbled against the porch railing, dumbstruck. Liam moved toward Ben with ease, his smile almost mocking. Eve waited for her father to bellow, to shout and yell and threaten him.

He did none of the above. Ben stared at Liam and, in the dark, Eve could see a glaze fall over his eyes. It faded away into recognition.

"Eve! Why didn't you say your cousin was here?" Ben clapped Liam hard on her shoulder. "Come in, come in. We were just sitting down for dinner."

"Cousin?" Eve choked out. Liam snickered, pressing a finger to his lips as he glanced back at her as if to say, *Don't say anything.* Ben ushered them inside, his voice announcing Liam's presence to the others.

Whatever confusion Eve witnessed from her family was brief. Pinched brows and uneasy glances melted away into excitement as Liam greeted them, his voice thick and honeyed with magic.

He's influencing them, Eve realized. She didn't know whether to be angry or relieved as he unwound the tension in the room. One by one, she watched her family members fawn over him, embrace him, welcome them into the family with more familiarity than they had ever spared for her.

"I'll... get another plate," Eve said. It was as if she didn't speak—no one spared her any attention as she slipped back into the kitchen to grab another table setting.

When she came out, everyone was already taking their seats at the table. Liam's cloak had been hung up with the others on the coat rack, revealing his slender waist. She joined the others at the table, forcing herself to sit close to Liam in case she needed to rein him in. Why did he have to show up *now?*

"Don't do anything stupid," she whispered to him under her breath. "More than you already have."

"I'd say I saved you from a dreadfully boring affair," Liam replied. "You're welcome."

Boring wasn't the word she would use for it, but Eve kept her mouth shut all the same. Nan settled into a chair beside her and squeezed Eve's arm tight. Eve smiled wanly back at her, slightly comforted by the gesture.

"I'm starved," Ben said, taking the seat across from Eve. "Why don't we get this show on the road?" His pleasant expression faltered when he met Liam's gaze, as if he were struggling to remember something.

"Liam," Liam said.

"Yes, Liam!" There was relief when Ben said his name. "Why don't you say grace?"

Several gazes turned to him expectantly.

"Grace," Liam said uncertainly. Eve was too stressed out to laugh.

"I'll do it," Nan said, giving Liam an encouraging smile from around Eve. He was as surprised as Eve, but the old woman clasped her fragile hands and bowed her head in prayer. "Dear Father..."

Once all was said and done, Ben carved into the turkey and their meal began. Liam observed each of the dishes passed his way with curiosity, sticking his finger into dishes and licking them off. He piled the ones he approved of onto his plate and, with a disgusted face, passed the rest. Whatever influence he had over her family was enough to prevent them from yelling at him about table manners, apparently.

"You need more greens on your plate," Sharon said, reaching over the table to scoop some additional green bean casserole onto her daughter's plate. Eve grimaced.

"Mom, you know I hate green beans." Then, glancing at Liam's plate, "Liam doesn't have any either."

"Don't worry about him," Sharon scolded. "Your cousin is healthy enough. You need the vegetables."

Liam snickered at her side, and Eve scowled. She tried to kick him under the table, but he slid away from her with ease.

"Was Eve always a picky eater?" Liam asked. "She barely eats anything when I see her."

Sharon thought about it for a moment. "No, not always. She's always fought me on green beans, though."

"Because they're gross," Eve muttered.

"Don't be a child, Eve."

Eve had to resist the urge to pout. She ate around the casserole on her plate instead, wrinkling her nose in disgust when green beans rolled onto her other dishes.

Nan leaned into her side and whispered, "They *are* gross."

Eve bit back a smile.

"What about stories?" Liam leaned back in his chair. "How was she growing up?"

Eve's smile vanished. He was approaching dangerous territory. Eve poked at the food on her plate, too distracted to have much of an appetite.

"Oh, we've got plenty of those," Ben said with a laugh. Nausea anchored in Eve's stomach. "There's the time she tried to learn how to ride a bike—" Sharon and Eve groaned. "She takes this thing to the top of a hill, and we practice a bit. It's going great until we try to take it back down. She's barely holding it, and the thing flies out of her hands and nearly crashes into her grandfather's car!"

"*While* he's driving," Sharon added. "My father nearly had a heart attack. Horrifying at the time, but hilarious now. We joke that it was a botched assassination."

"By a four-year-old." Ben laughed.

"Maybe don't give a four-year-old an entire bike to walk by herself then," Eve said sarcastically before she could think better of it. She knew her mistake the moment she saw her father's face.

Ben's smile twitched, but Sharon caught the switch in his mood and quickly cut in, "Remember when she thought the red ornaments on the Christmas tree were apples?"

"Oh, I remember," Ben said. He kept up his jovial attitude, but Eve could see the warning to her in his eyes. "That was an interesting time at the hospital..."

The stories continued on, elicited by Liam's curiosity. Eve's initial shame receded with each new memory. She'd heard these stories told countless times growing up. There had been a time she was embarrassed by them, but now she cherished them as some of the few good memories she could hold on to. She had almost forgotten that it was Liam who was prompting all of this.

"What about dancing?" he asked after another round of laughter died at the table. "Why does she hate it so much?"

He'd stepped on a landmine. Silence settled over the room. Whatever previous bond they'd shared had now shattered, and the thick, icy tension from before Liam's arrival resumed its place. Ben and Sharon exchanged a stony look, much to Liam's confusion.

"If we're all done eating, I think we should clean up," Sharon said, rising from the table. She picked up a few plates and stacked them in her arms.

"Sounds good to me," Ben agreed. "Bob and I need to catch up on the game, isn't that right?"

"I've been watching at the score on my phone all night," Uncle Bob said with a laugh.

Ben slung his arm around Liam's arm. "Come on, kid. You don't want to miss this."

Liam met Eve's gaze and mouthed, "*Help me.*"

She grinned back at him and responded in kind. "*No.*"

Eve only caught a glimpse of Liam's horror before he was dragged away into the living room, leaving Eve and the other women to clean up.

"You can go sit down, Nan," Eve insisted as she watched her grandmother carry in a set of dirty plates. "We can take care of it."

"No, no, Sam. It's the men's time." She patted Eve's hand with her own bony fingers. Eve frowned. Had her grandmother gotten thinner? She had been so busy helping prepare for guests that she hadn't noticed the way Nan's dress sagged on her shoulders, or how thin her wrists were. She could practically see the bone protruding.

Sharon and Aunt Amy stared at Nan the same way, worry creasing their foreheads. No one said anything, but Eve knew they were all thinking the same thing.

"How about I help you out?" Aunt Amy came to the rescue, hooking arms with Nan and leading her to the sink. Nan stared at her in confusion, glancing between Eve and Aunt Amy with uncertainty.

"Yes, that would be nice," Nan finally said, but Eve saw in her eyes that she didn't recognize her daughter-in-law.

Sharon set a pile of dishes on the countertop and nodded for Eve to follow her back into the dining room.

"Is your grandmother always this bad?" she whispered as soon as they were out of earshot. Sharon busied herself with collecting dirty napkins and silverware while Eve put away the leftover food in plastic containers.

"Not always. She recognizes a lot of people at church," Eve said. But lately that list had been dwindling down, too. How much longer until she didn't know anyone at all? The thought scared her more than she realized.

"I didn't realize it was like this." Sharon bit down on her lip and glanced back into the kitchen. Nan was cooing over baby Jimmy while Aunt Amy helped with the dishes. "I mean, I knew she was having trouble remembering, but your father said she wasn't bad when he talked to her on the phone."

"She's good at faking it," Eve whispered. "Mostly."

"She thinks you're your aunt."

Eve nodded. Sharon sighed pitifully. "Poor thing. I'll need to talk to your father, you know, about you staying here."

Eve tensed. "What do you mean?"

"If your grandmother is suffering, it's going to be impossible for her to watch you. Especially if something happens." *Especially if you try to kill yourself again,* her words implied. A stab of guilt tore at Eve's heart. It wasn't Nan she was worried about hurting herself, but Eve.

"I've been taking good care of her," Eve insisted. She didn't want to entertain the idea of moving back in with her parents. She hadn't even realized the option was there, but now that the possibility was before her, she would do anything to avoid it. Eve couldn't stomach the idea of sharing a roof with either of them again.

"You're still in high school. You'll have college to worry about soon." Eve didn't bother to tell her mom that she had no intention of going. Now wasn't the best time. "There won't be time in your schedule to give Nan the care she needs. We may need to consider a nursing home or see how much a live-in nurse may cost."

"It's fine, Mom. I can take care of her, I promise." Eve's throat was tight. She tried to push back the tears threatening to spill over. She couldn't move back—she *wouldn't* move back. Anything but that. "She's been doing better, and she's used to having me around. I think changing that routine is going to make things worse."

Her mother lowered her voice. "Listen to yourself. You can barely take care of yourself, and you want to be primarily responsible for another human being? What if you're tempted by the devil again?"

There it was—the slap in the face. Eve hadn't suffered from the urge in weeks now, but hearing her mother talk as if it was inevitable cut deep. It was almost worse than Sharon's belief that her daughter was going to hell.

"Please, Mom. I like it here." Eve didn't know what else to say. What could change Sharon's mind? What would make her accept that Eve belonged here and didn't need to go back home? "I-I've made friends."

Sharon paused, and Eve saw a flicker of relief in her eyes.

"Really? You're making friends?" Sharon was reluctant to believe it. Eve tried to hide her hurt as she forced a smile and nodded.

"Yeah. One of them is on a mission trip right now, but maybe you can meet them sometime." Eve had no intention of ever introducing Sage to Sharon, but her mother didn't need to know that.

"And what kind of stuff do you do together?" Suspicion seeped into her voice. "Do you see them outside of school?"

"I do." Eve told her mother about the sleepover at Hailey's house and their study sessions together. She didn't mention her poor grades, but if Sharon thought she was studying hard, maybe they wouldn't matter.

Sharon beamed at her daughter; it was the first time Eve saw a genuine smile from her in years. Somehow, it hurt. "I'm glad to see you're doing well, honey. See? I told you this move would be good for you."

"It has been, which is why I *really* want to stay," Eve pushed.

"I'll talk to your father. We'll consider it," Sharon promised. Eve tried not to show the disappointment on her face. Ben's opinion was basically law, and no matter how much she tried to butter up her mom, it would ultimately be her father's decision. "Let's try to get through the rest of the holidays first and we can discuss everything after."

"Thanks," Eve mumbled. Sharon turned and carried the dirty dishes into the kitchen, too pleased to notice Eve's solemn mood. Eve grabbed a few more dishes and followed after her.

Then she noticed it: a little turkey on her plate—a turkey made of butter.

A bird as soft as butter.

Could this be what Liam was searching for? It was surprisingly literal—Eve thought each item would be symbolic somehow—but maybe this quest was easier than she thought. Either way, it was worth a shot.

"Eve? Everything okay?" Sharon's panic was back. She peered at her daughter through the doorway, brows raised in concern.

Eve forced another smile and sealed the butter turkey in a small container. "Yeah. Everything's great."

Excited shouts from the other room caught her attention—Liam's voice included. That couldn't be good.

"Everything okay in here?" she asked, poking her head into the living room. The three men were ecstatic, cheering as a referee called a foul from the television screen.

Liam turned to her excitedly, pointing at an injured player on the screen. "You didn't tell me you had violent tournaments!"

Eve gave him a flat look. "You didn't ask." Then to Ben, "I'm going to see Liam out."

"What? No! He just got here!" Ben slapped Liam on the shoulder. "Can't leave while the game is still on!"

Liam was ready to agree, but the scowl on Eve's face must have convinced him otherwise. "Perhaps I *should* be going. My brother is waiting for me."

Ben gave him a blank stare for a brief moment, then nodded with a smile. "Of course. Great to see you, Liam. You'll have to come around more often."

Liam hummed noncommittally. He gestured for Eve to follow him out, and she did so without complaint. She never would have imagined preferring Liam's company over her parents, but the idea of having to put on another fake smile made her want to scream.

They stepped onto the front porch and the chaos of her family disappeared behind the front door.

The night had an empty stillness to it. Eve stared out over the yard, the first hints of snowfall clinging to the grass and pavement. Her breath came out in soft white clouds before they disappeared into the dark sky.

When she was little, Eve would stay up late to press her face against the glass and wait for the first snowfall of winter. The soft orange glow of the streetlights on a fresh bed of snow always put her at ease. She was in another world, somewhere soft and quiet, away from the rigorous rules that structured her life.

Here she was safe. She was home.

Her legs were also freezing. Eve knew she should go back inside and warm up—her tights weren't nearly thick enough to protect her from the wind—but she didn't want to. Peaceful nights were few and far between these days. She would take any moment she could get.

"Your family isn't what I expected," Liam said, his voice so quiet Eve almost mistook it for the wind. She hung back against the front door, the muffled noise of clinking dishware and the football game leaking through.

"Better or worse?" She asked.

Liam didn't answer. A calm silence stretched between them, with only the sound of the whistling wind interrupting. Eve glanced back at Liam—his slumped shoulders, solemn as he watched the swirling snow.

A soft *ribbet* caught her attention and Eve noticed a small green frog sitting beside her on the porch.

Isn't it too cold for you to be out here? She thought. She was pretty sure it was common for frogs to hibernate under the soil until spring came. More than that, she had no idea why this frog was out here in the first place; there wasn't any water around. Where had he come from?

Eve reached down to pick up the frog and carry him inside. Maybe she could try keeping him alive during the winter. As soon as her fingertips brushed his back, the frog cried out again and hopped off, disappearing between patches of dead grass amidst the snow.

"Why did you really come to my place tonight?" she asked finally.

"I was taking a walk with my brother and thought it would be a good time to check in," Liam said, sitting down on the porch stairs. "I didn't lie about Hailey's request."

"I didn't know you had a brother." Eve peered up and down the street, but the night was empty aside from the two of them. "Where is he?"

"He went ahead." Liam gestured vaguely toward the road. Eve still saw nothing. She settled on her grandmother's rickety porch swing, thumbing at the chipped white paint on one of the handles. It blew off into the wind, disappearing among the snow.

"I wanted to check in on your quest, too," he said, settling down on the porch steps. "Have you found any of the items yet?"

Eve rolled her eyes. Of course, that was his real reason for barging in on her Thanksgiving.

"Not all of them," Eve admitted with a sigh. "Wait here."

Eve snuck back into the house and returned with the carved bird in a plastic container. She offered it to him. "For you."

Liam stared at the Tupperware. "You're giving me used butter?"

"*A bird as soft as butter*. I'm surprised you didn't notice it at dinner," Eve clarified. Liam's eyes lit up in recognition and he took the container, marveling at the little carved bird. As he inspected it, his face fell.

"It's missing a wing," he complained. "And half a face."

"We all ate some of it," Eve said. "I didn't realize what it was—what it could be—until we were cleaning up."

Liam was disappointed but nodded, accepting the dish. *One down, three to go.* "Any luck on the others?"

"Not yet."

"Hmm." He kept glancing back at the forest, as if he could see something in its depths that she didn't. Liam scratched the back of his neck, fingers digging under his cloak to reach the spot.

"What do you even need this stuff for?" Eve asked with a yawn. She was tired and didn't care if he commanded her to shut up about it. If she was going to go on a wild goose chase for some cryptic grocery list, she wanted to know why.

"I merely do."

"That's not a reason."

"Perhaps I do not want to tell you mine."

"You keep scratching your neck." It was an observation, something she'd noticed over the past few months together. "Do you do that when you're nervous?"

Liam's fingers twitched, but he halted his movements. She expected some kind of snarky remark, maybe a cryptic command, but the tension in his body took her by surprise.

"I am unwell," he said.

"No shit." Eve snorted. Liam's lips pressed into a tight line. She immediately regretted her wisecrack as the gravity of the situation settled on her. "You're serious."

"There is someone that might know a cure," he continued. "She needs to identify it first, but she requires compensation."

"That's what the items are for," Eve realized. Liam nodded grimly.

"She says they will also help with my ailment, but there isn't much time." He clasped his hands in his lap. "You can see why I'm concerned about your progress."

She did understand. Guilt ached in her chest. Liam was an ass, but he'd been true to his word and hadn't commanded anything of her. It didn't make her situation any better, but Eve could see why Liam was desperate to ensure she held up her end of the bargain.

"Does Sage know?" she asked.

"No, and I will command you to keep quiet about this, if necessary," he said, but the threat didn't meet his eyes.

"Why keep it a secret from her? I'm sure she would help."

Liam laughed bitterly. "Clearly you don't know my sister."

"What's that supposed to mean?"

"Nothing you need to concern yourself with." He stood then, making his way off the porch.

"You're welcome," Eve called after him, annoyed. Liam ignored her. "If you're going to be cryptic about everything, you could at least say thank you when I help you out."

"A thank you implies I would owe you a favor in return," he said casually over his shoulder. "I have no intention of doing that."

"Ass." She couldn't help herself.

"I'll see you later, Evie." Liam flipped his hand at her in a poor attempt at a wave. She watched him go, disappearing between the forest's trees.

Twenty-One

The mission trip was all Hailey would talk about when she got home. It was *church-building* this and *culture clash* that all day long—between classes, during classes. Somehow, she even managed to wiggle it into their conversation on the Tudors in history. Eve tried to be happy for her, but by the time lunch had rolled around, her patience had worn thin.

"You would have loved it, Sage," Hailey gushed. Eve tried to bite back her exhaustion as they filed through the lunch line. "The trees, the weather—it was perfect."

"It sounds great," Sage said. Unlike Eve, her interest was genuine.

"I wish you could have been there! What did you end up doing on break?" Hailey asked, and Eve was thrilled about the topic change.

Sage's humor evaporated. "My brother was in town. We had some family stuff to deal with, and I wasn't allowed to leave."

Liam said the same thing, Eve thought, but he had still come to check up on her progress, at least. "We're glad to have you back."

"Isn't Liam always in town?" Hailey asked.

Sage stared at her. "My *older* brother. You know—Preece."

"I didn't know you had an older brother!" Hailey protested.

"I told you about him. You've *met* him," Sage said, taking a seat beside her at their usual lunch table. Hailey shook her head adamantly.

"No way. I would remember that."

"Clearly not," Sage muttered. Hailey opened her mouth to object. "We all went swimming in the lake this summer." There wasn't a thought behind Hailey's vacant eyes. "The lake? You panicked because a fish tried to swim in your clothes."

"We never did that." But Hailey didn't sound so sure. Her gaze was distant, as if she wasn't all there.

Something strange passed over Sage's face, subtle enough that Eve almost missed it. Was it anger? Hurt? It was so quick she couldn't tell, but the atmosphere at the table left her unnerved.

"I guess one of us is remembering it wrong," Sage finally said.

An awkward moment passed.

"What about you, Eve?" Hailey tried to change the subject with a forced smile. "Did you have a nice time with your family?"

"Sort of," Eve said carefully. She hadn't bothered to go into detail about Liam and his antics, pretending to be her cousin over Thanksgiving dinner. When Eve mentioned him to her family after he'd left, they had no idea who she was talking about.

She couldn't help but spare a glance at Sage, who had taken a sudden interest in poking at the food on her tray. Did Sage know Liam visited her? Would he mention it to his sister? Perhaps not. Based on her conversation with Liam that night, their relationship was a lot more strained than Eve realized.

Once lunch was over, Eve and Sage followed Hailey out into the hall, half paying attention to her stories.

"Before I forget," Hailey sped up ahead and gestured for the others to follow. "I got you both gifts from my trip!"

Hailey swung her green locker door open and dug through the top shelf. She presented the first gift to Sage—a black leather pouch with purple butterfly earrings inside.

"The earrings are made from coffee beans," Hailey said excitedly. "I know you don't have a lot of color in your wardrobe, but as soon as I saw these, they reminded me of you, and I *had* to get them."

Sage smiled, already removing her current piercings to place the earrings in. "Thanks."

"And for Eve," Hailey half-sang the words as she pulled out a small bundle from her locker: a pretty pale blue scarf and a small wooden toucan keychain. Eve wrapped the scarf over her shoulders and turned the toucan between her fingers, admiring the tiny painted details on its wings. "The scarf is made from bamboo. Crazy, right?"

"Amazing." Eve ran her hand down the blue scarf again, admiring the hints of pink and orange mixed in. A sunset. Other than her school uniforms, it was the first piece of clothing she owned that wasn't a hand-me-down or thrifted.

It must have cost a fortune, she worried. She would need to save up to get Hailey something nice for Christmas.

"They had clothes made from bananas, too," Hailey went on. "When I was in Costa Rica, I—" The bell rang, cutting her off. Hailey pouted and glared up at the sound system. "I guess I'll tell you about it later."

They bid each other farewell, and Eve walked back to her locker to tuck her souvenirs away; there was no way the staff would let her get away with wearing them around. She hung the scarf up on a hook in the back and ran her hand down the fabric again. It was soft and pale, reminiscent of the evening sky.

Cloth the shade of twilight.

Could this be what Liam needed? Twilight had plenty of phases and shades; was this the one he wanted? Her heart ached. Of course, the first time she would receive such a nice gift, and it had to go to Liam. That was typical, wasn't it?

At least I have my toucan, she thought, clasping the wooden figurine onto her backpack. It didn't bring her the same joy as the scarf.

He never said *when* she had to give him everything he requested. Maybe she could hold onto the scarf a little longer. It wouldn't be fair if Eve didn't get at least *some* use out of the gift, right?

She considered it for a moment, but shook the thought away. Liam had told her he was sick and, although she was inclined not to believe him, she'd seen his vulnerability when he told her about it. Even she couldn't bring herself to talk about her problems so freely.

With a sigh, Eve slammed her locker door shut.

Twenty-Two

The missing tabernacle—months after its disappearance—finally ended its gossiping reign over the church. Rumors had flown, fingers were pointed, but without proof, it was resigned to be another mystery to captivate the congregation's attention.

Little did they know, Eve had it set up on her desk, the brass painted over with a collage of forests painted to suit different times of day. It was the first thing Eve had painted in years, and she was rather proud of her work, barely disguising the church box as an interesting piece of artwork instead of a religious artifact.

She had removed a lot of the excess decor that had nicked at her fingers more than once, leaving her hands a bloody mess in the process. There was no changing the details on the box itself, though. She had to do her best when painting over them.

It had taken over an hour to pry the damn brass door open. Now that Eve had emptied out the tabernacle and cleaned its contents, she was still unsure of what to do with it.

If it hadn't been stolen, Eve wondered if Hailey would have liked it as a Christmas gift. It would certainly make up for the scarf.

"Damn it," she muttered as the door came swinging against her hand again when she turned the tabernacle. This time, as she moved, one of the loose pieces of brass she had been attempting to unsuccessfully rip off left a long bloody scrape against her wrist. Eve set her project down with a loud thump and marched back to the bathroom to clean the cut.

When she returned to her room, Eve used one hand to seal the paint while she used the other to scroll through the internet on her ancient computer. There wasn't exactly a forum for extra tabernacle uses, but lanterns were close enough, right?

"Fairy houses," she murmured, spotting a cute box that had been repurposed and stuffed between two books. It had been decorated into a miniature forest. Eve could easily do something similar with some materials from the craft store.

She was still scrolling through the reference images when Nan knocked on her bedroom door.

"Sammy?" she called through the thin wood.

"One second!" Eve carefully hid the tabernacle behind various cheap bottles of paint and brushes on her desk, even adjusting her lamp to sit in front of it. Even after painting the damned thing, she didn't trust her grandmother not to comment on it.

Satisfied with its placement, Eve turned to the door in time for Nan to push it open, a bob of gray curls peeking out from the other side.

"Everything okay, Nan?"

"You have a friend downstairs."

"Okay."

Nan steered toward her bedroom for a nap while Eve hurried down the steps. Sometimes it *was* Sage or Hailey showing up at her door, although they were usually there to pick her up and had never actually been in her house. Other times, older friends of her Aunt Sam would stop by. Usually, they were there to drop something off or check in on Nan, but since Eve moved in, their visits became sparse. She hoped it wasn't one of them today; the last woman had tried to get her to join a pyramid scheme selling makeup.

Sage waited in the tiny entryway, a black leather bag hanging over her shoulder. Sage never let her know if she was showing up; she would simply be there, ready to go. Eve glanced down at her paint-splattered jeans and a grimy old T-shirt. Hardly clothes to go out in.

"Hey," Eve said, wiping some of the paint and sealer from her hands on her jeans. They were ruined already, what would some more damage do? "I wasn't expecting you."

"I was in the neighborhood and thought I'd stop by." Sage raised an eyebrow at Eve's messy attire. "Are you busy?"

"No, I'm fine. I was thinking about going to the craft store. Wanna come with?"

"Sure."

Twenty minutes and a set of fresh clothes later, Eve and Sage found themselves amid rows of paint, blank canvases, and miniature craft supplies. Sage eyed everything with cautious interest, picking up and setting back down various unpainted supplies. Eve shoved a bag of fake moss into her basket.

"What are you working on?" Sage asked. She was especially interested in a pack of tiny miniature deer.

"I'm trying to make one of these." Eve showed her the forest book nook on her phone. Sage's lips quirked into a bemused grin.

"I didn't know you were creative."

Eve took a slight offense. "I'm usually not."

She wasn't sure what possessed her to paint the tabernacle. She hadn't touched her paintbrushes in years. She hadn't wanted to since the incident. And yet here she was, for once... excited? Yes, excited. Eve was smiling as she searched through the different miniatures and thought of what small details she could add inside the tabernacle. Maybe she would even be proud of it afterward.

Eve knew she was taking a long time picking out her supplies, but Sage didn't complain. She followed behind and helped Eve find whatever it was she needed in the thin aisles.

When they reached the checkout, and Eve handed her cash over to the elderly owner on the other side, she noticed Sage's gaze had latched onto her bandaged hands.

Sage waited until they were out of the store before asking, "How did that happen?"

Eve turned over her hands and smiled, embarrassed. "My project tried to fight back. Metal is harder to take apart than I thought. It's my first time working with brass."

"And that?"

Eve followed Sage's gaze. Her scars. A blush crept up her cheeks as she tugged her sweater's sleeves lower. Usually, her clothes did a good job at hiding them, but the scab from her earlier cut was visible, drawing Sage's attention.

She opened her mouth to answer but faltered. How do you tell someone that your life was so shitty that you wanted to end it? How do you confess your greatest moment of weakness to one of your first friends in years? Eve's mouth was suddenly dry, and raw panic crawled up her throat. *Don't cry.*

Eve tugged her sleeves lower, engulfing her hands entirely. "I had a rough couple of years."

She couldn't even say it aloud. What was there to hide? The scars on her wrists were more of a confession than whatever she could say.

"Did someone do that to you?" Sage asked quietly.

Eve shook her head. Her voice came out in a whisper. "I wanted to go away."

They walked in silence, and Eve knew an awkward wall had been built between them. She should have lied, should have said it was an accident, that she didn't want to go away, that it had been some freak mistake that she regretted. And sometimes she did regret it. Other times, she regretted that she didn't finish the job.

"Do you still want to go away?"

Sage's voice startled her. Eve gripped the inside of her sleeves, biting down hard on her lip.

"Sometimes," she admitted, ashamed. "Some days are better than others."

Sage nodded, not in passing, but in understanding. As if she had also considered the option of disappearing forever. Eve glanced at Sage's bare wrists—at the flawless, scar-free skin. But just because she didn't have scars didn't mean she didn't understand.

"I enjoy having you around," Sage said. "Hailey does, too."

Warmth inflated in Eve's chest, so sudden and consuming that Eve nearly choked out a sob. She bit down harder on her lip, tasting the iron of blood as her teeth tore into the skin, and she blinked back tears. Eve had no idea what to do with herself. This was such an opposite reaction from her parents, her community, that it was foreign to her. That she had friends, people that cared about her...

She had no idea how badly she needed to hear those words.

Sage didn't comment on Eve's sudden lack of composure, and Eve was grateful for that.

"Thanks," she managed, her throat tight. God, she hated crying. She had grown used to the constant numbing ache in her heart that any display of emotion left her vulnerable and ashamed.

Sage nodded and left it at that.

They slowed down as Eve's home came back into view. Dusk settled over her little home, shrouding the trees in shadow while the sky streaked in hues of orange and pink. Eve admired the vibrancy of it, the sharp contrast of light and dark. It was a time ripe with possibilities. When anything could happen.

Sage stopped short of the house and lingered by the road. This wasn't unusual—Sage rarely walked with Eve the whole way home—but something was off about her sudden stop. Eve paused a few paces ahead.

"You heading home?" Eve asked lamely. She wondered if she should invite Sage inside, but she couldn't think of anything to do if Sage took her up on that offer.

Sage nodded. "Yeah." A pause, then, "There's a party happening at my place this weekend. Hailey's invited; you should come, too."

"A party?" The words sounded hollow. Eve glanced sideways, reluctant to give an answer. "What kind of party?"

"Just a party." Sage's eyebrow raised. "You have been to parties before, right?"

"Sure, I have." But probably not the kind Sage was throwing. Did children's birthday parties count? Eve doubted any party by Sage would compare to the communions and baptisms she was used to. Sage stared at her, and Eve realized that she was waiting for an answer. "I'll have to see if someone can watch Nan."

"I'll let Hailey know." Sage gave a mock salute before walking back down the street, toward... wherever she lived. Did she live close by? Strange, the thought never occurred to her.

Eve ducked into her house, careful not to make too much noise lest she wake up Nan. She could hear the old woman's light snore from her bedroom.

The tabernacle was in a state of internal decomposition when Eve received an eager text from Hailey, begging her to attend Sage's party. Word had gotten out faster than she thought.

Hailey was relentless; for over an hour, Eve's phone lit up and buzzed with each new array of convincing texts her friend sent. God, how fast could this girl type? Was this normal?

Okay, I'll go, Eve texted back, turning her phone off immediately after. She hoped she wouldn't regret it.

Twenty-Three

This was a mistake.

Eve stared at herself in the mirror and attempted to fix her eyeliner for the third time this evening. It was the only thing keeping her mind away from the fact she was going to her first high school party. Ever.

Hailey mentioned there would be a lot of guests: friends, neighbors, people Eve had never met before. Eve didn't even know Sage and Liam *had* friends outside herself and Hailey. It wasn't as if they were particularly affectionate to anyone else in school.

Lucky me, I guess, she thought, and tried to quell the spike of anxiety that twisted in her stomach.

Was she dressed properly? Eve had no idea what other teens wore for parties outside of school dances; all her fashion knowledge came from storefront magazines and brief glimpses in the mall. She tugged at her beige sweater and tucked it into her long brown skirt. Her rumpled socks and shoes were pale and neutral, the only change of color coming from the tiny cross necklace at her collarbone. She was better prepared for a study session at the library than for a den of raging teenagers.

But it was too late to change it now. She heard the knock at the door and rushed downstairs, tucking Hailey's gifted scarf in her pocket. Eve checked once more that Nan was asleep before she slipped out into the night.

Hailey waited on the front porch, somehow more woman than girl. Hailey wore a tight orange crop top, a black bomber jacket, and some denim shorts that had clearly been longer before a pair of scissors tore them up. Black fishnets stretched down her legs into a pair of sneakers and a black choker clung to her neck.

A chill blew in, a nasty reminder of the late November season. Eve huddled in her sweater. How was Hailey not freezing to death?

"Ready to go?" Hailey chirped, a bright smile on her face. Eve considered excusing herself back upstairs to change, but what was there to change into? This was the most stylish outfit she had.

God, she was pathetic.

"Sure," Eve said with a smile that was more of a grimace. She locked the front door behind her, grateful that Mr. Stone had offered to keep an eye on the house in case Nan woke up in the middle of the night, and the girls padded down the wooden stairs.

Eve expected some admonishment for her attire, but nothing came. Hailey eagerly looped arms with her timid friend and led her on the path to Sage's home. Eve was glad Hailey had offered to take her because—from Sage's instructions—Eve had no clue where to go.

Through the cemetery and down the steps, Sage had said. It was the shadiest set of instructions Eve had ever received. Yet, the image of Sage and Liam living inside of some giant Gothic mansion in the middle of a graveyard made perfect sense to her.

The wide stone fence of the cemetery stood out between the trees, connecting to the side of the church and stretching back through the forest. The area inside had been mostly cleared for old graves, but it seemed as though nature was trying to take its land back; moss, vines, and tree roots broke through the cracked brick and over the slabs of engraved stone as if to pull it all under. The fence wasn't tall to begin with, but the way it crumbled under the foliage made it short enough for a child to climb over.

The wrought iron gate squeaked as Hailey pushed it open. It wasn't locked; in fact, the gate was close to falling off its hinges. Eve tiptoed behind her as they trespassed into the cemetery's grounds, and she was secretly pleased she didn't need to shimmy over the fence.

Did Sage really live around here? Eve found that hard to believe. She felt as if the eyes of the dead were watching her, judging her.

I should go back. The thought entered her head more than once. Eve found herself glancing back at the gate. The distance between her and the rusted metal stretched until she barely made out its shape in the distance.

Each step forward was damning. If not because of the tree roots trying to trip and kill her, then because of what she feared awaited her when she *did* arrive at Sage's house. *Would it be prom all over again?* The thought seized her. She hadn't tried to handle a dance in years. She wasn't sure she was ready to try. She didn't know if she would ever be ready.

Eve peered up at Hailey, surprised to find that she was undeterred by the unnerving atmosphere. Excitement gleamed in her eyes as she walked ahead with confidence. Hailey guided them with a small flashlight on her phone, focusing on the ground so they wouldn't break their necks on nature's traps.

If she asked, Eve knew Hailey would turn around and take her back home. But Hailey had been excited to bring Eve along to the party, and Sage was expecting her, too. She didn't want to let them down.

They slowed down as they reached a large stone archway. Eve wasn't sure if it was part of the cemetery or not—she couldn't see any graves, just tall trees and black shadows, and the arch wasn't connected to the fence. When had they left the cemetery? Or were they so far back that the graves no longer consisted of stone?

The archway loomed in front of them, out of place in the dense forest. Hailey let go of Eve's arm and walked forward, her flashlight trailing over the vines of wisteria settled at the top of the archway. She'd never seen wisteria grown up north—how was it surviving?

Hailey picked two of the purple flowers from the bush and handed one to Eve.

"What's this for?" she asked.

"You can't pass through without it." Hailey grinned and pointed.

She flashed the light over the arch's opening again and revealed a long, winding set of stone stairs descending into the darkness on the other side. The stairs appeared to go underground, although the arch was clearly in the middle of the forest. Eve was certain the stairs hadn't been there before. Was she anxious enough that her eyes were playing tricks on her?

Eve looked in askance at the flower in her hands.

"Are you coming?" Hailey was already through the arch's threshold, her footsteps quiet against the stairs. Eve reluctantly nodded, still clasping the flower in her palms as she followed behind.

Eve gasped as she stepped past the archway. The energy changed around her; there was a sudden pulsing through the air, raising the hairs on Eve's arms. It electrified her, energized her. She reached a hand out, as if she could grasp the energy in her palm. Everything was alive with it, from the ridges of the cavern walls to the cracks in the stone under her feet. It was as if anything could happen, that everything was possible.

It scared her. It excited her.

Hailey gave her a knowing smile from below. She understood the sensation, too.

Eve shuddered, overwhelmed. The change wasn't necessarily a *good* thing; it made her feel reckless, and that worried her. The last thing she wanted to be at a party was reckless.

"You coming?" Hailey asked.

Eve took a deep breath. "Yes."

The stairs themselves descended in a spiral, and the cavern Eve found herself in was large, with tall ceilings and was wide enough for two—maybe three—people to walk down side-by-side. Small lanterns hung on either side of the walls, illuminating the stairwell in pale green light. Eve tried to decipher what was fluttering around inside of the lanterns, but every time she got too close, the light went out.

Another archway stood at the bottom, and as soon as they passed its threshold, the wisteria disappeared. Eve stared at her hands, then at the floor and back up the stairs. Did she drop it? She would remember that, wouldn't she? But it was as though it had vanished into thin air.

Eve was still staring at her empty hands as Hailey led her to a waiting carriage.

She had never seen a carriage like this. The ornate box was white with a clouded window and brass hinges on the door. Skulls, bones, and other morbid designs were etched into the details on the carriage. There was not a speck of mud or dirt sullying the surface—even the wheels were pristine.

It was a stark contrast to the dark beasts maneuvering the vehicle. At first glance, Eve mistook their shape for horses. Upon closer inspection though, she noticed the strange, hollow void in their eyes and the twisting horns jutting out from the top of their heads. Even their legs dissipated into a black swirling mist.

Eve stared at the carriage with wide eyes, an uneasiness settling in. Every nerve in her body was alight, screaming at her to turn around and flee back home.

Hailey climbed into the carriage with ease, greeting the black-cloaked driver at the front. Eve could see the inside of the carriage had seats lined in plush black velvet. Hailey waited with a patient smile, patting the empty seat beside her.

Eve's trust in Hailey wavered as she, too, climbed into the carriage. She settled down in the seat across from her, hands folded neatly on top of her lap. The inside of the carriage was equally decorated, the skeletons and bones practically glowing from the carriage's outdoor lanterns.

"I'm pretty sure I saw this in a horror movie," Eve said as a joke, but the words came out low and scared. Hailey laughed.

"Right? I told Sage the same thing the first time she picked me up in it," Hailey agreed. She grinned out of the window as the carriage moved, the trees zipping past them in a blur. "I thought she was going to take me out to the middle of the woods for some kind of cult sacrifice."

Eve wasn't convinced that she *wasn't* going to be a sacrifice, but she kept her doubts to herself. She stared at the skulls, the flames of the lanterns flickering against their hollow eye sockets. Their jaws were slack, and Eve could almost picture them screaming in agony as they burned.

The trip to Sage's house was shorter than expected. The cloaked figure opened the door for them, his face hidden as he offered a gloved hand to the girls. Eve accepted his assistance, surprised to feel his sharp bones protruding against the dark fabric.

Sage's home was far from a house—it was an estate, with a wide expanding lawn and a dirt road that reminded Eve of driveways she saw in rich neighborhoods. The mansion was two stories tall and rounded, with white pillars arching along the outside in what might have been a massive ribcage. The solid pillars were carved with images of death similar to the carriage. Winding bark and tree roots formed the walls underneath, following the pillars' rounded arch.

A crest that Eve now realized matched one of the carriage's designs hung on the front door: a skull without its lower jaw in a ring of hemlock, a pile of berries resting under its teeth. Eve stared at its sunken eye sockets, a chill running through her body.

Strange flickering glass lanterns hung on arched tree branches, over bone-white rails, and lined up along the ground to the front door. The light spilled out of the estate and onto the grounds, casting a soft glow over its guests. If Eve was farther away, she might have assumed the building was on fire.

"This is where they *live?*" Eve whispered in disbelief. This house was the kind of blasphemy the church would condemn them for even visiting. She was sure her mother would faint at the sight of it. She could already see her father screaming at her now, demanding she turn around and march right back home.

A balcony stretched over the first floor and people were mingling on it, glasses of dark liquid splashing as they danced. They were dressed oddly, as though they were in strange costumes. Eve thought she saw the legs of a goat among them. The head of a fish on another.

Uneasiness pooled in her stomach. Wicked-looking faces glanced in their direction, their teeth sharp as nails. Up close, Eve struggled to see where the costumes ended, and the person underneath began.

If there was a hell, this had to be it. The Bible spoke of these creatures: demons with ill intent and a penchant for malicious deals. The longer Eve tried to wrap her mind around the mechanics behind the guests' attire, the less she believed it to be costumes at all. Her legs could not bend backward like that of the deer-legged man to her right, nor could her tongue flicker as the snake-like woman on her left. Eve found herself inching closer to Hailey.

"You didn't tell me this was a costume party," Eve said quietly.

"It's not."

"Oh." Eve struggled to swallow her nerves. A shirtless woman no larger than a scarab with luminescent wings yanked on a lock of Eve's hair as she flitted by, laughing as Eve flinched. Everything in her body screamed at her to get out of there, but Eve kept moving forward, too stunned to listen.

"I know what you're thinking," Hailey said. "Everything here is pretty extra. Some of Sage's friends are... unique, but they're a lot of fun."

Extra was an understatement. Eve couldn't tell if Hailey had any sense of danger or if she thought herself invincible. Hailey strode through the front door as though she owned the place, leaving Eve to stumble after her.

Hailey navigated the mansion with a familiarity that told Eve she had been there several times before. Eve had trouble picturing Hailey's cross-bearing mother being okay with that. She probably didn't know. It wasn't as if Eve told Nan where she was running off to, or who with.

Eve followed Hailey through the house and to the backyard, both terrified and fascinated by the strange relics she passed. Skulls and skeletons of a variety of creatures, none of them familiar. Jewel-encrusted weapons hanging on display. An entire chandelier made of bones. A cabinet full of strange muddled bottles caught her eye, but she didn't linger, afraid that she would be left behind.

Various flora and wildlife stretched out across the backyard, intermingling naturally with the enormous stone patio and decorative trees. Several plush cushions sat around the edges of the patio while couples danced in the center, billowing dresses swishing and long hair flowing as they spun and spun and spun. Instead of the loud pop music Eve had expected, a band of string and brass instruments stood in the corner, bellowing out an enchanting tune over the yard. Tables were prepared, their surfaces covered with golden plates of meats, cheeses, berries, fruits, and vegetables. There was a fountain beside one of the tables, a dark blue liquid pouring out of a skeleton's jaw and into the white basin below. Lanterns and sparkling lights swung from overhead, as though they, too, could participate in the dance.

"Jesus Christ," Eve breathed.

Hailey gauged her reaction with a smile, barely able to contain her excitement. "What do you think?"

What *did* she think? Eve didn't know what to say. Her mind struggled to grasp what it was looking at, let alone form words. Eve wondered if she'd stepped into a fairytale.

The dancers were not human. Many were *humanoid* to some extent, but Eve quickly realized that there was something off about them. Creatures of all sorts participated in the revelry, from goat-legged dancers to maidens with blue, scaly skin, to what she could only describe as goblins and trolls. Small figures flitted by, and while Eve had first mistaken them for fireflies, she saw now that they were tiny people with vibrantly colored skin and sparkling wings. A group of boys sat back on a bunch of pillows, their rough skin covered in spikes and brambles. Sharp teeth pointed over their upper lips from their lower jaws. One in particular caught her eye, his figure massive in comparison.

"Are those *horns?*" she whispered. She could not take her eyes off the tall, brawny man. As he turned to say something to his friend, she could see there were spikes poking out of his back, too.

"I told you they were unique."

"I don't understand," Eve said. "Where are we?"

"Sage's house."

Eve wanted to smack her. "*In what world?*"

Hailey opened her mouth to answer, but something in Eve's expression caused her to pause. Concern found its way onto her face as she glanced back at the party. "Maybe we should go home."

"I..." Eve hesitated. Hailey had been so excited about the party, and she went out of her way to include Eve, too. She didn't want to be the reason for ruining Hailey's night. "No, I'm fine."

"Are you sure?"

"Yes."

Hailey didn't seem convinced, but her eyes scanned the crowd, searching. "Sage! Over here!"

Eve was relieved to see that Sage was the same—no wings, no horns, no gills. It was almost suspicious how normal she was in comparison to her company. Even her dress screamed normal—tight and black with a pair of fishnets underneath and her signature combat boots. Sage held up a half-filled glass in greeting.

"There you are. What took you so long?" Sage wiped her lips with the back of her hand, leaving the navy-blue liquid to drip from her skin. Eve noticed that the drink was strange. Was it filled with glitter? Sage saw her staring and offered the glass. "Want some?"

"No thanks." Eve's response was immediate.

"Don't eat anything on the left side," Sage said, gesturing toward a set of tables. "Everything on the right side is safe."

Eve watched on in confusion as a group of leaf-haired women ate the berries on the left side of the yard. The food there was far more appetizing—the fruits ripe, the meats juicy—whereas the right side was plain.

She was about to ask why when a cloaked figure appeared at her side, his entire body shrouded in shadow as he wordlessly offered a platter of dark liquid glasses. Hailey plucked one from the tray, the glitter sparkling against her lips as she took a long sip.

"Do you want some water, Eve?" Sage offered. Before Eve could respond, Sage gestured the servant away, and he returned with a glass full of clear, plain water. Eve couldn't stop herself from sniffing it—just to be sure—before she took a light sip.

It was the best water she'd ever drank, but it was water all the same.

As Eve stared across the crowd, stories came to mind—stories of fairies with voices of bells and trolls hiding under bridges for unsuspecting children. They were creatures of fantasy, dreamed up concoctions of allegories and questionable punishments.

These were not the creatures of her picture books. They were real, with fangs and horns and tails and wings and everything else Eve thought didn't exist. Wasn't *supposed* to exist. Some were beautiful in a way that her mind struggled to comprehend it. Others were so ugly and grotesque that Eve knew they would reappear in her nightmares.

This was the world Liam belonged in. It made sense—his strange beauty, his arrogant attitude, the weird gold of his eyes—and yet she felt even further from the truth. None of this was supposed to exist, and yet here she was, sipping water alongside her human friends, surrounded by people that were not.

"Eve?" Hailey's hand pressed gently against her shoulder, her voice filled with concern. Eve hadn't realized her hands were trembling, the water splashing onto the ground. "Are you okay?"

"I'm fine," she said. And she was. Mostly. This should have scared her more than it did, but Eve felt... She didn't know how she felt. Her initial fear coming into the party had diminished the longer she observed the other guests. Eve found herself wondering how she might paint them on a canvas.

She could sense Hailey glancing anxiously in her direction, making sure she was alright; that she wasn't in shock and would run off screaming at a moment's notice. Maybe she *was* in shock. Eve grew used to the strange faces and the lullaby-like melody that floated over the yard. She was enchanted by it, and a part of her ached to be a part of it.

Eve stared back at the glass of water in her hand. Plain. Boring. She was out of place, an intruder among something magical. She almost wished she had one of those fancy, glitter-filled drinks—but that meant drinking, and even the smell of alcohol left her stomach churning. She could still smell it on Colton's—

Hailey's high-pitched giggle cut into her thoughts, and Eve took a deep breath, finishing off her glass. He wasn't here—he wasn't *anywhere*. Colton was dead. She never had to worry about him again.

"This song is so good!" Hailey yelled, her voice unnecessarily loud over the music. She swayed her hips back and forth and threw her hands up in the air, a strange juxtaposition to the whimsical tune that floated across the backyard. Sage smiled, her gaze drawn to Hailey's hips.

"Let's dance," she said, winding an arm around Hailey's waist. Hailey grinned stupidly; whatever she was drinking had hit her hard and fast.

Before Sage could steer her too far into the party, Hailey grabbed Eve's arm. "Do you wanna come?"

Eve shook her head. "I'm good, thanks."

"Come on," Hailey whined. "Loosen up! Shake those hips!" She jerked her hips back and forth for emphasis, accidentally ramming into Sage. Eve bit back a laugh.

"I don't think she wants to, Hay," Sage said gently. "Do you, Eve?"

"No, thanks. I'm good." Eve hoped her words were encouraging enough. She didn't mind accompanying Hailey to a party, but she wanted to stay as far from the dance floor as she could. There were too many unpleasant memories associated with it.

Hailey pouted, but Sage wasted no time dragging her into the crowd, their bodies already swaying to the rhythm by the time they disappeared. Eve watched them go, her smile fading.

What to do now? Eve glanced around the party, searching for something to dive into, maybe some group story she could hear or a game to join. There were plenty, but they were closed off, personal. She was not part of their clique. She was not one of *them*.

Eve migrated to the side of the house instead and lingered by the bottom of the stairs, out of sight from the rest of the party.

She watched the other graceful attendees, imagining how she would capture their essence on a fresh canvas. What hues would she use for a young woman's pale pink legs against the soft candlelight? How many times would she need to paint a pixie's shimmering wings until she found the right transparency? The revelry was a work of art, and Eve was dying to memorize even a small piece of it to recreate later. She hadn't been this inspired in years.

As Eve moved to get a better look at the way a goblin bent forward to whisper in his lover's ear, something hard knocked into her.

Eve gasped and stumbled, barely catching herself on the staircase's banister. A horned man swayed in and out of her personal space, mumbling to himself under his breath. He was clearly intoxicated, his hooves trotting unevenly across the ground as he teetered left and right in a poor attempt to catch his balance.

She wanted more than anything, for him to go away, to bother some other unfortunate creature, but she couldn't bring herself to tell him to leave. If she acknowledged him, then he might notice her—*really* notice her—and that was the last thing she wanted.

Still clutching the banister, Eve straightened herself and shrunk further against the stone wall. He was teetering to the right now—away from her—and Eve relaxed.

Until he swayed right back and rammed into her once more. Eve let out a small cry as his glass tilted over, the dark contents pouring out onto her clothes.

"Careful," the creature slurred, but Eve could not tell if he was speaking to her or to himself.

"It's alright—" Eve stopped, eyes growing wide.

The scent hit her all at once. The wine was cloyingly sweet and instantly recognizable. It soaked through her clothes and against her skin, trapping her there. There was no sting of alcohol, although she was sure it was present. Eve knew this scent, had tasted it before when she had been forced to lick the glistening droplets from Colton's lips.

How did it get here?

Eve whipped back around, but the creature was gone, lost in the crowd.

Large blue stains covered her sweater and skirt, completely ruining the beige fabric. Eve's stomach churned violently with each second the sweet scent invaded her nostrils. The memories hit her strongly, each one viler than the next.

She needed to get out of these clothes. Now.

Trying to contain her nausea, Eve pushed through the crowd and searched for a familiar face. She scanned the whirling dancers, everyone within it a blur.

"Sage? Sage!" she cried, her voice high-pitched. "Hailey!"

No one came. Not a single head even turned in her direction. Everyone was too swept up in their own enjoyment of the party to notice her. Panic clawed at her chest and throat, making it hard to breathe. She had to find someone. She had to get out of here.

Eve raced up the stairs with shaking legs, shoving anyone and everyone out of her way. She ignored the rude remarks and gestures in return. She couldn't be bothered with apologies right now; she needed to get out, get out, get *the fuck* out of here.

Eve caught a glimpse of one of the dark-cloaked servants watching her from the balcony. Maybe he would know where Sage ran off to.

"Excuse me, do you know—" She turned toward him, and the words died in her throat.

Colton Davis stared at her from under the cloak.

Twenty-Four

The world was tilting on its axis, tipping her over onto the floor like the spilled wine that stained her shirt. Colton, her rapist. Colton, right in front of her. Colton, very much not dead.

Colton, alive.

Her rapist was *alive*.

An anguished cry caught in her throat as she fell over, no better than a newborn fawn struggling to walk. She hit the ground hard. She couldn't stop staring, the blood draining from her face as if it had been siphoned out of her.

"Evie?"

She was afraid to move. If she moved, he could come closer. He could—

"Eve."

Liam was at her side, baffled as he took in Eve, crumpled on the ground. Shame colored her cheeks, but she couldn't bring herself to slap his hand away when he offered to help her up. She stood slowly without his help, and took a shaky step back, forcing distance between them. Liam shrugged and shoved his hands back in his pockets.

Eve turned back to the crowd. Colton was gone. Several black-robed attendants lurked around the revelry, but Eve didn't trust any of them now. Not when Colton was among them.

"You *reek*," Liam said, wrinkling his nose. Eve might have had a retort for that, but she was too shaken to think of one.

"I need to change," she said. The scent of the wine was nauseating. "Where's Sage?"

Liam scanned the dancers, then shrugged. "I don't see her." His gaze caught on the blotchy stains on Eve's clothes. "Follow me."

"Where are we going?" Eve stayed rooted in place as Liam strode to the doorway.

"Do you want to wear wine all night?"

"No." But she didn't want to go with him either.

He waved her forward. She didn't move.

"What is it?" he asked.

"I..." She couldn't explain to him *why* she was wary of following him inside. It was too similar to prom, following Nick all the way to the fourth floor.

Liam sighed dramatically, running a hand through his bright red hair.

"If you aren't coming, I'm going back to the party—"

"No!" She couldn't be left alone, not now that she knew one of her rapists was here. *Thought* he was here. Did she really see Colton, or was her mind playing tricks on her? Had the trauma gotten that bad? "I'm coming."

Eve followed Liam through the house, surprised at how many people had managed to squeeze themselves into each room. They kept coming, their warm bodies filling up the house and spilling out onto the lawn. She had never been anywhere so crowded before; her breath quickened, the desire to flee and get somewhere safe welled up inside of her. She glanced at the open front door where more strange people flowed in, their clothing as unusual as their faces.

Liam led her upstairs and down one of the enormous halls. Candles flickered dimly against the dark stone walls, hardly providing enough light to see her next step on the moss-carpeted floor. Eve kept her distance behind

Liam, tracing her fingers against the white appliqué along the door frames. The unusual texture and shapes kept her mind distracted from the cloying scent on her chest.

He must have noticed because Liam said, "Sage made most of these. She's as artistic as she can be annoying."

He was joking, Eve thought, but there was something unsettling about the way he avoided staring at the carved skulls for too long. Eve brushed the hollow appliqué with her fingers, unable to place the material.

"What is it made of?" she asked. It certainly wasn't wood, and porcelain wasn't right, either. There were chips and ridges in the carvings that were an inherent part of the material itself. If she squinted, Eve could see that the designs were made up of several pieces glued together in a strange white mosaic.

Liam didn't answer. They stopped at what could only be Sage's bedroom—the entire door had been carved with gaping faces and wilting flowers. A wreath of bones and dried leaves hung at the center. Without knocking, they stepped inside.

There was a disrobing couple on the bed, and Eve averted her eyes as Liam kicked them out, checking a few more spots to make sure they were alone. Eve stood beside the doorway, ready to run.

Liam stared at her, confused. "Is something wrong?"

"You're not going to stay here?" It came out as a question. Her stomach flipped. She should have known better than to come up here with him.

"Right," Liam drawled, stepping past her toward the hallway. Eve visibly relaxed. "Your kind is peculiar about privacy." He gestured toward a closed door across the room. "Clothes are in there. Knock on the door when you're finished."

Liam left, shutting the door behind him. Eve stared at the knob for a few more minutes, almost expecting him to go back on his word and enter, but the door remained firmly shut. With trembling hands, Eve held her breath and removed the wine-stained clothes. She tossed them into a dirty pile on the floor, relieved that her underwear had been spared, and peered around the room.

Sage's bedroom was large—twice the size of Eve's at least—with a canopy bed pressed against one of the plum walls. Dark velvet blankets spread out across the bed, half drooping onto the plush rug underneath. A desk sat in the corner, but its surface had been covered up by small tools and half-finished projects. Tiny nubs of a white-yellow material sat abandoned in an open jar. Eve leaned close, trying to decipher what they were.

A loud thump against the wall startled her. Eve crossed her arms, forming a cage against herself as she braced for the worst. Loud, drunken laughter leaked through the wall, and Eve waited until their footsteps faded away before withdrawing from the desk.

Every piece of clothing Eve shifted through in the closet was as dark and inky as the night sky itself. The styles, however, varied greatly. Some clothing she recognized—jeans, a leather jacket, t-shirts—but there was an even larger selection of breeches and billowing shirts with wide necklines and tight cuffs. Much of the attire was made of materials so raw that it was as if they were taken from nature itself.

A fleeting thought passed through her mind: *Is Sage one of them, too?* Eve thought of the unusual people she met tonight: creatures with horns on their head. Gills on their necks. Faces that were so contorted and alien that her human brain struggled to comprehend what she was viewing. Sage had looked nothing like them, but as Eve stared at a row of unique dresses stuffed in the back, she wondered who her friend was.

Eve was tempted to borrow one of the pretty dresses, but if something were to happen, she had no idea how to take care of it. With some reluctance, she grabbed a denim skirt and a T-shirt from the closet. She couldn't imagine Sage wearing the skirt, and, according to the tags still attached, it appeared that Sage *didn't* wear it.

Sorry, Sage, she thought, tucking the tags into the waistband and yanking the denim on.

The clothes were too big—the skirt sliding down to Eve's lower hips—and Eve shivered, unused to the exposure of her legs. She pulled on one of Sage's jackets, both for warmth and to hide the scars on her wrists, and hung her necklace back in place.

Eve frowned at the pile of dirty clothes on the floor. She didn't even want to try salvaging them—it would only remind her of this night, of Colton's face. *Maybe* his face.

It bothered her. Eve found herself constantly glancing around the room, out the window, wondering if he was there, silently watching her. Was he alive, or had it been in her head?

She swallowed hard. He was supposed to be dead. He had to be.

"I'm done," she called out, holding her breath as she picked up the pile of clothes. There was a pause before Liam opened the door, as if giving her time in case she changed her mind. She felt oddly grateful for that. Liam gave her a once over but said nothing, holding his arms out obediently for the pile of clothes in her arms. There was a physical relief when she deposited them and stepped away, getting the stink of sweet alcohol far away from her. "Thank you."

"You want me to put these in a bag?" He offered. She shook her head.

"Just throw them away. They're more trouble to clean than it's worth." Liam raised a brow but didn't object. Before he left, a thought struck her. "Ah, the scarf—the cloth. The one you wanted. It's in the skirt pocket." She hadn't wanted to give it up this soon, but she had no intention of wearing it if it reeked of wine, anyway.

Liam nodded and carried the bundle of soiled cloth out of the room.

When he returned, he held a dark bundle in his arms.

"Here. Sage will have a tantrum if anything happens to her jacket." Liam tossed her the bundle. Eve unfolded the cloth, surprised to see the large black cloak Liam had worn on Thanksgiving.

"Thank you."

"Think nothing of it."

She nodded, carefully avoiding the exposure of her scars as she exchanged Sage's jacket for the cloak. There were pockets inside and black stones had been sewn around a decorative copper clasp at the top.

Eve clutched the cloak closer to herself, finally taking in the sight of Liam under the dim bedroom candlelight. His ears were elongated and pointed back into sharp tips, and his eyes shone as bright as the topaz stones pierced into his left ear. His pupils were slitted and reminded Eve of a salamander.

The way he moved was different, as well—he was light on his toes, his bare feet barely making a sound across the wooden floorboards. His long, pointed fingers curled unnaturally with an extra joint she hadn't noticed before. Eve thought that even his body was different—sharper, more angular. Her gaze trailed to his neck where, behind thick patches of dark red freckles—no, *scales*—something rough and gray clung to the skin exposed underneath his shirt collar.

"You're different," she said stiffly.

"Am I?" Liam reached back and brushed his fingers over his ear. Understanding crossed his beautiful face. "I suppose you haven't seen my real face before. Surprise."

"You're the same as them," she whispered. Eve knew Liam wasn't human, but to have it confirmed with her own eyes was something else.

Liam followed her gaze to the window that overlooked the backyard. The party was still in full swing. Eve suspected it would continue to stay that way for some time, if it ever ended at all. "You figured it out. It's about time, honestly. I was getting tired of wearing that glamour all the time around you."

"What are you?"

Liam snorted. He smirked at her, his dilated eyes gleaming with amusement. "Perhaps not as smart as I thought."

Eve shook her head. "You're—you're like the books I read when I was little. You're—" She struggled to think of a word for it. Surely there was a name, but all she could say was, "Magic."

Liam didn't deny it. He strode about the room casually, as if this was his first time seeing Sage's quarters. He picked up a small white bear figurine from the shelf and toyed with it between his slender fingers. "We prefer to call ourselves the fair folk, but I have often heard mortals refer to us as the fae, or faeries."

Faeries. Eve had heard of them a long, long time ago. She had stumbled upon the subject during a research assignment, an article having connected old children's stories to different religions. It was unrelated to the assignment—and her father would have killed her if he found her reading about it—so she had dismissed the article.

In her defense, she never thought faeries would be real. She never thought she would be having a discussion with one in their *house*.

"And this is...?" She gestured vaguely toward the window.

"A window," Liam said. Then upon receiving a flat look, "Faerie. You're in the Kingdom of Faerie. I would guess that's where your kind came up with the name for us. But, more specifically, you are in the Unseelie Court."

She stared at him with bated breath, trying to sense a lie. There weren't any. This was the truth.

He said he couldn't lie, she recalled, her mind drifting back to when he'd used her True Name. But he'd pretended to be human; it appeared indirect lying didn't count. What else had he been indirect about? What more was he hiding from her?

Colton.

"I thought you got rid of them," Eve spoke calmly, but inside she was anything but. Liam stilled, the figurine nearly slipping between his fingers. She didn't need to specify what she meant. "You didn't, did you?"

Liam stood still. Eve could practically see the wheels turning in his head as he tried to find the right words. "You said you never wanted to see them again."

"You know what I meant."

"But that's not what you *said*." Liam turned to her, his tone almost patronizing. Eve squared her shoulders, fists tight at her sides. "So, what does it matter what I do with them? They aren't your concern anymore."

"I *did* see them again," Eve hissed. Liam's face paled. Oh, now he cared. "One of them tried to offer me water."

Liam's fingers tapped against the bear figurine. "That wasn't supposed to happen."

"Obviously." Eve wanted nothing more than to hit this stupid boy across the face. "So, you've decided to keep them as slaves? Do you even know what they're like?"

"Would you rather have me torture them instead?" he asked sarcastically. Eve didn't answer. He stared at her, mouth agape. "You're serious."

"It's better than *this*." She thought of her abusers strutting around, mingling into the party with ease.

"I don't particularly enjoy torturing men," Liam said coolly. Then, a smirk. "Unless they're a willing participant."

Eve was too angry to speak. She stomped over to the window and glared out of the thin glass, eyes scanning over the yard. Several figures bustled about, their features hidden behind the thick black cloaks. The uniform was designed to make them invisible, and it had an impressive effect. Eve had to truly search to find them, but they were there, carrying away plates or cleaning up messes the reckless guests left behind. A few were pulled into the revelry, forced to dance or entertain.

Liam's eyes were on her back, observing her. He thought her cruel, and maybe she was. But cruel things had been done to her, and she had little sympathy these days.

"Why didn't you kill them?" she asked, voice cold. She had to know.

"I found it to be beneficial. They have amused me on occasion."

She whirled on him, eyes wide with rage. "They *amuse* you?"

"Yes. The frightened one is an excellent juggler," Liam said, to Eve's disbelief. "I suspect that I've known them much longer than you have, Evie."

"Oh, I highly doubt—" She stopped.

No. *No.*

But she stared at Liam's face, and it all came together.

"The wine," she rasped. Of course. *Of course.* Where else would Colton and his friends have gotten that alcohol? It didn't exist outside of this other world—*Faerie.* "How did Colton get the wine?"

Liam didn't appear to understand the urgency of her question. "The Veil is thin in certain areas of Faerie. They connect all over your realm and ours; you could enter here from Vermont, leave in another gap in the Veil nearby, and step into Europe. I'm assuming he found one of the gaps."

Eve didn't care about that. "I want to know how he got the *wine.*"

"I might have given it to him. I give a lot of people wine," he said with a shrug. "My family runs the official supply for the Unseelie Court."

Betrayal sunk into her, deep and unyielding. Her body quaked in silent fury, nails digging painfully into the soft skin of her palms. The skin broke, blood pooling between her fingers. Eve hardly noticed.

"When?" she demanded. "When did you give them the wine?"

"You want the exact date?" Liam scoffed.

"*Yes.*"

Liam realized she was serious. "It had been a while since I'd last seen them. About two or three years ago, I would guess."

Two or three years ago. When Eve was still a naive freshman in high school. When she thought she could trust a group of senior boys at prom.

Time stopped. She didn't know what to say. What to *think*. Eve was sinking into a chasm of unwanted memories, her mind filled with such an onslaught of realizations that it left her dizzy. She staggered to the side, one hand pressing against the wall to root her in place.

"They came by often," Liam continued. He only further confirmed what she already knew. "They wanted a good time, and I gave it to them."

I knew it. Her heart ached. *I knew it.*

He ruined everything. Liam didn't care that he gave the alcohol to three power-hungry boys. It didn't matter to him what they did with the bottle, or what effect the mysterious liquid had on them, or what they did to others. What they did to *her*.

Tears sprung to her eyes. Were they from anger? From shame? Or was she back in that hole, so sick and tired of living? She had been doing better, even if she was reluctant to admit it to herself. She had been happy, she realized. Her abusers were off the streets. She had friends. She had family that appreciated her, even if Nan couldn't remember who she was speaking to most days. She didn't always see a future for herself, but maybe a part of her hoped for one.

Liam took that all away with his confession.

She was fifteen again. She had to walk by her abusers each day on her way to class. She had to see them laughing at the cafeteria, flirting with other girls in their grade, and eventually graduate with bright smiles and shining diplomas. She had to see their faces every day as she walked through the school—their class portrait hung up with every other previous graduating class for everyone to see.

She had to see them every day for almost three years and keep her mouth shut.

And Liam was letting them serve drinks at his party. He had been their *friend*.

Liam placed a hand on her shoulder. His touch made her want to crawl into a hole. "You should sit down. Sage will throw a fit if you throw up on—"

Eve slapped him across the face with every ounce of force in her body. Liam staggered back, jaw slacked. His left cheek bloomed with color. Eve's hand tingled, but she held it higher, ready to slap him again. It took Liam a moment to compose himself, but when he did, she could see the outrage in his eyes.

She saw his hand twitch at his side. Would he hit her back? Eve took a step away and lowered her arm.

"You callous, *arrogant*—" Her voice shook. She took a deep breath. "You have no idea what you've done."

Liam rubbed his jaw, his smile tight. "No, Evie, it appears I don't. Care to fill me in?"

"No."

His eyes narrowed. "Then want to explain what I did to deserve that?"

"No." She didn't owe him anything, especially not now.

A tense silence stretched between them. Liam's hands flexed at his side, and she could almost imagine him reaching up to choke out the air from her lungs. Eve's imagination showed her acting similarly. But neither moved, and eventually, Eve was the first to break the silence.

"Why do they obey you?"

"Do you truly think I'm going to tell you anything?" Liam laughed without mirth.

"You didn't fulfill your end of the deal. You owe me an explanation," Eve said, her body tense.

Liam's lips twisted as though he would argue, but he held it in. His eyes trailed out the window, although Eve was sure it was impossible to pick out her abusers from here.

"They're glamoured." Eve stared at him, waiting for the explanation. "They're happy to do whatever I tell them to, as long as I give the order."

Eve considered this. "Are they aware of what's happening?"

"Not entirely." Liam's eyes narrowed. "They won't forget everything that happened while they were under, though. This merely makes them more compliant."

Compliant. Thoughtless. Obedient. To leave them imprisoned in their own bodies, forced to carry out acts without even the option to object... Maybe this was the better option.

"Can you keep them trapped in that state forever?" Eve asked.

"That is the plan," Liam said. "Glamours aren't perfect, but they are sufficient. My father will make another one of his brews when he returns home and feed it to all of the servants as a precaution."

"I see."

Eve stared out of the window. She couldn't make out which figures were her abusers, but she was certain they were down there, locked in eternal servitude. The thought still left her anxious. She didn't trust Liam to keep them that way. Not after he'd twisted their deal to keep them alive.

"What did they do to you?" Liam asked. His voice was hard but quiet. Eve hated the way he stared at her, as if he could pull her secrets out if he guessed the right phrase.

"Wouldn't you like to know?" she muttered and turned to leave. The door swung open before she could.

"Lord Liam," a black-robed servant said, their voice monotone and indistinguishable. Eve's shoulders relaxed; it was not Colton. "There appears to be a problem in the courtyard."

Liam sighed and greeted the servant with an airy wave of his hand. "What do you need?"

"Someone is siphoning from the servants, my lord."

Liam's body went rigid. Eve could see the change in him at once. "Take me to them."

A group of servants were slumped carelessly against one of the bushes in the courtyard. Eve almost mistook their cloaks for bags of garbage. There were over two dozen of them, some pale as death while others carried a shallow breath. Eve recognized Nick's frame among them and physically recoiled, all of her senses screaming at her to find safety.

"It appears Killian's friends joined us this evening," Liam muttered as he crouched beside them, checking for life. The messenger servant stood motionless at his side, their hands clasped, still as a statue. "Are they still here?"

"We have escorted two off the property, my lord," the servant replied. "It is uncertain if there are more."

Liam muttered something under his breath and stood, wiping his palms on his pants. "I'll investigate myself. Alert Sage and have someone escort Eve and Hailey home."

"Yes, my lord."

"Wait." Eve moved out of the servant's reach. "What's going on? Are we in danger?"

"No. I'm merely dealing with a headache," Liam said and rubbed his temples for emphasis. A few more servants approached, but even under their shrouds, Eve could tell they were different from the messenger. Liam addressed them at once. "The living will need to be re-glamoured until my father returns. Separate them from the dead and dispose of the rest appropriately."

The servants bowed, immediately dropping to their knees to pry through the bodies.

Liam moved to leave, but Eve caught his sleeve, unable to disguise the growing panic in her voice. "I thought you said they would stay trapped."

"I also said glamours aren't perfect." Liam pried her hand from his arm. "There are ways to break them; drinking their blood included." Eve paled. "Don't be distraught. By the time they wake up, they'll already be glamoured again. Nothing will change."

"You promise?" There was a bitter note in her voice. Eve hardly trusted him now, but she needed some kind of confirmation. Something to hold on to.

Liam rolled his eyes. "I—"

Riotous laughter suddenly broke in, followed by the sound of glass shattering. Eve and Liam turned to see one of the horned people collapse into one of the servants. The tray in their hand had tilted over, throwing glass and starry liquid against the ground.

The guest in question was a boy not much older than Liam, with long black hair and onyx horns to match. She couldn't make out much of him from this far away, but he was obviously fae, and that was enough to deter her.

"I need to take care of this," Liam muttered, already stalking toward the guest. Eve gaped at him.

"Wait—You can't leave me here!"

"It'll only be a moment. Stand guard until I'm back," he said over his shoulder.

"I can't—Liam!" But he was gone, already hauling the horned man up by his rumpled shirt.

Eve directed her attention back to the crumpled servants.

She couldn't see their faces behind the dark shrouds, but she knew her abusers were among them. Their hazy voices gave them away, incoherent mumblings slipping past their lips as they struggled to resist Liam's glamour.

Her heart thundered in her chest. They were waking up, and she had no idea what to do.

"You—" Eve grabbed the arm of one of the servants that was separating bodies. They stopped, waiting for an order. The servant was human, with the same dazed look Colton had when she ran into him earlier, but the servant's face was gaunt and her arm too narrow. Eve could see the bones protruding against the thin stretch of her skin. "Watch these men."

The servant swayed but nodded. Liam would have to handle it himself. She couldn't stay here any longer. Not while her whole body trembled with the strength of a leaf caught in a storm.

Eve glanced once more at her abusers, their faces barely obscured by the dark fabric, before running back to the house. She would find Sage or Hailey and insist on going home. Her stomach flopped, nausea running twisting in her gut. If Liam had kept this word, none of this would have happened.

God, she could smell the spilled wine again, its scent on every breath she passed. Their bodies, their heat, their hands brushing past her, touching her, grabbing her—

Eve didn't reach the porch before she heaved into a nearby bush.

Twenty-Five

"You okay, Eve?" Hailey brushed the sweaty blond hair back from Eve's forehead. Her voice was soft and comforting. Eve tried to thank her but threw up more bile instead.

Eve didn't know when Hailey had arrived, but suddenly she was there, pulling Eve's hair away from her face while she rubbed soothing circles along her back. Eve had never known such a gentle friend before, but her heart ached for the kindness Hailey offered.

Exhausted, Eve fell back onto her calves, breathing heavily. Hailey continued to rub her back, pulling her close in a half-hug.

"Hey, it's alright," Hailey crooned. "You're all done now. Did you have any wine?"

Eve shook her head. Hailey moved her hand to stroke her hair instead. Eve was reminded of a mother comforting her child.

She couldn't help herself—Eve let out a pathetic sob, the tears rushing hard down her face. She couldn't get the words out to explain, to tell Hailey that she would be alright and to leave her alone. Eve *wasn't* alright, and maybe she didn't want to be alone.

"What's going on over here?" Sage appeared in front of her, a curious brow raised as she took in Eve crumpled on the floor in Liam's cloak. Eve sniffed, wiping her eyes on the thick fabric.

"Nothing, I'm fine," Eve said.

"Need to lie down?" Sage and Hailey helped Eve to her feet, reluctantly releasing her when they saw she could stand on her own again.

"No, I'll be okay," Eve reassured them. She was tempted to take up Sage's offer—Eve thought she would pass out at any moment—but if she laid down now, she wasn't sure she would get back up. "I think I should go home."

Sage nodded. "I'll get the driver."

Hailey helped Eve into the house while Sage disappeared. The girls wandered into a drawing room near the entryway, the room strangely abandoned despite the raging party. Hailey led Eve to a red couch near the large fireplace, its bronzework as detailed as every other aspect of the house. The fire roared in front of them, and Eve couldn't help thinking that the fireplace resembled a large animal's mouth, its jaw unhinged and roaring the flames to life. The heat dried the tears on her face and soothed the discomfort in her bones.

Almost three years and she still couldn't compose herself in front of her rapists. The realization sickened her. She had thought herself strong, but they left her feeling as pathetic and vulnerable as she did when she was fifteen.

But if Liam had done his job correctly in the first place, none of this would have happened.

I'll need to be more specific next time, she thought, then nearly laughed at the idea. There would not be a next time. She would tell Liam exactly what she wanted done with the men, down to the last detail, and that would be that. She would never have to see them again.

"Where were you all night?" Hailey asked quietly, startling Eve from her thoughts. "I haven't seen you since we got here."

Eve thought back to Colton and his friends sitting in a heap of dead bodies in the courtyard. Liam had said the glamour had been removed because their *blood* had been siphoned. She couldn't tell Hailey about that.

"Parties aren't really my thing," Eve said. When that didn't satisfy Hailey, she added, "I was with Liam for a while."

"Liam?" Hailey couldn't contain her surprise. She finally took in Eve's new attire—including the cloak. "I thought you two hated each other."

"We do." There was no doubt about that, especially after tonight. Hailey's lips slipped into a frown, clearly disappointed that her two friends were still at odds. Eve wasn't sure how to tell her that they would *always* be at odds and that she should give up hoping for anything different.

Sage slipped back into the room. "Liam sent someone home. The carriage won't be back for a while. Did you want to wait here?"

The drunken fae flashed in the back of Eve's mind. Liam must have kicked him out of the party—or hopefully removed the ones drinking blood. She shuddered.

The guests here were not kind, she had noticed. They were chaos incarnate, moving through the estate like a hurricane, leaving damage and violence in their wake. The severity of horns and spikes crawling along their skins didn't help their cause. She saw blood, wounds, and bruises from punches taken a stride too far. Then there were sloppy kisses on exposed ribs, bites on necks, and the sort of fondling that had been ingrained in Eve's mind as disgraceful, especially in a place so public. These people had no morals, no propriety. They did as they pleased when they pleased. A whirlwind of sin.

Eve tried not to think of the poor servants among them who would bear the brunt of their ire. That is, if they weren't guilty of participating themselves.

Hailey met Eve's gaze with a troubled expression. Whatever she saw there was enough for Hailey to stand and help Eve to her feet. "We can walk home; it isn't far."

Sage's eyebrows pinned together. "Are you sure?"

"Yeah, we'll be safe." Hailey leaned forward to give Sage a hug. Sage held on for a few seconds too long, and her face fell when Hailey eventually pulled away. "See you on Monday?"

"Sure," Sage said, with some disappointment. She led the girls out the front door, her gaze reserved for Hailey as they left the estate grounds.

While the mansion had been a beacon of light, the forest was pitch-black and disorienting. It was the kind of forest Eve imagined hid serial killers and child-eating witches. *Or blood-drinking faeries, apparently.* She could barely see her own hand in front of her face, let alone Hailey at her side. Her only comfort was in the sound of her friend's footsteps scuffing along the dirt path beside her.

"You know where we're going?" Eve was skeptical.

"Yeah, I've walked here dozens of times," Hailey reassured her. She seemed perfectly at ease, unconcerned about the creatures that lurked in the forest. Maybe they were all back at the estate. Eve hoped that was the case. Although none of them had done anything to *her*, she wasn't about to let her guard down.

Hailey noticed Eve's jumpiness and rummaged through her bag. She pressed something small into Eve's hand. Eve's eyes adjusted to the darkness, and she realized it was a small bundle of bright red berries with a four-leaf clover poking out at the top. A small pin was attached to the back: a brooch.

"What's this for?"

"Protection," Hailey said. "You just pin it on your person."

Eve doubted the little bundle of herbs—or even God himself—was going to protect her, but she pinned it to the cloak, anyway. The vibrant red berries gave her clothes a pop of color.

The girls trudged forward, completely encased in darkness now that the mansion was out of view. Eve couldn't help but think of what waited for her there. *Who* waited for her.

Then there was Liam. What was she going to do about him? Not only had he tricked her, but he was friends with the men that ruined her life.

I can't trust him.

"Where did you get this?" Eve asked, desperate for a distraction as she tugged at the brooch. Talking helped, she realized. At least, it kept her mind from wandering back to unwanted memories.

Hailey was quiet for a moment, pondering, and her answer came slower than Eve expected. "Sage gave it to me over the summer. I think she made it."

"Oh. Thanks for letting me borrow it, then." Eve brushed a finger along one of the vibrant berries. "I'll return it in the morning."

"Don't worry about it."

Hailey stared at the brooch with a blank expression. Even in the darkness, Eve could see a sort of hollowness in her eyes. *Like Colton's*, Eve thought with dread. Why did Hailey have that stare, too?

Hesitantly, Eve grabbed her friend's shoulder.

"Hailey?"

"Yeah?" Hailey tore her gaze away from the brooch, suddenly full of life. It was as if a switch flipped. Eve pulled her hand away, unnerved.

"Nothing," she said. The stone arch was in view now, the moonlight illuminating it against the depth of the trees. Eve hadn't noticed it upon her arrival, but wisteria hung from the arch and moss grew up over the sides at the bottom.

Hailey reached up and plucked two of the flowers. Eve stared through the arch, her eyes suddenly heavy with exhaustion. What time was it? She had meant to only leave Nan with Mr. Stone for a couple of hours, but she had completely lost track of time. Eve reached into her pocket and grabbed—

Nothing.

Shit.

"My phone," she moaned. Eve groped uselessly in Sage's empty pockets. "I think I left it at the party."

"Do you want us to go back and get it?" Hailey offered, glancing back at the path they'd walked. Eve saw the way her friend's shoulders sagged and her tired eyes snagged on the wisteria dangling above.

Eve's lips pressed into a tight line as she peered back down the road uncertainly. She wasn't comfortable going back on her own. She knew if she asked Hailey, her friend would follow her back in a heartbeat—but Hailey was exhausted, and Eve was tired of relying on others. She was tired of being weak.

"No, I'll go." *It wasn't that far of a walk*, she told herself. Maybe it would be best for Eve to make sure Liam actually finished the job, too.

"Are you sure?"

"I'm sure."

Hailey hesitated, but the temptation of sleep was too much, even for her. She dropped one of the flowers and stepped onto the first stair.

Before Eve could leave, Hailey spun around and said, "Call me as soon as you get home!"

"I will."

Hailey, although reluctant to believe her, nodded once and slowly trudged her way back up the stairs to the mortal world. To reality.

Eve turned and walked back to the estate.

The forest was darker without Hailey's presence—more violent, more menacing. The trees stretched up high, their branches closer to claws reaching for the sky. There were noises she hadn't noticed before—faint giggling that resembled wind chimes, whispers so light and airy that Eve almost mistook them for the winter breeze. Eyes watched her from behind the trees. She occasionally caught glimpses of their reflective yellow irises glowing in the dark.

Eve brushed the bundle of herbs attached to Liam's cloak and walked faster.

She could see the soft glow of the estate up ahead, a warm welcome compared to the daunting path behind her. Eve picked up the pace, practically running toward the mansion.

Something large slammed into her. Eve gasped as she was thrown to the side, crashing hard against the dirt road. She hissed through her teeth as she broke the fall on her palms. Long red scrapes burned against her skin. Disoriented, Eve blinked up at her attacker.

Nick Palenti stood with the brazen confidence of a fighting bull. His muscular body towered over her with an expression akin to hatred, his hands balled into fists at his side. The black robes had been discarded, revealing a stained wife beater and a ripped pair of jeans. He smelt as though he hadn't bathed in weeks.

Eve was going to be sick. Bile rose up in her throat, but she forced it down. She could hear her heart thundering in her ears, the threat of a panic attack worming its way through her stone-still body.

The servant was supposed to be watching him. Nick was supposed to be at the party awaiting a new glamour. Not here. Not with *her*.

Nick took a moment to regard her, a flicker of surprise flashing through his eyes as he recognized her. But if his recognition extended back to high school or remained from the party, Eve didn't know. He stepped forward. Eve scrambled back, forcing her shaking limbs to comply as she rose to her feet.

The estate was close, and yet it might as well have been a thousand miles away. She could see the lanterns winking in the distance, beckoning her closer.

Nick blocked the path there, his body a formidable wall. Her heart sank. There was no reaching the estate without getting past him.

He cracked his neck, his shoulders, his knuckles. Preparing for a fight.

She ran.

Through the trees, amid the darkness, Eve's legs pumped hard as she flung herself through foliage and twisting tree roots of the forest. She couldn't take the path back home—she couldn't risk bringing Nick back into her world.

She could hear him behind her, his movements lithe despite the lumbering weight of his body. Where Eve found herself stumbling and tripping over fallen branches and rocks, Nick glided over them with ease, gaining speed at an alarming rate.

Something shimmered ahead, and Eve raced forward, a surge of hope winding through her. A light—a home, somewhere with people. With witnesses.

Eve broke through the trees.

A pond stretched out before her: a dead end. Moonlight rippled over its surface, and Eve realized with despair that she had mistaken the shimmering waters for civilization. The water stretched out into the darkness between the trees. Eve considered running around the pond, dipping into another stretch of forest, but the deafening *crack* of a crushed branch forced her still.

Nick stepped out from between the trees, his broad arms clawed with scratches from debris. He lumbered toward her, and Eve knew that no matter which way she turned, he would easily be able to jump out and tackle her.

She was trapped.

Her heart raced as Nick approached. She squared her shoulders and tried to appear tall. Brave. But her body was shaking, her knees buckling under her.

"I know you," Nick said, his voice as low and rumbling as she remembered. She swallowed hard. He took another step closer, his thick eyebrows pushed together. "You were at the party."

The party. Not prom. Did he even remember that night? A bitter anger rose through her, outweighing the fear that had kept her quiet and timid. That singular night had changed her life forever. It had ruined who she was and thrown her down a hole so deep and meaningless that not even hell itself would spit her back out.

And he didn't even know who she was.

"And what else?" she snapped. "Where else have you seen me?"

Nick blinked, taken aback. Then, "You're one of *them*—those kidnapping fuckers that stole my life."

A faerie. He thought she was a *faerie*. Eve almost wanted to laugh at the ridiculousness of it all. She also wanted to puke.

She didn't hide the sting in her voice when she said, "You didn't mind it when they were letting you drink with them."

"They weren't kidnapping me then." Eve couldn't help shrinking back as Nick watched her with those dark, predatory eyes. Even when she tried to be strong, he found a way to break her down.

She had rehearsed in her head for years what she would say to her rapists if she ever saw them again. She thought of all the hurtful things she would yell, all the threats she would make. She wanted them to regret, to suffer. She wanted them to understand what it was to hate themselves enough that death became a reprieve.

But when faced with Nick, her speech changed entirely.

"You and your friends took me to your room during prom night. You raped me." She didn't want to cry. She wasn't supposed to cry, not in her little rehearsals by herself. But her voice was raw and thick with tears as she choked out, "*Why?*"

Nick stared back at her with an unreadable expression. She wondered if he even heard her—if she even said the words aloud, or if she had rehearsed them in the silence of her mind once more. Then, a small flicker of recognition passed his face.

"Art girl," he breathed. It was a punch to the gut. She was exposed, vulnerable, but she waited. She waited for the guilt to weigh down on him, for him to see the consequences of what he'd done. She waited for him to turn away in shame. She waited for an apology, a confession, *something* that proved he had some conscience for the sins he committed against her.

Nick smiled and lunged for her throat.

Eve caught the action and dodged, her shoes skidding against the muddy grass. Nick was faster. With one hand, he grabbed her by the shoulder and threw her down. She landed on her back with a loud thud, the breath knocked out of her. Eve gasped, pain coursing up her spine. She'd landed on a pile of rocks that barely stuck out against the dirt.

He was on top of her in an instant, his weight pinning her down. She lifted herself, only to be shoved back. Eve screamed, her limbs kicking and flailing as she struggled to push him off. It was no use; Nick was stronger.

Eve glanced down at the shiny red berries attached to her breast. *Protection*, Hailey had said.

But the brooch did not protect against humans.

Nick's meaty hands wrapped around her throat, and his thumbs pressed into her windpipe. She choked, eyes bulging and nails clawing into his fists as he squeezed the life from her. She had been here before, his hand around her throat as he stole what innocence she had left. But that time, he had been intending to scare her. Intimidate her.

Now he was trying to kill her.

Blood trickled from his hands as she scratched him, but Nick only squeezed harder with dead, empty eyes. The world blurred dizzily out of focus, the edges of her vision becoming fuzzy and black.

Was this how she would die, at the hands of one of the men who had already stolen what was left of her life? Part of her knew that this was what Nick had wanted three years ago; to unleash all that anger and desire for violence in the form of her dead body. She would never forget the look in

Nick's eyes as he held her life in his hands. There was no one to stop him now.

Eve's arms fell, fingers twitching at her sides. Something coarse and jagged brushed against her right hand. She didn't know what it was until she was holding onto it for dear life.

She lifted the sharp rock and bashed it against Nick's face.

Nick howled and his grip slipped as he reached for his bleeding brow. Eve panted and coughed, the air rushing back into her lungs all at once. One hand still pinned her down by her throat. Eve struck him again.

Again.

Again.

Adrenaline coursed through her as she beat him off, the tears in her eyes blurring his image. His hand loosened and tightened again around her neck, struggling to keep a steady hold on her. The only sign that she was still hitting him came in the form of the steady *crack-crack-crack* of rock against bone. Panic swelled inside of her and *get off, get off, get off* chanted in her mind in a tearful mantra.

Eve had wanted to die. Now she was fighting to live.

Red filled her vision and the thick stench of iron stretched up into the air. Nick rolled off her and Eve took every opportunity to scramble away, mud caking her knees and scraping under her nails as she stood to face him.

His head was a massacre. Eve hadn't realized how much damage she'd done. Her focus had been solely on getting him off her, but now she couldn't stop staring at the blood that poured out of the deep gashes in his face. He spit more blood onto the ground, red coating his teeth. Even for a man as large as Nick, there was no easy way to handle blunt force trauma to the head.

"You bitch," Nick growled, but his voice didn't carry the heavy threat it once did. He sounded distant and slurred. His gaze couldn't settle on her, and his head lolled like a deflating balloon on his neck.

Something in the pond caught her eye—a movement subtle enough that she almost missed it. The water rippled in a long stream; something was moving underneath it, coming toward them.

Eve stumbled back. The water sloshed, and suddenly, the tops of three dark-haired women popped out from its depths, their glowing yellow eyes locked on the bleeding man. Nick groaned, his eyes rolling in his head as he struggled for consciousness. Eve was frozen as she watched their webbed hands shoot up from the pond and grab his ankles. Nick screamed, clawing at the mud as he was pulled toward the pond's edge. They dove down and took him with them. A few bubbles floated to the top as he struggled for air.

Then, all was still.

Eve stared at the pond, waiting for him to return, but as the seconds ticked by, she realized no such thing would happen. The world froze, as if time itself had stopped.

Nick Palenti was dead.

And she would be too, if she didn't get out of there.

Her movements were sluggish as she turned back toward the forest and dove between the trees. Eve pictured the strange women of the pond crawling out and chasing after her, dragging her under the water's depths. She ran faster, breaking out into a sprint. She stumbled over tree roots more than she ran, but Eve didn't dare glance back, didn't dare consider what they were doing to Nick's body.

Eve nearly sobbed in relief when she saw the dirt road near the stone arch to the Unseelie Court. She didn't slow down as she snatched a bundle of wisteria and raced up the stairs, her footsteps echoing through the strange invisible tunnel. She didn't stop in the graveyard, or the road to Nan's, or even when she saw her grandmother's little house sitting silently behind the broken wooden fence. She ran up the stairs, to her room, and—once she was changed—flung herself under the covers of her bed.

And then she cried.

Twenty-Six

There was a lot to process.

Eve's throat ached as she blearily climbed out of her bed and proceeded through her daily routine. Mr. Stone was already gone by the time she'd gotten home, leaving a note to reassure Eve that everything had gone smoothly with Nan for the night. She supposed that was one good thing, at least.

But the knowledge of what happened after the party clung to her, constantly drawing her attention back to the memories of Nick's body being dragged into the water. To Colton's cruel face hidden under his dark cloak.

It should have been suffocating. It should have broken her down, rendered her useless and traumatized. Eve guessed she was in shock; that was the only way to explain how she was able to keep going through her life as if nothing happened. But as the days passed and Monday rolled around once again, Eve still had not fallen apart, and now she doubted that she would.

Hailey and Sage met her at her locker Monday morning before classes began. Hailey was visibly relieved, one hand clutching the fabric of her sweater over her heart.

"Eve! Why didn't you text me when you got home?" Hailey yanked Eve into a tight hug. "I was calling you all weekend!"

"My phone?" Eve paled, suddenly remembering the device's existence. That's right; she'd left it at Sage's house. That was the whole reason she had walked back, after all. *I didn't even make it back to the house.* "Oh. I uh, I couldn't find it."

"Seriously? That's awful. I'm sorry. I should have walked back to help you find it." Eve shook her head. The idea of Hailey being involved in what happened with Nick made her sick to her stomach.

"No, it's okay," Eve reassured her. "I'm sure it's around there somewhere. It was a long night and I wanted to get home."

"I'll see if I find it when I get home," Sage offered.

"Thanks, I'd appreciate it. Oh, and," Eve added, "If you happen to see my necklace anywhere—"

"You lost it?" Hailey's voice filled with despair.

"I think I lost it when I was changing clothes," Eve said. She'd searched for it all weekend, but it was the only place she could think of. *I could have sworn I had it on the whole time, though.*

"I'll see if it's in my room anywhere," Sage promised.

"Thanks." Eve pulled out a bundle of clean clothes from her locker. "Thanks for letting me borrow these. If you could make sure Liam gets his cloak back..."

"Sure. I forgot about them, to be honest." Sage shoved the folded bundle under her arm, but her eyebrows pushed together when she noticed the berry pin attached to Eve's bag inside of her locker. "What's that?"

"Oh, Hailey gave this to me." Eve held out the bag for Sage to see.

"You gave that to her?" There was irritation in Sage's voice as she addressed Hailey. If Hailey noticed it, she didn't let on. Guilt crept up on Eve as she eyed the broach. She knew Sage had made it for Hailey, but she didn't realize there was an attachment to it. "That was supposed to be for you."

"Eve needed it," Hailey said with a simple shrug. Sage's lips pressed into a tight line.

"I don't mind giving it back," Eve said, already reaching to unclasp it from her bag. Sage grabbed her wrist, stopping her.

"It's fine; you can use it." She looked pointedly at Hailey. "I'll make another one."

Hailey smiled at her, and although Sage didn't return the gesture, she did soften a little.

She's got it bad, Eve thought pitifully. Even when Hailey hurt her, Sage's anger never lasted long. Did Hailey even realize what she was doing?

Eve shook her head. She had bigger things to worry about than her friends' love lives. Two of her rapists were still out there, and Eve was going to make sure they met the same fate as their friend.

Eve found Liam lingering by the cemetery's forest on her walk home. He had restored his glamour, appearing no more out of place than herself. Briefly, she wondered why he was by himself near the forest, then decided she didn't care. There were plenty of strange things he did that she didn't understand.

"I was wondering where you were," she said upon greeting. Liam peered up from the tree stump he had been huddled over. A small green frog stared up at her from atop the bark, as though offended by her presence. It hopped away when she got too close, disappearing into the foliage. A part of her wondered if it was the same frog she'd seen on his shoulder during the field trip.

"Conversing with frogs again?" Eve asked with a raised eyebrow. Liam stood upright. "I can't imagine they'd have much to say."

"You'd be surprised," Liam said, shoving his hands in his pockets. Eve wondered if he got cold the same way humans did. She wondered if he felt *anything* the same way humans did.

"Is he a good conversationalist?"

"Rarely. He tends to ramble," Liam joked with a wry grin.

"Hm." She ran a hand over the stump where the frog had sat. Ordinary wood, nothing magical about it. After the party, Eve had started to doubt anything was ordinary, though. Eve cleared her throat, jumping straight into her point. "I want you to take me to the men you captured."

Liam hesitated. "I don't have them."

Eve blinked. Did she hear him wrong? "You let them go?"

"They ran off," Liam explained, exasperated. "Without the glamour, they regained consciousness and walked off."

"You were supposed to re-glamour them before that happened," she snapped.

"There was a lot going on that night!" Liam threw his hands up in defense. "Dealing with Killian and his men isn't exactly my idea of a good time, I'll have you know."

"That—" Eve sucked the air between her teeth. She needed to calm down. "I told one of your servants to watch them."

"*Just* watch them?" Liam ran a hand down his exhausted face. "Oh, I'm sure they fulfilled that request splendidly. They watched them walk away."

The ground swayed from under her. She grabbed onto a nearby trunk for balance. She knew Nick had managed to sneak off, but *all three of them?* And if Colton or Logan found out about what she did to Nick...

Shit.

"It's fine," she said. Nothing was fine. Nothing was ever fine. "I'll take care of it myself."

"What do you mean by that?" Liam regarded her suspiciously.

"Not that it's any of your concern," Eve said coolly. "But since you proved to be incompetent, someone has to get the job done."

She let as much acid leak into the words as she could, but Liam didn't react.

"You're going to handle it on your own? Oh, Evie." He laughed in disbelief. Eve bristled. "You couldn't even capture them in the first place. Give me a few days, and I'll make sure they stay out of your life. I'm sure they won't be hard to find—there's only three places nearby where they can get fresh water, and leaving the Unseelie Court is a lot harder than entering it."

I haven't had any trouble, she thought, but chose not to say it aloud. She wanted to believe what Liam said, that these men would be trapped in the Unseelie Court, but she had trouble believing anything he said anymore.

"It doesn't matter," she decided. "I'm going to kill them."

Liam blinked, processing what she had said. The words came out naturally. Even Eve was surprised by how casual she sounded, how sure of herself she was. But this is what she wanted, wasn't it?

"You're going to *kill* them."

"Did I stutter?"

Liam shook his head, a mixture of outrage and confusion on his face. What right did he have to be upset? He couldn't uphold his end of the deal, anyway.

"Why do you want them dead?" he demanded.

Her heart dropped. She hadn't expected him to ask her to justify herself.

"That's my business," Eve murmured. None of her friends knew what happened that night, and she sure as hell wasn't going to confess to *Liam,* of all people.

"You're dragging me into murder," Liam said. "I believe it would be common courtesy to give me the reasoning behind it."

"No one's dragging you into anything. I can do this on my own." She would have to, since Liam was useless to her.

"You say that quite often for someone who's had to rely on me to handle all of their dirty work," Liam said sardonically. "Unlike the rest of the Unseelie Court, I don't enjoy murdering without good reason, Evie. If you would just—"

"I have a good reason," she snapped.

"Then *tell* me." His voice was commanding, but he didn't use her name. He easily could have—she could hear the frustration in his voice, his temper rising—but he didn't. Why?

"Make me." Eve glared up at him. It didn't register until now that they were standing inches apart, their matched anger a live wire between them, ready to erupt into flames. *Prove me right,* she thought. *Prove to me you're the same as every other man I've met.*

Liam was silent. His breath caught. He stared down at her, and she could see the temptation in his eyes. On his tongue. His lips curled back, ready to form her name in his mouth. *Evelyn.*

It terrified her. This invisible power, this dynamic where she was left at the mercy of someone that wanted more than she was willing to give—*that* scared her more than anything.

Liam said nothing.

Eve turned away, welcoming the cold distance she put between them. She threw her bag over her shoulder and left, refusing to let him see how relieved she was that he had not used her True Name.

Twenty-Seven

Eve's neighbors did not wait to celebrate the holiday season. Cornucopias and wheat wreaths were replaced by jolly, red-faced Santas propped up in yards, and glittering fairy lights hung on awnings. By the time December came in full, the town was decorated in its own mini winter wonderland.

Aside from Nan's house. Her family had insisted on doing some light decorating before leaving: a few lights around the porch. Some old, melted plastic popcorn decorations that they'd procured from the basement. But the house was largely empty, devoid of much celebration. Ben promised they would get a tree and decorate it together when they all returned for Christmas break. Eve was dreading it.

Guilt needled at her as she passed by Wilson's Toy Store. The windows were lit up with stuffed reindeer, blinking baby dolls, and shiny red sleighs. Stacks of board games propped up the holiday-themed toys, showcasing a vintage aesthetic versus what Eve had seen in every department store advertisement for as long as she could remember.

There was a time when Eve loved the holidays. She would long for the strong smell of pine as Ben lugged in the Christmas tree. Her favorite memories were of Christmas morning, when her family would tiredly get together to exchange gifts and play games after staying up late for midnight Mass the night before.

Those days were long gone now, replaced by a smothering anxiety in her chest every time she had to see her family's faces.

Clutching her scarf tightly, Eve braced against the next gust of wind as she continued down the street. Eve watched the flurries dance by, tiny snowflakes clinging to the wool of her jacket and the curls of her hair. It wasn't even technically winter yet, but the weather had decided to jump-start the holiday.

Scanning the storefronts, Eve ducked into Greenfield Hardware Store. Presents were the furthest thing from her mind as she slowly paced the aisles, eyeing up the tools and boxes displayed against dark wood paneling. After scouring documentaries and true crime articles in the days following the party, Eve realized her options for handling Colton and Logan were limited. Bear traps required a license, and she was too young to buy a gun.

Which meant she had to get creative.

Several wicked-looking tools sat in rows along the aisles. Serrated edges glinted like sharp teeth and pointed saws promised clean cuts. Eve picked up one of the hammers and weighed it in her hands. She savored how it felt: heavy, powerful.

She tossed it into her red plastic basket, then added a drywall saw for good measure. The hammer was more than enough, she thought, but if something went wrong, she didn't want to be empty-handed.

Grabbing a few more miscellaneous things as not to appear suspicious, Eve carried the basket to the register. The cashier was in his fifties, with a short, patchy, gray beard and a hairline that receded back into his denim baseball cap. *JOE JR* was stitched into his vest in place of a name tag, and there was a hint of amusement in his smile. Eve was certain he thought she was lost.

"You helping out on a project at home?" he asked. Eve nodded, uninterested in small talk. He didn't pick up the hint. "That's nice. I wish my kids would help out once in a while. Say, you know how to use one of these?"

Eve nodded politely through his unwanted explanation. Then, she slapped her cash on the counter and snatched the plastic bag, retreating from the store as fast as she could. She didn't want to risk leaving Colton and Logan out in the woods any longer than necessary. There was no guarantee they wouldn't find their way back to her world, and Eve didn't want to take that risk.

Eve trudged into the cemetery, huddling up in her scarf and hat as the cold cut through her jacket. It had snowed overnight, enough to leave a fresh sheen of white across the ground, but it barely stuck. As she crunched past the gravestones, a realization dawned on her. She glanced back at the obvious trail of her footsteps through the light snow and cursed under her breath. She was leaving a perfect path behind.

She shuffled her feet in an attempt to hide the distinct pattern of her shoes. Pieces clumped up, exposing more grass than snow, but her shoe prints were gone, at least. Eve adapted an awkward shuffle as she made her descent into the Unseelie Court.

The forest was different in the daytime, but no less threatening. Invisible eyes watched her through the branches, and Eve glimpsed shadows and wings out of the corner of her vision. Shoving the plastic bag into her pocket, Eve carefully tucked the hammer and drywall saw under her sleeves, gripping the handles so they wouldn't scrape against her. It was reassuring to have something to protect herself with.

Only a few days had passed since the party, but Eve came to Faerie every chance she got, memorizing the winding paths and marks of forest trees. At first, it had been purely for her own safety; she needed to get a sense of the land in case she had to make a quick escape. Then, Eve found herself taking longer treks home, admiring the extra shimmer of snow against pine and the soft melodic humming that occasionally whispered through the air. She'd even noticed a few homes—tiny doors at the base of trees, burrows with lit candles in nearly invisible windows—but kept her distance. There were monsters in these woods, but at least she could expect it from the fair folk. Humans were another story.

Eve reached the edge of a familiar bend in the road and paused. Liam had mentioned fresh water during their fight. If Colton and Logan were smart, it would make sense to stick to somewhere that would keep them hydrated while they tried to escape the forest. The pond flickered in the back of her mind. Eve shuddered at the thought. She hated the idea of facing those creatures again, with their webbed claws and hungry yellow eyes.

But did she have any other choice?

Glancing above the trees, Eve frowned at the cloudy sky. She didn't have a clear indicator for when the sun would set, but she knew she didn't want to be in the forest alone after nightfall. Eve tried to check her phone—Sage had kindly returned it after a quick search at home—but the clock didn't tick forward. *Maybe time works differently here.*

She couldn't decide if that was a good thing or not.

Gripping the handles of her weapons, Eve marched toward the pond. At least, where she thought it was—it was dark the night she'd fled, and Eve didn't pay much attention to where she'd gone. It was a miracle she'd found her way out of the forest at all that night.

It took longer than she'd hoped to find. Eve stumbled over raised tree roots and caught her hair on branches until the sound of water caught her attention. The pond stretched out farther than she realized. It was a lake, spread out in an hourglass shape with a tail end that carried off into a bubbling creek further in the forest's depths.

Eve peered into the water. She couldn't even see how deep it went.

She shuddered, taking a generous step back. The water was unusually still, and Eve couldn't help glancing back in every so often to see if she would catch a glimpse of the webbed creatures. Could they walk? Would they reach up and drag her in, too? Eve shifted further away from the bed of water. She hadn't seen any footprints coming in, but maybe there were other signs they'd stopped here.

Pushing back her nerves, Eve paced the length of the lake, keeping her eyes peeled for signs of life. It turned out there *were* footprints, but nothing she recognized. They varied from the size of her knuckle to the length of her entire leg, with a heavy mixture of animal tracks she could barely recognize. If Colton did pass through here, his footsteps were lost in the throng of others who had done the same.

Eve checked for other signs: discarded robes, food, signs of a fire or campsite. Nothing. She carefully avoided the spot she'd fought with Nick, despite her better judgment. She didn't want to see if they'd left anything of him behind for her to find.

The clouds darkened overhead. Maybe they were already dead. It had been freezing all week; without shelter and a fire to keep warm, it wouldn't take long for them to freeze to death—if nothing else got to them first.

Eve bit down on her lip. She couldn't jump to conclusions yet—there was still a lot of forest to check.

Crack!

The snap of a branch echoed through the woods. She froze. Her anxiety kicked into overdrive as she peered between the trees. She gripped the handles of her hammer and saw tighter, her palms breaking into a sweat through her gloves.

The forest was still. Had Colton and Logan come to get some water before it got dark? Did they see her there? Or was it a stray animal that caught her attention?

A sense of being watched hung over her. Eve struggled to keep her breathing even as she moved away from the noise in the forest and closer to the lake. The frantic beat of her heart surely gave her away, but she wouldn't be caught off guard. When they appeared through the trees, Eve would be ready. ◻

A creature skittered into her field of vision. Shame colored her face when she saw the small red salamander on the ground staring up at her. Not an enemy—a lost amphibian. Eve closed her eyes and took a deep breath to calm her nerves.

God, I'm losing it.

Something grabbed her shoulder from behind.

Eve didn't think—she swung. Her hammer slid from her sleeve, glinting in the daylight as it tore through the sky.

Whoever—whatever—had grabbed her ducked with a faint exclamation of surprise. She missed, the weight of the hammer yanking her to the side—

Directly into the lake.

Eve gasped as the frigid pull of the water enveloped her. It was colder than ice, cutting through her clothes with a burning chill that stunned her. It was so dark, darker than the lake had any right to be. Her eyes stung as Eve frantically searched for the surface, her arms and legs kicking out in a panic.

Fear gripped her with its steel claws. She knew how to swim, but the weight of her winter clothes pulled her down, sinking her toward the bottom. Eve let go of the hammer, allowing it to drag away as her numb hands fumbled with the buttons on her coat. The drywall saw scraped against her arm, slicing open the skin. The water mixed with her wound, drawing the blood out. Eve ground her teeth together to keep from crying out in pain.

Her lungs already ached, begging for more air. She wiggled in her coat, one shaky hand snatching off the hat and scarf. But she was losing steam quickly. The frigid temperature of the lake paired with the weight of her clothes was bringing her down, and Eve didn't have the energy to keep up.

Don't stop. She had to keep going. Who was going to watch Nan if she wasn't around? Who would enact justice on her behalf?

Fighting against her exhaustion, Eve shimmied out of her coat, the sleeves catching on her cardigan underneath. She tried to unbutton this too, but her fingers were too numb to work. She had to keep going. She had to—

Eve shivered as something scaly brushed against her leg. There was movement in the water, circling her. A predator sizing up their prey.

Shit. Her mind worked too slowly in the frigid water, but it now dawned on her that drowning was not the worst of her problems.

Especially not when a pair of slitted yellow eyes blinked in front of her.

Eve kicked away as the creature sped forward, their jaw unhinged wide to show off their horrifying pointed teeth. It reached for her with webbed hands, its fingers stretching out into long, menacing claws. Eve wanted to scream, but she had little breath left. Her energy waned with each second underwater. How much longer before her body gave up?

She managed to kick the creature in the side, but it recovered fast, spinning its body to attack from another angle. Eve's coat still hung on her elbows, refusing to fall off—along with the saw stuck inside.

Gripping the saw's handle, Eve thrust it out toward the beast. It was a pathetic stab, slowed down by the pressure of the water and the awkward hang of her jacket, but it sliced a thin line across the creature's face. The beast recoiled, hissing as dark blood leaked out into the lake.

When their eyes met, Eve knew she was doomed. The creature rushed forward. Eve squeezed her eyes shut, her arm lagging as she pathetically waved the saw in the beast's direction.

There was no pain. Eve felt the movement in front of her, the splashing of fins and limbs, but nothing touched her. Drowsily, Eve opened her eyes.

Another figure moved in the water—one without fins, an outsider. Eve tried to see who it was, but her body was shutting down. She couldn't keep up the fight any longer—against the creature, or the lake. Her vision blurred, black spots creeping in as she sank lower.

It was ironic, she supposed, that she would die in the place she killed a man. Death had a sense of humor, at least.

Something tugged on her sleeve. Then, she was pulled under.

Twenty-Eight

Eve awoke to fire. The flames blazed in the open carved jaw of a beast, the heat slapping against Eve's dry cheeks. Compared to the chill in her bones, the warmth was delightful.

Maybe hell isn't so bad after all.

Someone cleared their throat nearby. Eve glanced over to see Liam sipping a cup of tea from a settee beside the hearth, his long legs dangling over the edge.

I spoke too soon.

Eve squinted at him. Cloth the color of twilight hung around his neck. "Are you wearing my scarf?"

Liam glanced up from his cup, finally taking notice of her.

"My scarf, you mean," he corrected. "Glad to see you've sorted out your priorities upon waking up."

Eve grumbled but tried to sit up, immediately falling back against the couch as vertigo kicked in. A thick blanket had been laid out over her, and Eve held it tighter, clinging to its warmth.

"What happened?" she whispered.

"You nearly died," Liam said. "Who knew you'd overreact to a little poke?"

"It was *you* who grabbed my shoulder," Eve realized quietly. Her head was swimming, fuzzy memories of the lake.

"Were you expecting someone else?" There was a suggestion in his voice—then frustration. "What were you doing with the asrai? Are you trying to get yourself killed?"

"Asrai?" Her brain was still muddled with sleep and the lack of oxygen. Eve blinked slowly, putting a name to the horrific face in the water.

"That lake is their home," Liam explained, with no shortage of exhaustion. "You would have been dead if I hadn't shown up."

He didn't need to tell her twice. Her lungs burned with each breath; the cut on her arm was a dull ache. Eve avoided his gaze as she worked to sort out her thoughts. "How did you know I was there?"

"I didn't. I was meeting with Ophelia—that is, until you attacked her." Eve recalled the slash across the creature's cheek. Huh. So, the monster had a name; it sounded much too lovely for what she'd witnessed underwater.

"She tried to eat me first," Eve said stubbornly.

"You were in her lake," Liam pointed out, as if that justified everything. "Which brings us back to my question: what were you doing out there?"

As her senses returned, Eve's cheeks burned with mortification. She couldn't admit to him that she'd been hunting down Colton and Logan—not after it had gone so disastrously. She would never hear the end of it. It would only confirm she needed his help. Eve would rather Ophelia drown her in the lake.

"That's none of your business," she croaked, immediately clearing her throat after. She sat up on the couch slowly, squeezing her eyes shut at the pain that surfaced through her head. Liam reached toward her but immediately pulled his hand away.

"I suppose I can make a few guesses on my own." It took a moment for Eve to register the tool he held up to her: the drywall saw. He flipped it over lazily in his hand. "How primitive."

"Give that back." Eve tried to reach for it, but Liam held it out of reach. "I need it."

"Not for stabbing anyone, I hope." Liam gazed at her pitifully. "You won't do much damage with a toy."

"It cut Ophelia," she spat back.

"And that's all it did. You can't kill us so easily, Evie." Liam flung the drywall saw into the fire pit. Whatever enchantment was placed on the fire, it melted the saw into a tiny silver pool as if it were nothing. "Although, I suspect it's not the fair folk you were searching for, was it?" Eve glared back at him. Liam sighed. "Are you still set on doing this by yourself?"

"I don't need your help," Eve ground out. It hurt to speak.

"Clearly," he drawled flatly. Eve's fists tightened on her blanket. Liam rose from his chair, wiping his hands on his pants. "Your clothes are drying on the hearth. Ophelia kept your coat."

"My clothes?" Eve glanced under the blanket. She'd been changed into a dry white shift, and her arm had been bandaged with a strange green paste leaking through. Her voice came out strangled. "Did you—"

"Please, Evie, we have servants for that," Liam cut her off before her thoughts could carry her any further. "Female ones. Wouldn't want you to get too excited."

"You'd be surprised," Eve muttered before she could catch herself. Liam cracked a smile.

"And don't worry," he added in a teasing voice, pausing in the doorway. "Saving your life will only be a small cost. Be careful not to rack up too much debt, alright?"

Eve gaped at him as he slipped out of the den. Of course, he would find a way to take advantage of this situation. She could only imagine what he would make her do now that she carried a *life debt*.

Eve sunk back down into the couch with a groan. How had everything gone so horribly wrong? She wasn't any closer to killing Colton and Logan. She couldn't even defend *herself*. How was she going to take down two grown men?

She felt a souring disappointment that her plan had gone awry. Eve had hoped to end it quickly with a hammer to the head and a saw to the heart, something personal but efficient. Or maybe not so efficient, she realized. In her fantasy, she'd imagined them coming up to the pond to get water, already weak from dehydration, and she would attack from behind. Eve imagined pushing them in if things got too difficult, watching the asrai pull them under for a feast.

But what would she have done if they saw her first? Nick had recognized her from the party—would Colton and Logan do the same? What if they recognized her from school? A new fear struck her to her core. What if they were searching for her, too?

How much time did she have before they found her?

"Eve?" Sage's voice trailed in from the doorway. Eve looked up, her greeting dying on her lips.

It was Sage, but it also wasn't. The Sage Eve knew didn't have luminescent wings or hair that faded from a deep purple to a lavender so pale it was almost white. This Sage's eyes were bright, almost glowing, and Eve knew deep down that they were not contacts as she had assumed. Sage cocked her head to the side, drinking in Eve's expression with a wide, pointed smile. Her hair moved on its own, showing off the same pointed ears Liam had.

She shouldn't have been surprised, yet Eve found herself staring as Sage floated toward the couch, admiring Eve's reaction to the vivid change as her wings flapped silently behind her.

"What are you doing here?" Sage asked, breaking the stunned silence. Eve swallowed hard, wincing at the painful burn in her throat.

"It's a long story," Eve said. She worked to quell the surge of panic rising in her chest. Sage didn't need to know about her near-death experience. Forcing a smile on her face, Eve added, "Your hair is pretty."

Sage beamed, and her hair floated higher. Eve wondered if it was the first genuine smile she'd ever seen her make. "It's your first time seeing it, isn't it? It can be exhausting keeping the glamour up all the time." Sage sat cross-legged in the air, as if on an invisible chair. "But you humans tend to throw a fit otherwise."

"Has Hailey seen...?" Eve gestured vaguely toward Sage's wings. She couldn't imagine such a secret being kept between them.

"Yes," Sage replied. Her expression fell. "Once."

An uncomfortable silence followed. Eve glanced out the window; the clouds had parted, revealing a sky streaked in sunset. She swung her heavy legs over the side of the couch and pushed the blanket to the side.

"I should be getting back," Eve said, reaching for her clothes. Sage grabbed her hand, stopping her.

"You can stay with me for a few more minutes," Sage said sweetly, her voice carrying a strange, honeyed lilt that instantly calmed her. Eve's anxiety ebbed away as Sage watched her, a placid smile on her face. Maybe Nan could handle a few more minutes by herself. Why was she even worried?

Everything was fine. Everything was perfectly fine.

"Okay."

"Follow me." Sage unwound her limbs as she tugged Eve to the backyard. Eve followed without complaint, her feet practically moving on their own. Sage led her barefoot through the yard and through a gap in the hedges to the side. Eve noticed a strange chill from the snow brushing her feet but didn't think too hard about it, as she was compelled to squeeze through the gap.

On the other side, Eve stepped out into a small meadow. Flowers perked up unnaturally in the field despite the thin layer of snow covering the dead grass. Sage noticed Eve's confusion and offered a small smile. "No one else comes out here. I wanted it to remind me of home."

"Home?" Sage's smile lost some of its humor.

"I'm from the Seelie High Court, along the Lily Meadow. I moved here when I was a child."

Sage plucked one of the flowers from the field, twirling it around between her thumb and forefinger. Its already white petals appeared crystallized under the thin sheen of snow. She continued, "Things aren't meant to grow here. I can't keep plants alive as I could in the Seelie Court. My father had a powerful gnome make this space for me when I arrived—nothing lasts forlong, though."

She touched her fingers against the petals. The snow melted away instantly.

Eve thought of the wisteria hanging over the archway. Sage must have been responsible for that as well, or someone similar to her. There was no way it would survive the harsh winters otherwise.

Eve shifted beside her, the frost leaving her toes numb. "How many courts are there?"

"Several," Sage said with some exhaustion. "There are the high courts, lesser courts, and some individual courts. The Bone Court is a lesser court—they're part of the Unseelie High Court, along with the Blood Court. You probably heard about their little prank on the servants at the party."

Blood Court. The Bone Court had sounded worrying enough, but the idea of a court centered around blood sent a chill down her spine. No wonder Liam was frustrated that night.

"Do you know the people who run this court?" Eve wondered if it was more dangerous for her to be wandering between worlds than she thought.

"We do," Sage said with a smirk. She plopped down onto the snow, ignoring the wet stain it left on her pants. Eve sat beside her, the dampness clinging to her shift. "Technically, Evren does, but eventually it will fall to one of us."

"Who's Evren?" Eve asked.

"My father," Sage explained. Eve thought she heard an undertone of displeasure in her voice.

"And your mother?"

Sage stared at her small field of flowers. "My mother is dead."

"I'm sorry," Eve said softly. She felt stupid for having asked, but Sage waved her off.

"You don't need to apologize. These things happen." But Eve could see the hurt in her eyes. She tried to picture Sage's mother, but every time she considered the fact they were from the Lily Meadow, her imagination faltered. Sage was always in black, as if part of an endless funeral procession. The Bone Court was the perfect place for her.

"Is Liam from the Seelie Court, too?" Eve asked, searching for a change in subject. Sage shook her head.

"He's from the Unseelie Court, but his mother comes from a lesser court atop the Burning Mountains." Sage saw the question in her eyes. "She's not around anymore. He's been here for a long time." There was a bitterness to Sage's voice that Eve couldn't quite place.

"You have another brother too, right? What about him?"

This made Sage smile. "Preece is from the Seelie Court. He stays there when he can. Evren has been requesting his presence more often lately, though."

Sage paused, her expression troubled. Eve wondered if she was only half-understanding their conversation.

"Can I ask some more questions?" Eve asked hesitantly. If this conversation was upsetting Sage, she didn't want to keep bothering her about it.

Sage shrugged, displeasure vanishing from her face. "Sure."

Eve racked her brain, trying to decide what topic to touch first—what was *safe* to touch. There was so much she wanted to know—so much she didn't understand—that it was overwhelming. If she asked everything she wanted to, they would be here for another week, at least.

Sage laughed as the silence between them stretched on. "This isn't the last time you'll see me, Eve. There's plenty of time to ask whatever you want."

So, she did. And Sage explained it all—how they glamoured themselves, why they attended school (Sage for Hailey's company and Liam for entertainment). The most fascinating for Eve was the differences between the courts and her own reality.

"It's dangerous for humans if they don't know what they're doing. One moment you could be eating our food, and the next you'll starve to death because nothing will ever satisfy your cravings the same," Sage said with unnerving excitement. "Or you'll be drawn into a dance, and you'll never be able to stop on your own."

"You've seen this happen before?" Eve asked.

"All the time." Sage laughed. "You humans are so incredibly gullible."

Eve shifted uncomfortably. *You humans.* It was hard to forget that Sage *wasn't* human, but now, more than ever, Eve was painfully aware of the difference between them. Her attention drifted to Sage's pointed ears, the translucent green wings, the beauty of her face and body that was anything *but* human. Her brain struggled to understand what she was looking at, filling in gaps for what her addled mind couldn't comprehend.

"Are there ways to avoid it? Falling for tricks?"

"There are some." Sage hedged around her answer. "Those berries I put together for Hailey—the brooch you wore. They protect against our magic."

Eve touched her chest—the place she'd kept the brooch pinned to her cardigan—but brushed the white shift instead. "Does it work against monsters?"

Sage cocked her head. "It'll protect against glamours, not teeth. Why do you ask?"

"No reason," Eve said too quickly. Sage raised a brow, the mannerism strikingly similar to Liam. She pushed the thought to the back of her mind, quickly adding, "What about weapons?"

"What *about* weapons?" This interested Sage. Her eyes were brighter now, shimmering with the gleam of gemstones. It was disorienting.

"Do you have any magical weapons?" Eve asked. *Something better than a hammer and a saw?*

A bemused expression flickered across Sage's face. She tilted her head to the side, her long hair flowing around her elbows. "What do you want a weapon for, Eve?" When Eve didn't answer, Sage's grin widened. "I have a few. They're not the same as any of the toys you humans make, though. It would be stupid to travel around the Unseelie Court without them. There are too many dangers in the forest."

Sage's gaze focused on the trees at the edge of the clearing. Eve glanced back, her anxiety creeping up on her. Did Sage see something she didn't? Eve searched between the trees, sure she would find Colton or Logan staring back at her. All she saw was forest.

"I see," Eve managed.

"Do you want to see one?" Sage asked suddenly. Eve turned to her, taken aback.

"Sure," she finally said. Sage reached into her boot and pulled out a sheathed dagger; the handle was gold, with nature motifs and shining purple gems embedded at the hilt. When she unsheathed it, a silver blade stared back at Eve, its point freshly sharpened.

"Evren gave this to me on my sixth birthday," Sage said, admiring the blade. "He said if I wanted to inherit the Bone Court, I would need to learn to use it."

"Are you inheriting the Bone Court?" Eve asked as Sage sheathed the dagger once more, hiding it beneath the black leather of her boot.

"That's to be decided." With a stretch of her arms, Sage floated into a standing position. It appeared their game of questions-and-answers was coming to an end. Eve climbed to her feet, uncomfortable as the wet shift clung to her behind.

"I have a question for you now," Sage said suddenly. "Did you make a deal with Liam?" It sounded as if she already knew the answer.

Eve bit her lip, peeling the shift away from her skin. "I did."

If Sage was surprised, she didn't show it. "Did your deal have something to do with your interest in weapons?"

"Something to do with it." She didn't want to explain further. The embarrassment of her failure—and the weight of her life debt to Liam—was too much for her to take in.

"What did you trade?"

"My name." Sage's attention snapped to her, but Eve couldn't bring herself to meet her friend's gaze. Shame heated her face. She hadn't known it at the time, but now she understood the depths of her own stupidity. Liam's words came back to haunt her, playing in a taunting cycle at the back of her mind.

Names have power, Evie. You should be careful who you give yours to.

She had given her power to Liam without a second thought. Granted, she didn't *know* she was doing it, but that was even worse.

"Why would you give him *that?*" Sage asked in disbelief. "What did you want him to do? It must have been important." Her shock gave way to curiosity.

Eve pushed through the gap in the hedges, a few dead leaves sticking to her hair. "It was."

"You humans are truly foolish," Sage said with a laugh. Eve's cheeks flushed in shame. "Your mistake was making a deal with Liam in the first place. If you want a job done, you have to go to someone capable." Sage's amber eyes glinted with mischievous delight. "I would be happy to help you in his stead."

"You would help me?" Eve asked. They made their way to the den, where Eve's clothes were spread out across the hearth. She quickly shoved her displayed panties to the bottom of the pile as she gathered them up in her arms.

"Of course," Sage said slowly. "As a favor."

Before her deal with Liam, Eve wouldn't have given a second thought to the favor—humans did things for each other all the time—but the word latched onto Eve's mind. *A life for a life*. She had already given Liam her True Name—would Sage want the same?

"What would you want in return?" Eve asked hesitantly. A creeping sense of unease settled in Eve's stomach, but she chalked it up to her failed contract with Liam. She had been burned before, and her debt to him was only increasing.

"That depends on what you're asking me to do."

Eve swallowed hard. If she wanted Sage's help, she would need to tell her exactly what she wanted. Her heart beat unevenly in her chest as she deliberated on what to say. Would Sage ask questions? Would she tell Hailey?

"Something happened a few years ago." Eve tried to keep her tone casual as she followed Sage to a spare room to change. Her throat swelled with the memory. "I want the men responsible to pay for it. There are three—two of them, and I want them dead."

Excitement gleamed in Sage's eyes. "I never took you for a murderer."

Eve didn't know what to say to that. "Would you do it?"

"Sure," Sage said flippantly. "The Unseelie Court is not a kind place, Eve. The fair folk here are brutal. There aren't many exceptions to that."

They stopped in front of a spare room, and Eve took the extra time to think while she changed by herself. The exhaustion hit her all at once.

Eve sluggishly pulled her clothes back on, pleased to find the brooch still attached to her cardigan. The wool coat was a lost cause, but if that's all it cost to keep from being eaten by lake monsters, Eve was happy to pay the price.

Sage was waiting for her when she stepped out of the guest room. Without a word, Eve followed her to the front door where the stark white carriage was waiting. It was only in the last glimpses of daylight that Eve realized it was not carved from marble or any precious stone. The carriage was composed of bones that intricately fit together to create a myriad of faces and figures against the candlelight. A mosaic of death.

Silence stretched between them as Eve hesitated to climb in.

"What do you want in exchange?" she asked. "If we were to go through with it."

Sage thought it over. "I haven't decided yet. I'll call on you when the time comes."

It was a non-answer, if any. Eve shifted, the cold seeping through her winter boots. "I'd rather know now. I don't want to be tricked again."

Eve expected Sage to be angry, but she was intrigued. "You think I would trick you?"

"I don't know," Eve admitted. "But I don't want to take the risk."

"I'm not my brother," Sage said, offended by the comparison.

"But you're still fae."

Sage pressed her lips together in a tight line, a hint of irritation seeping through. But Eve would not budge on this. Sage seemed to think her options over carefully. "I promise I won't take your True Name." Then, when it was clear Eve wasn't persuaded, "I would request your help to claim the Bone Court."

"How would I do that?"

Sage smiled. "I can think of something."

It was a vague request but came as a huge relief all the same. Eve weighed her options; she hated not knowing what that entailed, but Eve doubted it would be as bad as giving away her True Name could have been. *That* power, at least, was off the table.

And Sage was her friend. Eve wanted to trust her.

"Alright," Eve breathed, the air coming out in a puff of white smoke from the cold.

Sage smiled. They shook on it.

Eve settled into the carriage and glanced out the window, a thousand questions on her lips, but Sage had already disappeared back into the manor. Back into her world.

Twenty-Nine

The cold bit through Eve's gloves as she shuffled in front of Parkside Mall. The automatic doors opened often as Christmas shoppers passed by, blowing a wave of taunting heat toward her. She probably could have waited inside, but with how crowded it was, Eve decided it would be easier for Hailey to spot her out front.

Eve scrolled through her texts with Hailey again, confirming she had the right place. Hailey had texted the night before, begging Eve to accompany her for some Christmas shopping while her parents were out of town for a conference. Luckily, Mr. Stone had some shopping to do himself, and he was happy to drop her off while his wife watched over Nan.

But fifteen minutes had passed, and Hailey still wasn't here.

Eve bit her lip. Her thumb hovered over the call button, reluctant to commit.

Thankfully, she didn't need to; a bright orange scarf caught her eye, and Hailey waved in greeting as she rushed to meet her.

"You didn't have to wait outside," she said, her breath coming out in white puffs.

"I don't mind." Eve glanced beside Hailey, unsurprised to see Sage right behind her. She *was* surprised to see Liam dragging behind, his attention focused on Eve.

Son of a—

"I need to get my mom this fondue set, and my dad asked for a new radio," Hailey listed off the items from her phone as they entered the mall. "I have no idea what to get my brother. Michael can be a pain in the ass with presents. Any ideas?"

"What is he interested in?" Eve asked, relishing in the central heating. She kept herself close to the wall, away from the bustle of shoppers.

Parkside Mall was outdated, with a few empty storefronts and fading signs on the department stores. Someone had tried to spread a little holiday cheer with inflatable decorations of giant presents and reindeer in the middle of the hallways. Banners hung over boarded windows wishing a happy holiday, but it did little to hide the fact the mall needed an upgrade. With as many people as there were crowded in the stores, Eve wondered why they hadn't fixed it up already.

"I don't know. Hockey, skiing, winter sports mostly." Hailey sighed. "He's proposing to his girlfriend on New Year's. Depending on how that goes, I'll need to get him and his fiancée an engagement gift, too. And a wedding present. He's getting real expensive, real fast."

Eve glanced at a large display of new cookware in a nearby shop window. "Why don't you make him something?"

"I suck at making gifts," Hailey said. "Trust me, they'll *definitely* want something store-bought from me."

"I don't understand why you need to get him anything anyway," Sage said, her attention drawn to a jolly-faced Santa by the food court. A cheery teenager dressed as an elf ushered a group of kids to his lap. "You told me the holiday has something to do with a baby. What does a baby have to do with gifts?"

"It's complicated." Hailey pursed her lips. Then said to Eve, "What are you getting your family?"

"I'm not sure." Eve had been careful to avoid the subject of Christmas since her parents left after Thanksgiving. She didn't have money to buy them anything fancy; homemade would have to do. "I haven't thought about it."

As if reading her mind, Sage suggested, "You could paint something for them."

"Probably not—" Eve started, but Hailey immediately interrupted with, "You can paint?!"

"Sort of." Eve cast an annoyed glance at Sage. Having avoided the hobby for so long, she knew her parents would be overly analytical with anything she created for them.

"I'm *jealous*," Hailey whined. "You and Sage are so creative. It's seriously unfair."

"Basketball is sort of an art," Sage said. Hailey wrinkled her nose in disagreement.

"It's not like I can give someone a game of basketball for Christmas," she muttered. "Are you doing homemade gifts then, Eve?"

"I don't know." She immediately thought of her conversation with Nan. Maybe she would paint a picture of James Dean. She wasn't skilled at painting humans, but it was the thought that counts, right? *Even if she hates it, she probably won't remember where she got it from, anyway.* She bit her lip, guilty for the thought.

"How do you usually celebrate Christmas?" Hailey continued. "It must be hard with your birthday being so close."

Eve hesitated. "How do you know when my birthday is?"

"It's on your Facebook. Your page is seriously out of date, by the way. Do you have a TikTok or something instead?"

"No." She wasn't even supposed to have a Facebook, but Eve kept that secret to herself. She thought she'd been careful enough by avoiding posting pictures of herself on it, but clearly she hadn't done enough.

"*So,* what do you want to do for your birthday?" Hailey leaned against her friend with a conspiring smirk.

"We don't need to do anything," Eve reassured her.

"We have to do *something*," Hailey argued. "You're going to be an adult! That's huge!"

Eighteen. Adulthood. Eve never thought she'd see the day, and yet December fifteenth was creeping closer with each passing second. A sense of panic squeezed at her chest; she was never supposed to be around this long. What was she going to do?

"Don't try to fight me on this Eve," Hailey argued when Eve didn't respond, jabbing a finger against her shoulder. "I'll end up planning something anyway, and you'll have to suffer through it whether you want to or not."

"How about we throw a party?" Sage suggested. Hailey latched onto the idea before Eve could register what had been said.

"That's a great idea! We could throw it at your place, couldn't we, Sage? My parents will go nuts if I have a bunch of people over."

"Sure, if Eve's fine with it." The girls waited expectantly. Eve's stomach churned. Sage's last party still haunted her; she wasn't exactly excited to repeat the event.

But what choice did she have? They were her only friends; Eve didn't want to disappoint them.

"Yeah, I guess we could do that." *Then we can plan my funeral afterward.*

"We're having a party?" Liam drawled from behind.

"We never said you were invited," Sage said, but Liam ignored her, turning to Hailey for confirmation.

"The fifteenth is on a Friday, right? Let's do it next weekend after school," she said, then emphasized, "It's for Eve's birthday, so you can't be an ass."

"I'm never an ass, Hailey." Liam faked offense. "But a party would be wasted on her. We should celebrate something else instead. My beauty, for example. That's enough to have a party over, isn't it?"

"Beauty isn't the word I'd use," Eve muttered. Sage stifled a laugh.

"The only reason we're having a party is *for* Eve," Hailey argued with a sigh. "Don't be a jerk."

"Isn't that the radio you wanted, Hay?" Sage pointed to one of the storefronts: a vintage-style tech store filled with themed record players, lamps, and other neat devices. At the front, a group of vintage radios sat on display. Hailey's face lit up.

"That's it!" Her face fell as she took in the long line stretching out of the front doors. "Crap."

"I'll wait with you," Sage reassured her. Hailey beamed. Eve grimaced at the crowded store, her chest tight. She didn't hate crowds, but people were packed inside, closer than sardines, barely managing to squirm around one another as they snatched electronics off the shelves.

Noticing Eve's reluctance, Hailey said, "It's going to be kind of crazy around here. It might be better if we split up. Sage and I can meet you guys back at the food court once we're done?"

Pack herself into a crowded store or spend time alone with Liam? Maybe joining the sardines wouldn't be so bad. "I don't mind waiting—"

"It's fine," Liam answered for her. Eve bit back the harsh remark that lingered on the edge of her tongue. "We'll see you there."

Hailey glanced at Eve for confirmation. Eve forced a plastic smile. "Yeah, we can meet you back at the food court."

Relief flashed across Hailey's face. "Thanks! We'll meet up with you then. It shouldn't take more than"—Hailey sized up the crowd—"Twenty minutes? I hope."

"Good luck."

Eve tried to ignore the twisting ache in her gut as she and Liam turned back toward the busy mall. She tried even harder to blatantly ignore the annoying faerie at her side as she scanned the crowded storefronts. Maybe she could lose him in one of the stores until they were supposed to meet back up.

"Why did you agree to the party?" Liam asked once they were out of hearing range. Eve was tempted to ignore him, but the question took her off guard.

"They wanted to throw one for me. It would be rude to say no."

"But you hate them."

"I never said I *hated* them."

"You didn't have to." Liam yawned, stretching his arms above his head momentarily. Eve pressed her lips together tight. It discomforted her to know how easily Liam saw through her.

"It'll make them happy. It's fine."

"What would make *you* happy?"

Eve paused by the escalators, meeting his gaze. The way he watched her made Eve self-conscious. She stepped onto the escalator, eager to remove her face from his line of sight before he could see the heat spreading up her neck.

"You fulfilling your end of the bargain would be a start," she retorted a beat too late. "But I'm not holding my breath."

Their conversation lapsed as they wandered the lower level of the mall. Eve pretended to be interested in the display windows, giving herself something else to focus on.

"What are you going to buy?" Liam asked.

"I haven't decided," Eve said. Gifts had been the last thing on her mind, but she supposed that was the whole point of coming out today. She needed to get it done, eventually. Eve glanced at a nearby display of winter wear decorated on faceless mannequins. Even with their end-of-year sales, Eve had trouble justifying paying the prices marked on the little white tags.

What did she get for her mother last year? A charm bracelet? *Maybe I can get her a necklace to match.*

That left her father. She didn't want to spend any money on him—which was unfortunate, because she didn't want to make him anything, either. What would the man even want? She couldn't afford any of his hunting gear, and she didn't want to deal with his irritation if she got him something he took offense to. Ben was easily offended.

Maybe she would get them both a tin of popcorn and call it a day.

I should get Hailey and Sage something too, she thought. It was only fair since Hailey brought her back souvenirs from Costa Rica. Hailey was pretty easy to shop for, but Sage... Eve didn't know where to start. *I guess I could always try Hot Topic.*

Eve started toward the Gothic chain, but a small figurine in a nearby window caught her eye: a baby deer sleeping atop a bed of grass. A purple butterfly made of amethyst brushed its ear, its wings glittering under the lamplight.

Liam followed her gaze. "What a boring trinket."

"You're a boring trinket," Eve grumbled for lack of a better insult. She ducked into the storefront, squeezing between tired mothers in turtlenecks and fussy children. The shop was filled with greeting cards and hand-blown glass ornaments under signs which read *BUY TWO, GET ONE FREE!*—a deal that many customers were taking advantage of. Eve managed to sneak between them and snatch up the figurine, purchasing it before she could change her mind.

Liam peered over her shoulder into the bag. "Who's that for?"

"None of your business," Eve said, pinching the bag shut.

"Are you always this charming?"

"Only when you're here." Eve shot him a withering smile. She made it all of three feet out of the store without paying attention before her shoulder bumped into someone. "Oh, sorry—"

Her apology cut off as she met Eric's awkward grin.

"Hey," Eric said. "I didn't expect to run into you here."

"Neither did I." Eve gripped the handles of her bag tighter. She glimpsed Liam observing her from behind, his attention drawn to the potential entertainment, but when she turned back, he was gone. *Invisible*, she guessed.

She needed to get out of here. Fast.

Eve tried to step around him, but Eric took a step to the side at the same time, following her movement. "Hey, I want to make sure there are no hard feelings." Eve gave him a dumbfounded look, forcing him to clarify. "Because I went out with Hailey."

"Oh. No, I don't mind," she said quickly.

"It's just that you weren't interested—" Eric continued. Eve was disappointed to hear the hope in his voice.

"Yeah, I wasn't." She winced as the words came out too fast. Hurt flashed across Eric's face. "Sorry."

"It's fine," Eric said. He shifted awkwardly; their silence made even more uncomfortable by the static pop cover of *Jingle Bell Rock* playing over the mall's stereo system. "I guess I should let you go. I still have a lot of presents to sneak home before my mom finishes work."

"Me too," Eve agreed, more to the departure than presents. Eric nodded stiffly, his nylon coat rustling as he turned away. Eve released a sigh of relief.

"The human is interested in you?" Eve jumped as Liam's breath brushed against the back of her neck. She reached back to smack him, but Liam was already hopping out of the way with a playful grin. "I guess that answers my question."

"Leave me alone," Eve snapped, harsher than she'd meant to. She didn't apologize, keeping her stride even as she walked to the food court.

"Are you interested in him, too?" Liam raised an eyebrow at her.

"No."

"I can't blame you. I've met toadstools with more personality." Eve bit back an involuntary smile. The only thing she hated more than thinking he was—very rarely and extremely mildly—amusing, was Liam knowing about it. "I'll bet he's a poor kisser, too. I've never seen dryer lips in my life."

"I wouldn't know."

Liam stopped in the middle of the walkway, nearly causing a collision with the group of teenagers behind him. "You haven't kissed him?"

Unease crept inside of her, pressing against doors she'd rather leave shut. "Why would I?"

A genuine curiosity sparked in his eyes. "Have you ever kissed anyone?"

There it was, the pain in her chest. She had, but she hadn't wanted to. Where was the answer for girls who had their first kiss stolen, left with bitter memories that would rather be forgotten? "I think Hailey and Sage should be done by now."

"You didn't answer my question."

Eve's fists tightened around the handles of her bag. "Are you going to make me answer?"

"Do you want me to?" Liam asked with a smirk. Eve shot him a glare, and the amusement died from his face. "It was a jest."

"You're not funny."

Liam frowned. She waited for some kind of retort, but he seemed troubled instead. She was reminded of the way he had behaved on her porch—solemn and faraway.

"I'm sorry." He tested the words, as if he'd never spoken them before in his life. Eve had certainly never heard an apology from him. "I don't intend to hurt you."

The anger inside of her simmered down, replaced with... what? An unfamiliar warmth and discomfort clashed inside of her, and Eve found herself at a loss.

"It's fine," she finally said. "Just—don't make jokes like that. About controlling me. Even if you don't actually do it, the jokes still bother me."

Liam nodded, his face serious. "Very well. I won't do it again."

"Okay." Eve shuffled awkwardly. She found it hard to meet his gaze. "Anyway, let's go to the food court. I'm starving."

Sage and Hailey were already waiting at the food court when Eve and Liam arrived, and an extra chair had been pulled aside to hold Hailey's bags. They didn't waste any time hurrying back into the shops, browsing through books, jewelry, perfumes, shampoo—anything that Hailey thought might be a fun Christmas gift.

Liam lingered at her side, asking questions about certain items in the stores, while Eve helped him browse for items related to his quest. Since his earlier promise, Eve found her anger lessening as she talked to him. He still royally botched the disposal of her abusers, but at least being in his presence wasn't completely unbearable.

Halfway through their trip, Hailey decided it was time to try on some clothes.

"Just wait out here," she told Liam. "We won't be long."

"What am I supposed to do?" Liam asked, annoyed.

"Figure it out," Sage said, following Hailey to the dressing rooms. Hailey had pulled some clothes for Eve to try on, and even though she couldn't afford them, Eve had a hard time saying no to her.

After Hailey was already situated in her dressing room and Eve was about to enter hers, Sage pressed a hand on her shoulder.

"I know how you can help me."

Thirty

It was past midnight when Eve snuck out of Nan's home. The old woman had been asleep for a few hours by now, and Eve trusted her to rest throughout the night.

Eve found herself glancing over her shoulder on her way to the cemetery, squinting back at the shadows that played across her neighbors' houses. Even if someone was hiding among them, there was no way she'd be able to tell.

That didn't stop Eve from checking.

The temperature dipped low overnight. Eve huddled in her coat and scarf, quietly wishing that she'd worn more than a pair of sweatpants out. But that was all she'd had time to grab.

Sage waited for her near the stone archway; there was no disguise tonight, no trace of human touch. Her luminescent wings twinkled against the falling snow, her elongated limbs somehow even more beautiful in her natural form. Even her clothes were different—a long fur cloak hung over a heavy dress—although they were still in her signature coal shade. She turned with Eve's approach, pieces of snow clinging to her lilac hair.

Eve felt even sillier in her puffy nylon jacket and old sweatpants.

"I was starting to think you wouldn't come," Sage said. She rose a brow at Eve's appearance but said nothing more.

"Sorry," Eve apologized. Sage shrugged and plucked a piece of wisteria from the arch. A new one grew in its place.

"I've had some time to think about it, and I think I know how you can assist me. That is, if you're still interested in keeping our deal?" Sage played with the flower in her hand, new vines growing over her palm and down her arm. Eve watched in awe. Sage's eyes flickered up to meet hers, waiting.

"Yes, of course," Eve answered a beat too late. She couldn't take her eyes off the flower. New buds popped up along the vine, the thin green line twisting around Sage's arm and intertwining through her hair. *Magic.*

Sage gauged her response, her head tilted gracefully to the side. "Have you ever killed anyone before?"

Eve was taken aback, but reluctantly nodded.

"Yes." The confession came with a heavy weight on Eve's chest. Technicalities didn't matter here; Eve wanted Nick dead, and now he was. If the asrai hadn't dragged him under, Eve might have delivered the final blow herself.

Sage's expression remained neutral. Despite Eve's familiarity with Sage's calm composure, in this instance, it left her uneasy. As if she were being evaluated.

"My father is fond of playing favorites as much as he is fond of playing games," Sage continued. She let the wisteria grow out to Eve, offering her a bundle. Eve took it cautiously. "I know he has something big planned to decide who will inherit his court, but I'm certain he's already decided who the winner will be."

Eve didn't like where this was going. "You want me to make sure they can't participate?"

"I want you to kill Liam."

Eve nearly dropped her flower.

"What?" She couldn't believe what she was hearing. Eve knew Sage and Liam had issues, but to kill him? Eve anxiously dug her nails into the wisteria's stem. She had her own complicated relationship with Liam, but even when he'd failed to kill her rapists, she didn't plan on *murdering* him.

"I doubt Preece will care for the title," Sage said. "He has his own place in the Seelie Court to attend to, so his willing participation isn't anticipated. My father thinks I'm soft because of my mother's roots in the Seelie Court, and thus he doesn't consider me a serious contender, either. Liam, on the other hand, was born entirely in the Unseelie Court, and thus is the favorite. If we remove him"—Sage snipped a bundle of wisteria off her arm. It tumbled to the ground and wilted instantly—"then there is nothing left to worry about."

Eve didn't know what to say. Sage spoke calmly, as if plotting the murder of her brother was the most natural thing in the world. How long had she been planning this?

"I... I'm not sure if..." Eve struggled to find something to say. This was too much. She wasn't a killer for fun—she wanted revenge, and that was the end of it.

"You want me to kill those men for you, don't you?" Sage pushed. Eve bit down on her lip.

"Yes." *More than anything.* More than Liam's life? She wasn't sure.

Sage floated closer, lowering herself to Eve's eye level. "I'm offering two men's lives in exchange for one. That's a better deal than anyone else would offer, you know. Besides, you aren't fond of Liam, are you?"

Eve wasn't sure what to say. She hadn't been, initially, but Eve—despite everything—was growing accustomed to him.

Sensing her hesitation, Sage pushed, "He still has your True Name."

"He promised not to use it."

Sage scoffed. "And you truly believe that? Didn't he also promise to get rid of these men for you?" Eve had nothing to say to that. "It sounds to me that he isn't capable of keeping his word. How long do you think it'll take before he gets bored and decides you get to be his next toy?"

Eve inhaled sharply. How many times had she wondered about that herself? As his sister, Sage knew Liam better than anyone. Eve doubted she was the first foolish mortal to give her True Name over to him; what became of the others?

"Don't let it get to that point." Sage said, her voice sweet as honey. "He can't use your True Name if he's dead. You don't have to live in fear forever—you can go back to having control over yourself again."

The thought sank into Eve's mind. She never thought she could take that power back. Eve had resigned herself to Liam having that control forever, despite what promises he made. But if there was an alternative...

"I didn't know I could do that," Eve whispered.

"Every deal has its loopholes, Eve. You aren't trapped with him."

It was almost too good to be true. She could be free, never having to worry about if Liam might use her True Name again. Never having to suffer through his horrible jokes about the power he wielded over her. *And her rapists would be dead; she wouldn't even need to hunt them down.*

All you have to do is kill him.

"Why me?" Eve asked. "Why not kill him yourself?"

"There aren't rules against it in the Unseelie Court," Sage admitted. "But Evren would be displeased. He would rather not give his title to anyone than let the murderer of his favorite son have it."

"And he wouldn't take it out on me?" Eve asked skeptically.

"Not if I'm in charge." Sage beamed. "You would be immune. Evren couldn't do anything to you. Those men would be dead, Liam wouldn't have control over you anymore, and you wouldn't have to worry about my father taking revenge. Isn't it perfect?"

It was—or it would have been—if Eve had not been getting along with Liam. If he had not saved her life from the asrai. She owed him a life debt, and she would repay him in his own blood.

But Colton and Logan would be dead. She couldn't get the thought out of her head. She had already seen how badly going after them herself had gone; Eve could use the help.

"Alright," Eve said, ignoring the seed of doubt that crept into her chest. "I'll do it."

Sage smiled with a full set of pointed teeth. "Excellent."

Thirty-One

Eve was brushing her teeth when she heard a sharp knock at the door, followed by Sage and Hailey's chatter carrying up the stairwell. Eve stepped out of the bathroom, confused. "What are you doing here?"

"We need to get you ready for the party," Sage said, as if it were obvious. She eyed Eve's plaid cotton shorts and rumpled T-shirt curiously. Eve covered her wrists with her hands, self-conscious.

"I thought the party wasn't until this weekend," Eve said. She subtly tried to stretch out the length of her shorts. It did nothing. "I can't go anywhere; I need to watch my nan."

Hailey peeked into the living room. Nan was probably still sitting in her rocking chair, either watching a series of game shows or passed out in her blanket.

"I'll take care of it," Hailey offered. "Michael's off work from the hospital tonight. I'll ask him to watch her for a bit."

"You don't need to do that," Eve objected, but Hailey already had her phone pressed to her ear for the call. Eve hesitated, then bit the bullet and walked to her room. If they were going to drag her out, she ought to get dressed.

By the time Eve shimmied into one of her skirt and sweater combos, Hailey's brother was already on his way. Eve wondered what that was like, to have someone you could trust at the drop of a hat. It was almost impossible to think about.

Eve joined her friends in the living room. She was surprised to find them relaxed on the couch, mid-conversation with her grandmother. Nan was smiling, but it was more than the empty, confused grin she usually had—this was genuine. Eve frowned. What was she doing wrong?

"I see you've met my friends," Eve said. She took up one of the empty chairs in the room, curling in on herself.

"Yes, yes. They're such nice girls." Nan smiled at Hailey and Sage from the safety of her rocking chair.

"We were talking about the flowers," Hailey said with a gesture toward one of the potted plants in the room. There were many, all fake, but Eve could see the wet rim where her grandma had tried to water them. She would have to clean that later.

"Yes, my garden." Nan's eyes lit up as she gestured between the plastic arrangements. "I've been taking care of them for years. Aren't they lovely?"

She was so proud. Eve didn't have the heart to tell her that they weren't real. It appeared neither did Sage nor Hailey.

"They're beautiful," Hailey agreed, brushing her fingers across one of the fabric petals nearby. Eve caught her questioning glance and nodded. Hailey frowned as understanding passed between them.

Another knock at the door. Hailey bolted up from her chair. "That must be Michael."

She wasted no time greeting her brother at the door and leading him inside. He was slightly older than the family photos suggested, but Eve could see the resemblance between the siblings instantly.

"Hey, Eve. I'm Michael." He introduced himself with a strong handshake and a smile. "Hay here will give us each other's numbers in case there are any emergencies. Would you mind running the situation by me before you head out?"

"Sure." Eve led Michael into the kitchen, where the notepad full of instructions from Nan's doctor was. Normally she wouldn't be comfortable leaving Nan alone here with a stranger, but she trusted Hailey. "Thank you for doing this. How much do I owe you?"

"No charge. I owe Hay a favor, so this one's on her." He smiled pointedly at Hailey, as though physically to say *we're even.* Hailey grinned back at him.

"Thanks again, Mikey," she sang, already skipping out the door. Sage followed after her and, once Eve was bundled in her coat and scarf, the trio made their way to the cemetery.

The headstones were even more grim between the snow and slush, their gray surfaces sticking out against the clouded sky. Fresh flakes fell from above and piled onto the inch already covering the ground. The girls' boots crunched against the new snow, leaving a straight trail between the graves.

"What did you do for your brother?" Eve asked after a long moment of silence. The quiet unsettled her. It gave her too much time with her thoughts, ones she wanted long buried.

"I caught him smoking weed in our parents' garage last year," Hailey whispered with a mischievous grin. "I had to distract my dad so Michael could air it out and take a shower. Don't tell him I told you that, though."

"I won't," Eve said. Another beat of silence. "So, what are we doing out here?"

"Going to my house," Sage replied from up ahead.

"*Why* are we going to your house in the middle of the night? What did you need for the party?" Eve glanced back at the woods. The further they got from the cemetery, the more paranoid she became. Was that a head or a pile of rocks? Were those noises a part of the local wildlife or something more sinister? Could the three of them survive an attack by two grown men? How much experience did Sage and Hailey have in fighting?

"You need a new dress," Sage said. That caught Eve's attention.

"A dress?"

"For your party. You didn't think I was going to let you wear your usual clothes, did you?" Sage raised an eyebrow. A rush of heat climbed up Eve's neck to her face. Was there something wrong with the way she dressed?

"You'll love it, Eve. Sage had a dress made for me for a party over the summer, and it was amazing," Hailey gushed, clinging onto Sage's arm. Sage's lips twitched up into a proud smile.

"I'm sure it'll be great," Eve said. She loved pretty dresses, but she found their use wasted on her. The fabric always hung strangely on her flat chest, and anything that clung to her hips felt too sexual, too inviting. She knew that wasn't how things were, but it was hard to get rid of that conditioned mentality. Creating a gown for her was as useless as trying to put a hat on a bird. It was cute for a bit, but the charm would eventually wear off.

As they crossed the threshold into the Bone Court, Eve couldn't resist glancing at Hailey and wondering what she knew about Faerie. Did she know that Sage was a faerie from the Seelie Court? What had Hailey wanted desperately enough that she decided to make a contract for it with Liam—and had she fulfilled it?

Eve kept the thoughts to herself as they approached the estate. They passed several smaller houses that Eve recognized from her private treks through the forest, their structures made of different natural materials from stone to wood to sloped, mossy roofs. As Sage's home came into view, Eve realized the estate appeared smaller between the snow-capped trees. There was a haunted look to it, as if someone had left a birdcage out long enough for nature to take it over. The garden stretched out on either side of them; some blooms that Eve had never seen before reached out toward her from their thick bushes. A dusting of snow coated the blossoms like powdered sugar. Sage paid no heed to the landscape—one she surely had seen a thousand times—and led her friends inside.

Eve noticed a short woman waiting patiently beside the open parlor doors. She did her best to suppress a yawn as she turned to greet the girls.

"This is Dunla, our seamstress," Sage said with a broad gesture to the dwarf woman. Dunla was short and squat, with a large bonnet covering most of her white hair and jet-black eyes. A pair of small, round spectacles hung on a chain around her neck, seemingly too fragile against her rough hands. She was not of the same ethereal beauty Sage and Liam were, but there was still something about Dunla that drew Eve in, made her want to know more.

These creatures are dangerous.

"It's nice to meet you," Eve said politely. Dunla nodded, appraising the three girls with a keen eye. She gestured for them to follow her into the parlor, the room already set up and arranged for their fittings.

If Eve hadn't been here once before, she never would have guessed this room belonged to the estate. The seamstress had completely taken it over, covering the furniture and walls with as many textiles as she could. Pools of fabric draped over the couches and chairs. They were fine, shimmering fabrics made of materials that Eve had never seen before in her life. Some were as light as air, while others hung heavily, weighed down by the embellishments that decorated the trim. One bolt was as dark as midnight with silver embedded in the thread like stars. There was another as velvety as real rose petals, and one with silk so bright and reflective that she wondered if it was made from diamonds. Eve gaped at the selection in awe.

Sage had no trouble picking out her fabric, immediately gravitating to a dark bundle as deep as onyx. There were streaks in the fabric: twisted black vines made of jewels. Sage paired it with another bundle of black feathers and detailed out the gown with the seamstress.

Hailey and Eve wandered through the room, not nearly as settled on their attire. Eve had never worn anything half as expensive before—and she was certain these were expensive—let alone had a dress *custom made* for her. Even though Sage had insisted that she would take care of any expenses on the way there, Eve found herself gripping the wallet in her pocket. She wouldn't have nearly enough money to cover this, but if Sage mentioned anything, Eve would be prepared to offer her what she could.

"Do you girls see anything to your liking?" Dunla asked, stepping between the two.

"Everything is beautiful. I'm not sure how to decide," Hailey said with a nervous laugh. Dunla smiled.

"Of course. They are all originals," she boasted. Dunla pulled off a nude fabric from the couch. Light neutral feathers clung to the fabric, intermingling with the shimmering embroidery underneath. "I have just the thing for you."

Eve awkwardly shuffled through the rows of fabrics as Hailey and the seamstress went over details for the gown. From what Eve overheard, it wouldn't be too far off from Sage's.

"And for you, my dear, what about this?" Dunla held out a blush fabric covered in soft floral accents. "It would suit your complexion wonderfully."

Eve stared at the fabric, unconvinced. The dress she wore to prom wasn't nearly as lovely, but the color was too close for her comfort.

A bundle of white on the couch caught her eye. The fabric was as pale as freshly fallen snow, with bright red winter berries sewn into intricate patterns across it. *Like the brooch,* Eve thought, glancing down at the pin attached to her jacket. She hadn't left anywhere without it.

"What about that one?" she asked. Dunla followed her gaze.

"Ah, I see you've found my newest creation!" Dunla picked up the bundle—it was lighter than Eve had anticipated—and allowed her to observe from a closer distance. It was exquisite.

Dunla explained how the fabric was made—what woods she scoured to acquire the berries, the mountains she had to climb for the snow-white fabric. She led Eve to a stool in the center of the room and prepared to take her measurements.

"I'll be needing you to strip down, dearie," Dunla said.

"I have nothing to change into," Eve said cautiously. The parlor doors were wide open and so were the windows. What if someone saw?

"You won't be needing nothing, your underclothes is fine," Dunla said. When Eve didn't move, she raised an eyebrow. "You *have* underclothes on, don't you? No shame if you don't, I've measured them all—"

"Yes, I have underwear," Eve said hurriedly. She looked to Sage and Hailey for help, but neither girl understood the urgency of her situation.

"You'll be alright," Dunla promised, but once she saw the apprehensiveness on Eve's face, she gestured for the girls to cover up the room.

"Don't worry, people are pretty loose with clothes around here. You'll see at the party." Sage chuckled, but Eve's stomach churned.

"My *birthday* party?" Eve folded her clothes into a neat pile at her feet and tried to ignore the blush creeping up her neck. Dunla offered a thin silk chemise to place over her. Eve pulled the dress on, nodding thankfully to the dwarf.

"Yeah. It's going to be fun," Sage said with a sharp grin.

"You don't need to worry about getting into that stuff, though," Hailey quickly jumped in. "Just enjoy your party."

Although Hailey meant to be encouraging, Eve felt sick. She had seen the strange intoxication of the last party here, but somehow, she had assumed her birthday would be different. Was that how all faerie parties were?

She was one to talk. Eve was going to celebrate her birthday not with kisses and alcohol, but with murder.

I don't have a choice, she told herself.

Dunla circled Eve, wrapping the measuring tape around her limbs and jotting down measurements. She asked Eve a series of questions relating to her dress—what length, the cut, the shape, the extra details—but Eve had no idea what she wanted. She could sense Dunla growing irritated as Eve responded with a series of "I don't know" or "Whatever you think is best."

"At this rate, you won't be wearing anything at all."

Eve jumped at the sound of Liam's voice, her hands fumbling to cover herself up. She rested her arms over her chest, trying to ignore the way Liam's gaze trailed to her legs and back up again with an unreadable expression.

"Aren't you supposed to be out?" Sage asked tightly.

"This is my home. I don't need to be anywhere." Liam raised an eyebrow at Eve's thin chemise. "Is that what you'll be wearing?"

"Why do you think she's here?" Sage interrupted before Eve could respond. "We're getting dresses. Get out."

"So hostile." Liam clicked his tongue. "I need to be fitted too, you know."

"Are you coming to the party, Liam?" Hailey asked. A small part of Eve, the part that didn't want to kill anyone else, hoped he would say no.

As if he could read her mind, Liam smirked at Eve, his light eyes dancing.

"Of course. I wouldn't miss it."

Thirty-Two

When she was nine, Eve had her first period. It was the earliest among the girls in her grade—many hadn't even had *the talk* yet. She had run to her father sobbing, blood trickling between her legs, and begged to be taken to the hospital.

Disgusted, Benjamin locked her in her room.

"He didn't mean it badly." Sharon tried to console her. She brought two books in the room with her—*Your Body is a Temple for Jesus* and the Holy Bible. "Your body is going through some changes. This is an exciting time!"

It was not exciting. It was a nightmare.

More changes came in the following years: hair in places that itched, foul smells that materialized when dawn broke, lumps of fat that were too obscene for her parents and too small for the boys in her grade.

The books Sharon gave her didn't help. *Abstinence!* they screamed in bold letters, threatening the fires of hell if these girls could not be bothered to protect the purity of their bodies.

But by the end of middle school, almost every girl had their first kiss—and many had gone further. It was only through the gossip in school, and a few private internet searches, that Eve truly learned about the joys of puberty. Boys didn't look at her with disgust—she was a prize, and the number of dates she'd been on dictated what place she stood in. Was she a first-place virgin waiting to be sacrificed on her marriage night? Or was she a consolation, the girl that had been through so many kisses and touches that it didn't matter whose hands it belonged to anymore?

Eve hadn't gone on dates, but it wasn't for lack of trying. She was too skinny, her boobs too small to appease the boys—and the girls—her age. Yet, somehow still too large to wear tank tops when her father's friends visited. There were no right answers; only a constant cycle of change that never seemed to be good enough for anyone.

The worst was the way her father looked at her. Gone was the sweet, innocent princess he'd swung over his shoulders and ate ice cream with. Eve was a foreign language, written in an alphabet her father couldn't understand and didn't care to learn.

Eve sat outside now, cold rain trickling off the edge of the porch roof as her stomach twisted and tore in a series of painful cramps. It was too hot inside, but the cold winter in Vermont wasn't any better. Eve wrapped the blue cardigan tighter around her shoulders.

One more day, and the pain would stop. One more day, and it wouldn't be her blood that spilled—it would be Liam's. That didn't make her feel any better.

"I hate you," she groaned to her lower abdomen, her knees pressed up to her chest as she swayed on the porch swing.

Ribbet.

Eve was surprised to find a small frog perched on the edge of the porch's railing. It watched her through half-lidded eyes, as if offended.

"Not you," she reassured him, then gestured toward her stomach. "Period cramps."

She felt this satisfied the frog. It edged closer to the swing, hopping up to rest sideways on the column supporting the roof.

"What are you doing out here?" she asked. "Aren't you supposed to be hibernating?"

Ribbet.

"I see. Trying to get some winter snacks?" Eve peered out over the rainy landscape. It was supposed to turn to snow overnight, but not without turning to ice first. "I don't know how many you'll find out here, buddy. The ground's going to freeze solid. You might want to get back home to your family."

Ribbet, said the frog. He sounded indignant. Could a frog sound indignant?

"Do you have a family?"

Ribbet.

"A wife? Kids?"

Silence. The frog watched her. She watched him, too.

"Okay, none of that. Brothers? Sisters?"

Ribbet.

"Ah, lucky. I'm an only child."

The frog croaked. He didn't sound as if this pleased him, but Eve didn't speak frog. Maybe he was telling her she was crazy for talking to him. How would she know?

Look at me, I'm turning into Liam, Eve thought with some disdain. How he'd laugh if he saw her now.

But the frog was cute, and Eve couldn't help but worry. Winter was almost there in full—what if it starved before going into hibernation? Was it already too late?

"Are you hungry?" she asked. Before it could answer, she rose from the swing. "Wait here."

She expected the frog to hop away as soon as she got up, but to her surprise, it remained in place while she ducked out into the rain.

The yard was not even, and Eve easily found small patches of puddles and drenched soil filled with wiggling, fat worms. The frog watched her with eager black eyes as she set them down in front of him. He waited until she was seated back on the porch before his tongue shot out, sucking one of the worms between his green lips. Eve half-smiled and half-grimaced, equally grossed out and pleased.

The frog rested on the banister, his eyes slitted and content. The swing creaked as Eve swung back and forth gently. Then came another surge of pain in her lower belly.

"Crap," she grumbled, clutching her stomach. The frog opened its eyes, alert. "This sucks."

The frog surveyed her for a moment, its chest bulging out with another croak, before he leaped from the banister and disappeared into a nearby bush. Eve craned her neck to find him again, but he was gone. With a sigh, she rose from the swing. She needed some medicine, stat.

Ribbet.

Eve turned. Sitting on the top step, as if it'd been placed there, was a lump of fresh ginger.

"Little buddy?" she called out. There was no sign of the frog. *Weird.*

But she wasn't about to turn down some free ginger—not when her stomach was revolting against her. If her mother taught her anything, it was how helpful ginger was for stomach pain. Eve picked up the herb and carried it inside.

Thirty-Three

"Happy birthday!" Hailey's voice carried too loudly over the cafeteria. Eve shrank back a little, embarrassed, but smiled. It reminded her of the birthday mornings when her mother would wake her up with the smell of boxed birthday cake. She wouldn't be allowed to eat it until later that night, but the familiar smell of vanilla batter and store-bought icing always made her smile.

A cupcake of the same batter was presented before her in Hailey's hands, the icing smudged from whatever container it had been held in. A little candle stuck up from the top, although it was not lit. Eve took the cupcake gratefully, joining the girls at their usual table by the window. The window clings had been exchanged for a nativity scene of construction paper, although the angel's wings were lopsided.

"I wasn't sure what flavor was your favorite. Is this okay?" Hailey eyed the cupcake with concern.

"I bet it'll be delicious. Thanks," Eve grinned and took a large bite. This was even better than the kind her mother made.

Hailey beamed and pulled out a small container of cupcakes from her lunch box. She distributed two more between herself and Sage before putting the container back. Sage took a bite, struggling to hide the disappointment on her face. Before, Eve had assumed Sage was a picky eater, but now that she knew her friend was one of the fair folk, it made sense. Why bother to play along if she didn't enjoy human food, though? Looking at the way Sage stared at Hailey, Eve thought she knew the answer.

They sat in silence as they devoured their cupcakes. Despite not liking it, Sage finished hers first and immediately complimented Hailey's skills afterward. Her friend grinned, oblivious to the meaning behind it.

"Are you excited for your party tonight?" Hailey asked, turning in her chair to face Eve.

Right. The party.

Sage had gone over the plan to take out Liam a hundred times, and yet Eve couldn't stop herself from panicking. What if she forgot a step? What if she chickened out, or worse, what if she *failed?*

No matter how she felt about his death, killing Nick had been an accident. This was different.

"Yeah. Can't wait," she said with a polite smile. Eve hoped it would hide the dread in her gut. Sage eyed her but said nothing. Maybe she could see the way Eve paled whenever she thought of taking Liam's life. He hadn't hurt her in the same way her rapists did, but if she didn't do something, she would be on her own.

Colton and Logan will die, too, she thought to herself, but the thought was less comforting than she'd hoped.

Sage and Hailey picked Eve up from her house at sunset. Nan was already in bed and, although Eve couldn't find anyone to watch her through the night, Eve suspected her grandmother wouldn't notice her granddaughter missing for a few hours.

The steps down into the Bone Court felt charged. Magical. It was in the air around her, electric and alive with promises for the night ahead.

Eve only caught a glimpse of the ballroom before Sage and Hailey were ushering her upstairs and locking her in one of the many available guest rooms. Eve couldn't imagine anyone needing this many rooms, but she supposed she never tried to guess what Sage's family's life was like in the Unseelie Court.

A large wooden box sat on the center of the bed. Eve lifted the lid.

It was the same fabric Eve had picked out when Dunla visited, but the dress was another work of magic. The skirt was large and full, with piles of berries sewn at the bottom, their thin branches stretching up in enchanting designs toward her waist. The fabric had been doubled to give the dress more depth. The top was similar, with bunches of berries trailing across her off-the-shoulder neckline and long translucent sleeves, the sticks pulling down to the skirt. It gave off the illusion that there was nothing to hold up the gown but the berries themselves.

And there were *pockets*.

"Oh, bless you Dunla," Eve breathed, eager to exchange her ruddy day clothes for the new gown.

A few more details were included in the box: a small comb, a choker, and some heels had been tossed in, all accented with berries. Eve's hair was short, but she managed to pull it into a half-up style with the comb. When she put on the necklace, she realized that the dripping berries made it appear as if she were bleeding.

She reached down and unpinned the brooch from her cardigan—the final touch, a *real* amulet of protection. She pinned it to her breast, admiring the splash of green from the clover against the rest of the red and white ensemble.

Eve stared at herself in the full-length mirror, spinning a few times to get the full effect of the gown.

For the first time in a very long time, Eve found herself beautiful.

"Are you ready?" Sage appeared in the doorway, a perfect vision in her black feathered gown and cape. If Eve stared at her for too long, she wondered if Sage would sprout wings and fly away. Sage tilted her head, her bone jewelry rattling together. Eve could hear the early sounds of the party downstairs, a joyous mixture of laughter and music.

Sage's presence was a reminder of what tonight was really about. This was not a birthday party—it was an execution.

Eve examined herself once more in the mirror. Lovely. Gentle. Deadly.

"I'm ready."

Thirty-Four

An electric energy hovered in the air, as if something truly magical and equally dreadful was about to happen.

Sage led Eve through the ballroom past faces both frightening and enchanting. Loud melodies consisting of harps, lyres, and fiddles set the eccentric guests into a flurry of dance, their inhuman features less grotesque under the candlelight. Their attire was even more outlandish; shoes made of tree bark, skirts as fluid as water, feathers and bones and leaves appearing at every turn. Eve searched for a hint of webbed hands or monstrous teeth, but none of the guests fit that description.

Hailey waited for them near the musicians, her feathered gown swishing at her feet as she swayed to the music. Sage walked faster, dragging Eve along with her.

"Wow, Eve, you look amazing!" Hailey gasped as she took in Eve's white and crimson gown.

"You too," Eve said with a grin. Hailey's attitude was contagious.

Hailey's dress was near identical to Sage's, except it was in a beautiful shade of rose-gold and ivory. Her feathered cape deflected any dirt Eve assumed it would pick up.

More magic, she guessed.

"Have you seen the buffet yet?" Hailey glanced over to three large tables that were filled with various meals and hors d'oeuvres that left Eve's stomach grumbling. A large cake sat in the center, its tiers decorated with a thin layer of frosting and several different berries and jam. "Everything looks amazing; the cooks went all out."

"I can see that," Eve said. Several guests had already taken pieces of cake and plates from the buffet, but there was still plenty to grab—and it seemed that servants were bringing out more. "Have you guys seen Liam yet?"

Sage met her gaze but shook her head. "Not yet. I'm sure he'll show up soon."

Eve nodded. Patience, then. Patience was key. She turned back toward the ballroom, searching and failing to find something to do. Why were parties almost exclusively reserved for drinking, eating, and dancing? Eve had no interest in any of that.

The song changed then, and Hailey was practically jumping in excitement as she pulled Sage toward the dance floor. Eve watched them go. For once, she was happy to be left alone.

She couldn't exactly kill Liam with an audience.

Picking up one of the goblets, Eve sniffed the liquid to make sure it was water before passing through the crowd. No one paid her any attention; they were solely there to party, no matter the occasion. It wasn't exactly Eve's ideal plan for a birthday, but at least someone was having fun.

Still no sign of Liam. Did he decide not to attend?

Sweat formed on her palms, but Eve discreetly wiped it off on her skirt. She wanted to get this over with. Doubt was creeping in, curling at the edges of her mind. She was no killer. Eve took another sip from her goblet.

"You appear to be troubled."

A lilting voice caught her off guard. Eve turned, the goblet gripped awkwardly in her hands as she craned her neck to look up at the tall, slender intruder. His features were as sharp as the points of his ears, his long hair a fiery red. He wore a white-spotted black coat in the pattern of a magpie fungus, and trousers to match. Eve was certain she'd never met him before, and yet there was something strikingly familiar about him.

"I didn't intend to startle you," he said after a moment. "But I find it rather disheartening that the guest of honor isn't enjoying her party."

A quiet alarm bell rang in the back of her head. "Have we met?"

"No, I don't believe we've had the pleasure." He smiled. A chill ran down Eve's spine. "I am Lord Evren Fogtree, but perhaps Evren is enough. I've heard many things about you, Miss Carter. Unfortunate they were only in passing."

"You've heard of *me?* I guess you're close with Liam and Sage, then?" she asked politely, taking a sip of her water.

"I'm their father."

Eve choked on her drink, dropping her goblet to the floor. Evren's eyes twinkled with amusement as he watched her struggle before finally waving one of the black-robed servants over.

"You're not dying, I hope," Evren said, although Eve had an inkling he didn't care either way.

"I'm fine." Heat rushed to her face. "I didn't mean—you look young, I mean."

Evren chuckled. "How old do you think I am?"

"I—" Eve coughed again into her arm. Evren swiped two goblets off the tray from the servant. "Forty-something?" Even that sounded too old. She hoped he took it as a compliment.

"Try three hundred and ninety-seven." Eve nearly choked again, but Evren quickly offered the goblet to her. Eve nodded her thanks. "How are you liking Faerie thus far? Does it compare to what you're familiar with?"

"It's better than that," Eve said, surprised by her own answer. A small part of her knew it was true; even amid the horror she'd seen, there was beauty in the Bone Court. She thought of her strolls through the forest, quiet and peaceful in the light of day.

She took a small sip from the goblet, and Evren did the same from his. A warm, honey-sweet taste filled her mouth, with notes of almost-soured citrus and nutmeg and something else she couldn't pin down. Eve pulled the goblet back, noticing a slight amber sheen to the liquid.

"You don't prefer gallivanting amongst mortals?" He said it teasingly, but there was curiosity in his eyes.

"Not really." She thought of Nan and Hailey, catching herself. "I don't *hate* it."

"But?"

Eve hesitated. There was no easy way to sum up how miserable her life in the human realm was. There were countless expectations she had to live up to, roles she needed to fill, and Eve had failed in every way. She couldn't even imagine a future for herself. She was a diver running out of oxygen, too deep in the ocean's trenches to swim back.

"Sometimes I wish I didn't have to go back," she spoke quietly, more to herself than to Evren. The confession shocked her; Eve didn't want to talk about these things, especially not with strangers. She stared into her goblet. "What is this?"

"My newest brew; I thought I would test it out at the party." Evren's gaze flickered to her goblet. Eve didn't take another sip. "You aren't fond of it?"

"No, it's not that." Quite the opposite; it was the best thing she'd ever had in her life. She stared at the amber liquid, tempted to drink more. Her mouth watered at the thought. "I don't drink alcohol."

"There's a first time for everything, isn't there?"

Eve opened her mouth to object—or to take another sip, she couldn't decide—when she spotted Liam stalking toward them. Evren followed her gaze, something eager flickering across his face.

"Ah, there you are," Evren said, opening his arms in a welcoming gesture. Liam sidestepped him.

"What are you doing here?" Liam demanded of his father. "I thought you had important business in the Seelie Court."

Evren waved off his concerns. "Not so important that I would miss your friend's birthday. We are her hosts, after all."

"I didn't know you'd heard about it." Liam played with an idle string on his sleeve, the gold thread making up a larger pattern of embroidered skulls and twisting vines against a silky black fabric. Liam had opted for a matching high-collared tunic and trousers, the unusual threaded designs spreading down to the tips of his pointed boots. Eve couldn't decide if it was elegant or gaudy.

"I know about everything that happens in my court." Evren's voice was playful, but there was an underlying threat settled beneath it. "Now, there's no need to be tense. We were having a friendly chat." He flashed his son another smile, one that Liam did not return.

"I've been looking for you." Liam didn't address Evren, his attention focused on Eve. "We need to talk."

Her heart leaped into her throat. There was no way he could know about her planned attempt on his life, and yet, what if?

"I'm sure it can wait. I was about to ask Miss Carter for a dance." Evren bowed slightly and held out his free hand to her, stealthily slipping his goblet onto the tray of a passing servant. It would be a way for her to avoid Liam's confrontation, but there was something unsettling about the way Evren leered at her.

Before Eve could accept, Liam snatched her hand away.

"What a great idea," Liam mused, with false enthusiasm. "Mind if I take the first spin?"

Liam didn't give either of them a chance to object. He dragged Eve to the dance floor, taking her goblet and tossing it carelessly over his shoulder for some poor servant to pick up. She stumbled after him, nearly tripping over her dress.

"I don't want to dance," Eve hissed under her breath. She tried to wrench her arm away, but Liam's grip was steel. "Let me go."

"I know you hate it, but I promise it will only be until my father finds something else to stare at," he said.

Eve craned her neck to see if what he said was true, but a new song began and Liam yanked her into position, his hands finding their way to hers as they entered the large circle of dancers.

She had never formally danced before, but somehow Eve's feet managed to move to the music, as if the melody was compelling her body to move on its own. She tried to wriggle away from him, but even that was futile; once the dance had started, she couldn't stop.

"What are you doing to me?" she demanded.

"It's the music," he said under his breath. "I'll make sure you stop. Trust me."

"Maybe make yourself trustworthy first," she snapped, but there wasn't as much bite behind it as she intended. The dance itself wasn't terrible. Eve actually found herself enjoying the sweeping motions, the way her skirt flared when she spun. She never did get to dance at prom, and this was different to anything she had experienced before. It was... kind of fun.

Not that she would ever tell Liam that.

He didn't seem inclined to listen, anyway. Liam was distracted, his gaze scanning the edge of the dance floor in quiet distress.

"What's wrong?"

"Time is running out," he said, keeping his voice low. "Where are the last two items?"

"Does it look like I have them in my hands?" She held up their joined hands for emphasis. He didn't find her sarcasm amusing. "I'm working on it. It would be easier if I knew what I was trying to find."

"I already told you: *hair as liquid as ink* and *a name as fleeting as the sun.*"

"Yes, let me go pick those up at the grocery store," Eve muttered, but behind his frustration, she could see the worry in his eyes. Liam was sick—she never asked *how* sick, but the implication was there. "Okay, *a name as fleeting as the sun.* Have you tried using a True Name?"

"That's hardly fleeting," Liam huffed. Then, "Yes, I tried it."

"Nicknames?"

"They can last a while, too."

"Middle names?"

"Still permanent."

Eve thought hard. She had been tossing this riddle over in particular for a while. "Confirmation name?"

Liam eyed her. "What's that?"

"It's a name you get in eighth grade if you're Catholic," Eve explained. "You choose a saint to emulate and add their name to yours. I'm not Catholic anymore, so I don't count it as part of my name."

"That... might work." He didn't sound so sure, but they were both out of ideas. "What was your name?"

"I chose Mary," Eve said. It was a pretty common choice, but Eve had admired the Mother Mary for years. "I only used it for a year before I gave up on Catholicism for good."

"I'll give it a try." Liam's body relaxed a little. Guilt crept through Eve's nerves. No matter what little hope she gave him, it meant nothing if she was going to take it all away. "What were you talking to my father about?"

The question took her by surprise. "Nothing much. Why? Are you afraid he said embarrassing stories about you? Serves you right for egging my parents on at Thanksgiving."

"Embarrassing stories are the least of my worries." Liam sighed in aggravation. "My father is not a kind person."

"And you think my dad is?" Eve snorted. "I can handle him."

"Because you did so well with the asrai." He chuckled, but the sound was strained. Was he actually worried about her? Impossible. "Have you found those men you were searching for?"

"One of them found me."

"And?"

Eve said nothing. Liam met her eyes, confused. A beat passed, and with it dawned a new understanding.

"You killed him." He sounded as if he didn't believe it. Liam stared at her—with respect? Disgust? She couldn't tell, but Eve forced herself to meet him with a level gaze.

"I told you I would."

He had nothing to say to that. For once, Eve relished in being the predator instead of the prey. The song ended, and, as promised, Liam halted their dance. Eve pulled herself from the dance circle, the spell of the music suddenly broken, leaving her legs achy and tired.

"What? Did you think I couldn't do it?" she asked.

Liam didn't respond right away. He cocked his head at her with an expression she couldn't read and, although he appeared aloof, there was an edge to his voice. "Did he deserve it?"

"Yes." Eve had never been so certain about anything in her life. It was just another sin to add to the endless list that damned her for eternity.

In the distance, a familiar face caught her attention.

Sage was a blot of ink amid the rustling sea of papery wings on the dance floor. Eve only caught a glimpse of her hard, golden eyes before she turned toward the hall. A silent understanding passed between them.

It was time.

Eve went over the plan again in her head, the words all but engraved in her skull. She could feel the jeweled dagger weighing down her pocket, its poison-coated blade sheathed and waiting.

She would kill Liam. She *had* to kill Liam.

She didn't want to kill Liam.

I owe him my life, she thought. Sickness twisted in her gut. God, why did *he* have to save her from the asrai? If it had been anyone else...

No, even then, she didn't want to kill him.

But what else can I do? Despair held her hostage. Colton and Logan needed to die, and this was her best chance.

"I need some fresh air," Eve said before she could change her mind. Sage had already gone over their plan a hundred times. She had to get him out to the balcony, away from everyone else. "Come with me."

Eve had told Sage this part of the plan wouldn't work; there was no way Liam would want to follow her outside for any reason. Sage insisted, claiming that the entire house would be filled with witnesses. As long as they were outside while the music was playing, no one would hear what was about to happen.

"Very well," Liam said. Eve froze in shock. She'd never expected it to be that easy.

"Okay," she said, composing herself. She nodded stiffly and walked toward the balcony. Eve didn't dare to see if he followed—she didn't want to give away the doubt in her eyes.

The cold mid-December air bit her skin, the sounds of the party muffled behind her as Liam shut the large stained-glass doors.

Flurries of snow fluttered down from the sky, sticking to the bare tree branches. She gripped the balcony's railing and took a deep breath. Now wasn't the time to panic.

It was simple: she would stab Liam with the poisoned dagger, push him over the balcony, and Sage would be waiting at the bottom with a fallen tree branch. They would say he was impaled, that it had been an accident. If he didn't die right away, the poison would take care of it. No one needed to know that Sage and Eve were involved. No one *would* know.

"Feeling better?" Liam leaned on the railing beside her. Small flakes of snow clung to his red hair, glinting in the soft light from the ballroom.

"No," Eve answered, surprised by her own honesty. It was only a sip, but maybe the wine was affecting her.

"Take as much time as you need," he said. "I might freeze to death first, though."

"Good. We don't need any of your spawn running around in the world," Eve said sarcastically.

"Oh no, we couldn't have that. There's only room for one dangerously handsome face in this world," Liam mused, rubbing his chin for effect.

"If only it was yours."

"You don't think I'm handsome?" Liam leaned toward her with a mischievous glint in his eyes. Eve gripped the railing tighter.

"I think you should brush your teeth. Your breath stinks," she said, but it wasn't true. Liam smelled nice tonight, a strange mix of fresh dew on the earth with a hint of smoke. She could almost picture him in a cottage somewhere, tending to a fireplace at dusk.

Or maybe that was what she wanted for herself—to be far away from the rest of the world. Somewhere she could tell monsters apart by their pointed teeth instead of manipulative smiles.

That's not going to happen, she thought. The dagger in her pocket was a grim reminder of the only future she had left.

"What's this?" Liam asked. It took Eve a moment to follow his gaze, even longer to understand that he'd seen her scars through the mesh fabric of her sleeves. Panic gripped her as Liam reached forward and rubbed his thumb over the mark, tracing the pale line of skin through the thin sleeve.

Eve flinched, tripping backward on her heel as she tried to get away. She crossed her arms firmly over her chest. Liam stood there in shock, hand still raised to caress the air before he let it fall. He turned to look out over the balcony, giving Eve the sliver of privacy she needed to regain her composure.

"The party appears to be a success," she said, abruptly changing the subject. Eve could feel his eyes on her, on her wrists.

"Sage will find any excuse to show off."

"I think it was more for Hailey than me." The words came out before she could stop them, but Eve realized how true they were. She and Sage were friends, but everything Sage did was for Hailey's attention. How else could their matching dresses be explained? Or stalking Hailey on her date? Or any of the other small touches and longing stares she had given when Hailey so much as entered a room?

"She thinks she can fix things if she forces it enough. That isn't how this works," Liam sighed, pressing most of his weight on his elbows as he leaned back against the railing.

"Fix things?" Eve's brows pushed together.

She knew she was supposed to be killing him now, but something nagged at her, drove her curiosity. Maybe it was the guilt of knowing she would be a *real* murderer once she went through with it. Maybe it was her own concern for her friends. Either way, Eve didn't mind wasting a few more minutes, if only so she could have more time to prepare herself for what she was about to do.

Liam hesitated, and, for a moment, Eve feared he would make an excuse and leave her there, all of her efforts wasted. Lowering his voice, Liam explained, "Sage and Hailey had a quiet affair going on over the summer; that's the whole reason Sage decided to go to school with her. But a couple days before school started, something happened—"

There was a crash against the glass door. The frame rattled against the hinges but was otherwise left unmarked as a rowdy guest collapsed against it, their laughter muffled on the other side. Eve and Liam both glared at the interruption, but the guest wandered off, leaving them alone once more.

"Anyway," Liam continued, "Hailey came to me one day in tears. I don't entirely understand what happened." Guilt pulled at Liam's features. "She was begging me to make a deal with her. She wanted her memories erased; everything involving her recent romantic pursuits." He paused. "I didn't know she was dating Sage until after the deal was done."

So, that was why Hailey's parents were so weird with her having girls over; they must have known about their daughter's preference. Was that why Hailey had begged to stop feeling that way in the first place? What had happened to make her want to get rid of her memories altogether?

"Why didn't you give her the memories back then?" Eve asked. She understood the desire to forget—she too desperately wished to erase her own past. But forgetting meant letting those who hurt her walk free. She couldn't allow that.

"I can't. Once a deal is done, it's done." Liam met her gaze, his golden eyes boring into hers. "You can't go back from it, not without making a new deal. She would have to ask me to give her those memories back in exchange for something else."

You would need to make another deal to make me forget your True Name, was what he implied. But what was more powerful than that? She had nothing to offer him.

"Hailey hasn't asked for them back because she doesn't know they're missing," Eve said, her irritation with him rising. Sage was suffering in her attempts to get Hailey to feel something for her that she simply *couldn't*—not because she wasn't interested, but because Hailey had wanted to feel nothing at all. "How is she supposed to break the contract without knowing?"

Liam shrugged. "That's for her to figure out."

His callousness made her want to scream. How could be so nonchalant about his friend?

Unless he didn't see Hailey as his friend, Eve realized. Why would he? She was a human. He was fae. They came from entirely different worlds.

"What did she give you in return?" Eve asked. Liam didn't answer. A sickening sensation settled in her gut as she realized what it might be. "How many names do you have?"

"It's not her True Name," he said, dissuading her of any further thoughts. His gaze cast out over the ballroom, unseeing. "Hailey was kind to me. I didn't want to take something that would hurt her. I decided to take away her ability to experience any romantic acclimation at all. She can still love, but it will not be a romantic kind of love."

"And Hailey accepted those terms?"

"She did."

Liam nodded, but the gesture was half-hearted. He was distracted again, his focus drawn to the ballroom.

"Are you ready to return to the party?" he asked after a moment. Her chest ached, and Eve swallowed hard.

"Almost."

Eve knew that her time was running out. He could excuse himself to the ballroom any minute, and any chance of getting Sage's help would be ruined. Colton and Logan would still be free. Eve would be on her own.

I have to do this, she thought, pushing back the rising guilt in her throat. Eve slipped her hand into her pocket and gripped the dagger's pommel. It was slippery in her palm. *I have to.*

She could hear the thunderous beat of her heart and wondered if Liam could hear the same. But he stared at the ballroom, eyes unfocused and lost in thought.

I'm sorry, she thought, and drove the dagger into his neck.

Thirty-Five

The dagger halted against his neck, scraping with the sound of metal against stone. It didn't even break the skin.

Liam's eyes shot open with awareness, and he stumbled back, pressing a hand protectively against the unmarred skin. He took in Eve's panic, then the dagger in her hand.

"Did you just try to *stab me?*" Liam gaped at her.

"No," she said automatically. The dagger glinted in her hand.

"You—" Several emotions flickered across Liam's face, everything from anger to confusion to hurt, but the one that confused her the most was intrigue. For a brief moment, he looked almost *fascinated* that he'd nearly been assassinated on his own balcony.

He composed himself, and Eve saw a quiet rage burn in his eyes. Whatever interest he had was gone.

"*Evelyn Marie—*"

The electric power of his command tingled through her. He'd promised not to use her True Name for anything else. *He promised.*

Eve threw herself at him, shoving a hand over his lips to muffle the sound. They collapsed into a heap on the stone floor, Liam's back breaking the fall. Liam yelled her last name through the cup of her hand, but it came out muffled and wrong: ineffective.

The dagger slipped from her hold. It slid across the ground, one of the jewels cracking against the stone. Both pairs of eyes followed it, Eve's breath hitching when it stopped precariously close to the balcony's ledge.

What to do? Her grip over his mouth tightened. She pressed her other hand against his shoulder, holding him down, although she was convinced the weight of her dress was doing most of the job. She couldn't get the knife without letting him speak. She couldn't kill him without it. What the hell *could* she do?

Liam moved under her. She was taking too long—her advantage was slipping, his strength overpowering hers as Liam made for his escape.

She had to improvise.

Eve's hands slipped to his throat; she squeezed. Liam's hands shot up and grasped hers, prying at the fingers around his throat.

There was an odd texture at the back and sides of his neck—it wasn't the soft flesh she expected. It was hard. Rough. Was this why she couldn't stab him?

As she squeezed harder, fighting hard against Liam's hands, she saw it—solid gray stone, as if makeup had been smudged out of the way.

Not makeup, she realized. A glamour. The stone wrapped around the back and sides of his neck, stretching down in ash-colored patches to his shoulders and down his arms. Eve vaguely recalled the sight of the stone at the party, but it had hardly registered in her mind.

She never even took it into account.

His illness, she remembered. Was this a part of it?

Her grip loosened. Liam seized the opportunity.

She was thrown onto her back without a second thought. Eve gasped as pain shot up her spine.

"Not as much fun when you're the victim, is it?" Liam spat. He settled on top of her, his hands like iron clamps around her wrists.

Eve thrashed under him. His weight crushed down on her, pinning her to the ground. For someone as lithe as Liam, he was surprisingly heavy. Eve coughed, a new panic seizing her. *It's Liam, it's Liam,* she told herself, but she could feel their phantom hands, their bodies, pressing against her. Her breathing came out in short, panicked gasps.

"Get off me." Eve didn't have time to worry about the quake in her voice—tears pooled at the corners of her eyes as she struggled to contain her hyperventilation.

"You just tried to kill me," Liam scoffed. "And now you want me to let you go? Have you lost your mind?"

"I said *get off!*" Eve wiggled an arm free. She jabbed her elbow as hard as she could against his face.

A sickening crunch sounded, followed by a warm pool of blood dripping from his face and onto her dress. Liam cursed loudly and instinctively reached for the wound. The sharp scent of metal invaded her nose, but Eve scrambled out from under him and grabbed the dagger.

When she turned back, Liam was climbing to his feet. His nose was broken—a deep gush of crimson poured out over his hand and onto his clothes. She wasn't sure how they were going to explain that away with a fall over a balcony. Not that it mattered anymore. Her plan had gone as far south as it could possibly go.

Eve rose to her feet, the dagger clutched so tightly in her hands that the indents of the handle cut into her palms. She wasn't going to let it slip out of her grasp this time.

Liam glanced toward the doors—then made a run for it. Eve launched after him, tripping over her heels. She managed to grasp the back of his shirt, pulling him down with her.

They struggled, rolling back and forth across the balcony with each hit, kick, and jab. Liam punched Eve in the chest. She kneed him between the legs.

"You owe me a *life debt!*" Liam gasped out, his bloody hands clutching his crotch. Eve cringed at the sight of his broken nose but held down the bile in her throat.

"I didn't ask to be saved!" she shouted back, the feral rage built up inside of her flowing out like a broken dam.

Disbelief clouded his features. Liam spat, "I should have let the asrai have you."

"That was your first mistake," Eve hissed. Liam's gaze flickered to the dagger in her hand, his confidence staggering.

"You owe me," he said.

"I'll repay you by making it quick," she promised him. Liam threw his head back against the stone floor.

"What's worth *killing* me for? I can't be *that* bad."

"Do you want me to make a list?" Eve was stalling. Her hands shook; her mouth was dry. Each second that passed, her willingness to keep her deal with Sage wavered. She didn't want to kill him any more than he wanted to die.

Perhaps she had some humanity left in her after all.

Liam met her gaze. "What is it you desire? What will make you change your mind?"

"I want my name back—" she started, but Liam interrupted.

"I told you, I can't *give it back.* That's not how it works."

"I know." She pressed the dagger to the exposed flesh of his throat.

"But I can give you something else." Desperation edged into his voice. Liam swallowed hard, wincing as the blade scraped his Adam's apple. "Those men—there's still two more, right? I'll take care of them."

"You had your chance with them."

"Anything else, then. What do you want? Money? Clothes? You could use them, your skirts are hideous—"

Eve ignored the jab. "Why should I bother making another deal with you? You couldn't even keep your word on the last one."

"I think I can be persuaded," he said sourly.

"Not interested." The poison left a clear sheen against his neck. One flick of her wrist and it would all be over. Why couldn't she do it?

"I won't trick you this time. You have my word," he promised, but Eve's face showed how little it meant to her. "I swear on my mother's death. There has to be something else I can give you besides my life."

Eve paused. She couldn't kill him. She knew, deep in her soul, that it had been futile all along. He was not the man she wanted dead, and killing him would only make things harder.

But Liam didn't know his life had been spared. Eve might be breaking off her deal with Sage, but she would not be left entirely defenseless—not if she had anything to say about it.

"Your name," she demanded through heavy breaths. God, her chest ached. "I want your True Name."

Liam's eyebrows shot up, appalled by the suggestion. "Absolutely not."

"Then you're going to die." Eve shrugged. "A life for a life, remember?"

"Don't throw my own words back at me in such a condescending tone."

"Should I throw them back in a cheerier tone? A life for a life," Eve sang. Liam scowled.

"If I give it to you, I'll make you forget it," he said through gritted teeth. "Perhaps I'll make you forget how to hold your bladder while I'm at it."

"Do you want to try that? I'm the one with the knife." She tapped the tip against his skin for emphasis. Liam cleared his throat uncomfortably.

"Yes, I'm aware." Liam licked his lips. He tried to remain calm and aloof, but Eve could see his nerves betray him every time he glanced down at the blade. "Do you mind getting off me? I'm losing circulation in my arm."

"Not until you tell me your True Name."

"Oh, that." He rolled his eyes. "Are you sure there's nothing else you want? Something more interesting, perhaps?"

"No, but maybe I need to find a better way to persuade *you*." Eve moved the dagger down his neck to his chest, the point pressed taut against his skin. Liam flinched as it pressed against the spot over his heart. Eve grinned. "I thought so." She pursed her lips, considering. "Or I could cut out your tongue; you can't use my name if you don't have a tongue."

"You wouldn't do that," Liam said, but he didn't sound certain. "You're not cruel."

"You have no idea what I am." Her voice was cold, deadly. Eve pressed the tip of the blade against Liam's bottom lip. But he was right; she wouldn't do it. She couldn't.

She moved the blade back to his chest.

Liam started to lick his lips again but stopped, his eyes growing wide. "It's poisoned."

"I needed to make sure the job got done."

That rattled something in him, more than her confession to killing Nick. This was proof of her lethality, her ruthlessness. She was going to hell, and she was going to do it efficiently.

"Liam Thistle Fogtree." He ground the words out as if it physically pained him, keeping his voice barely above a whisper. Even Eve struggled to hear what he had to say.

"Your name is Liam *Thistle Fogtree?*" Eve stared at him, incredulous. It was the stupidest name she'd ever heard of.

Liam pulled back, offended. "It's certainly better than whatever a *Carter* is."

"Okay, whatever, but Thistle Fogtree? Seriously?" The name reminded her of some fantastical storybook character she would have read as a child.

"We can't all be named after nonsense, Evie." Liam shifted, his brows pushed together in frustration. "My arm is *asleep.*"

With caution, Eve lifted herself off him. She almost expected Liam to dive at her—to steal the dagger and slice her throat instead—but he simply stood up and brushed the dust from his clothes. Eve sheathed the dagger in her pocket.

"*Evelyn Marie Carter.*" The words sent a jolt through her. Eve's body stilled, rigid. She inwardly cursed herself for not taking more precautions against whatever commands he had in mind. "You are not to kill or maim me for as long as you live. Don't think I'll take tonight's events lightly; consider this a mercy. If I were to bring you forward to the higher courts, you would wish for death."

Her heart dropped. She hadn't considered Liam's status—he was never supposed to survive in the first place. What was Sage going to say? She was waiting below, still anticipating her brother's body to come crashing down. Would she be mad about how things turned out?

"What are you searching for?" Liam asked. Eve tore her gaze away from the balcony's ledge.

"Nothing," she lied. Liam's lips parted to issue another command, but Eve had a command of her own. "*Liam Thistle Fogtree,* you are not to kill or maim me for as long as I live. In fact, you are to protect me against any harm."

Liam guffawed. "I didn't add *that* to your duties."

"No, but I added it to yours. So do it." This night wasn't a total loss; if things got messy with her abusers, she could always call on Liam to come running to her aid. Having a magical bodyguard would have its benefits.

"Fine." Liam's jaw clenched, and he spoke in the way of command, "Then you're responsible for protecting me, too. Believe it or not, you're not the only enemy I have in these lands."

Eve made a face. She wasn't sure how useful she would be in protecting him against other fae creatures, but it was only fair.

"Fine." She paused. Liam moved to leave. "Wait."

Eve tried to speak but found herself hesitating. *I'm sorry,* she wanted to say. *It wasn't supposed to happen this way.* Eve hadn't realized what a frail companionship they'd built together until she stabbed him in the back. Now that she was staring at the ashes, she wondered if her deal with Sage had even been worth it.

"Are you going to stand there or say something?" Liam asked impatiently.

"What is your illness doing to you?" Eve asked instead and couldn't help running her own hand against the back of her neck. The sight of the hard stone embedded in his skin was burned into her brain.

Liam stared at her, his expression carefully controlled and blank. "Are you going to command me to tell you?"

"No."

Liam scoffed and reentered the party, disappearing between the lights and crowd. Eve didn't go after him; she walked back to the edge of the balcony and took a deep, shaky breath. She peered over the edge of the balcony and into the darkness below. She could barely make out the side lawn, its snowy fields engulfed in deep shadows.

"Sage?" she whispered. It only occurred to her now that, if Sage was indeed waiting down there, she would have heard everything. She would know Eve had failed in killing Liam, and she would know about the deal they'd made in exchange for his life.

There was no response other than the rustling of the last bit of dead leaves against the winter wind.

Thirty-Six

The party ended too late. Or maybe it was too early. Eve couldn't tell; everything was a blur in the mass of dancing goat-legged men and moss-haired women. Too soon, the birds chirped, and the sun lazily rose over the horizon, painting the snowy forest in glistening shades of pink and purple that felt unnatural.

She hadn't seen Sage for the rest of the night. Or Liam, for that matter. Eve had searched the ballroom high and low, but the faeries were nowhere to be found. When dawn approached, Evren kindly offered her one of the spare rooms, but Eve declined. She hadn't meant to be out this late—if she didn't get home soon, Nan would worry.

Eve barely remembered getting into the carriage home, weary and tired as she stumbled out of the white box and onto the familiar dirt path. She was still wearing the ball gown from her party, the white ends dirtied and smeared with mortal grime and mud and Liam's blood. It was close to a Cinderella ending—the spell broken, everything less glamorous and exciting now that she'd left the ball—except Eve was lucky enough to still have both of her shoes.

The carriage had barely left when a hand clamped over her mouth from behind, silencing her scream as she was dragged back into the forest's shadows.

Sage pressed her back against the bark of a snow-capped pine tree, her lips curled up into a snarl. She was taller than usual and—in Eve's panic—she realized Sage was floating. Her translucent wings flapped silently in the air as they held their owner up above. Sage's hand over Eve's mouth slipped to her throat, the unnatural length of her fingers curling around the soft flesh. Eve felt the sting of a cut, followed by the warm trickle of blood down her back.

In her tired mind, Eve understood why this was happening: Liam was alive. She'd failed. But she didn't realize it would incur this kind of wrath from her friend.

"Sage," Eve choked out the name. She reacted too slowly, her fingers prying uselessly at Sage's long fingers. It was easy to see the stark difference between them—the mortality that addled Eve, her instincts too slow and sluggish to fight against Sage's inhuman strength. "Sage—"

"He was supposed to be *dead*. That was our deal," Sage ground out through clenched teeth. Eve grew lightheaded. "What happened?"

Sage's grip loosened enough for Eve to respond. "I don't know."

"You don't *know?*"

"He had some kind of armor." Eve recalled the flash of stone, its imperviousness to the blade gripped in her hand. "My knife wouldn't go through."

"He knew?" Surprise flashed across Sage's face. She released her and Eve collapsed to her knees in a fit of coughs. Sage paid her no mind as she floated back and forth in thought. She hadn't changed out of her attire from the party either, Eve realized.

"He didn't know," Eve said while rubbing her throat. Blood smeared over her skin and dress, dousing the white fabric in crimson.

"How are you sure he didn't know?" Sage turned to Eve with a sharp glare. "Why else would he wear armor?"

Eve shrugged meekly. She wasn't sure why, but something inside of her didn't want Sage to know that it had been a part of his skin. Sage truly wanted him dead, and the less she knew of him, the better.

"Of course. I should have known better than to leave this to a human," Sage muttered. "I thought you wanted those men dead."

"I do," Eve said.

"Not badly enough." Sage's temper flared, her wings spreading out as if they would envelop Eve and suffocate her.

Eve cringed away, her nails digging into the bark behind her. Sage took a deep breath to calm herself.

"No matter," Sage said with the shake of her head. "We will simply need to go back to the drawing board. We can—"

Eve cleared her throat. "Liam and I can't kill or maim each other. That was the deal."

Sage pursed her lips, her lilac hair falling to the side as she cocked her head.

"And how did you get Liam to agree to such a dangerous bargain?" Sage spoke softly, sweetly, with the sort of undertone of magic Eve recognized in Liam's glamours. Another threat—Eve could tell her what happened, or Sage would pry it out from her. Eve doubted the experience would be pleasant.

"On the balcony, we exchanged it after... everything. I can't hurt him." Eve didn't trust Sage enough to tell her that she held Liam's True Name. Something about the way Sage stared at her left her uneasy, like she was nothing more than a tool used to carve up the future. Eve wished she'd never said anything at all.

"That changes things."

Eve bit her lip. "I'm sorry. I know—"

"Our deal is off," Sage decided with a flippant wave of her hand. "I'll handle Liam. If you want something done right, I suppose you need to do it yourself."

"You still want Liam dead?" Eve couldn't contain the shock in her voice.

"Of course. The tide always turns in the art of war, Evie." Eve cringed at Liam's nickname for her. It sounded sour and mocking coming from Sage's lips. The faerie reached forward, twining a short stray piece of Eve's blond hair around her long finger. "Liam took Hailey away from me, so I'll take everything from him."

Eve started. "You knew about—"

"His deal with her?" Sage interrupted. "Of course I did. Inheriting the court is one thing, but I can never forgive him for what he did to Hailey. Now there's the matter of you, however."

"What about me?" The dead-eyed stare Sage gave Eve sent a chill down her spine.

"You can run off to Liam and tell him about our deal," Sage said. "I doubt he trusts you now, but my brother isn't *entirely* idiotic, and it's more trouble to me than it's worth leaving you alive."

Eve backed up against the tree. "You're going to kill me? I thought we were friends."

"So did I, but friends don't back down on their promises." Sage eyed Eve, her lips curled into a sneer, and Eve could almost see every deadly plot running through her mind.

Panic struck Eve fast and hard. Even if she called on Liam for protection, he couldn't possibly arrive in time. She needed a distraction—a persuasion. She had to convince Sage to keep her alive.

"H-Hailey would be upset if I died," Eve said. "She would never forgive you if she found out."

Sage shrugged. "I can make it appear an accidental."

Damn it. Sage was hovering closer now, her eyes focused. Her decision was made.

"You could make me promise not to say anything," Eve offered desperately. "We could make a deal."

"You're not very good at keeping deals, Eve."

"I'd keep this one." She needed to. Her life depended on it. "I won't say a word. You—You could even use that glamour thing on me if you want."

Sage paused, and Eve could see the wheels turning in her head as she weighed her options.

"You're willing to be glamoured?" Sage cocked her head to the side, testing her.

"So that I don't say anything to him about our deal," Eve said. "In exchange, you don't kill me."

Sage stared at her for a long time, her eyes growing warm like honey as she considered Eve's proposal.

"I don't kill you right now," Sage amended. Eve shook her head.

"You don't kill me at all," Eve pushed. Sage's eyes narrowed.

"You're not in a good bargaining position, Eve."

"Hailey would still be upset," Eve pushed. "And Liam will know something happened to me. What's the point of me keeping quiet if you kill me in five minutes instead of right now?"

Sage's wings flapped in irritation. "I will not kill you for this at any time now or in the future. That will have to be enough. I cannot make promises for future acts of stupidity on your part."

It wasn't enough, but Eve had no more bargaining power to offer. She nodded slowly, accepting the terms.

"Good," Sage said, satisfied. "Remove your brooch." Eve did so. "And the dress."

"The—"

"The berries in there protect you from glamours," Sage said hotly. "Don't think you can trick me by wearing it."

"I didn't intend to." Eve's fingers shook as she unbuttoned her dress. It fell into a heap at her feet, a splotch of red on the fresh white snow. Eve shivered against the cold, clinging to the thin silk chemise she'd worn underneath.

"*Eve*," Sage's voice was honeyed and sweet, the same as it had been before Eve accompanied her to the meadow. Somewhere, in the back of Eve's mind, she realized that she had been glamoured—but that did not matter now. What mattered was Sage's order and how to best fulfill it. A warmth spread through her body, eager to please. "You will not breathe a word of our deal to another living soul. Should you try, words will fail you. Do you agree to these terms?"

"Yes," Eve breathed. White frost trailed from her lips, and it was only when Sage pulled away that the cold settled back in.

"I hope that leaving him alive was worth it" Sage said, her tone full of mockery. "He—"

A harsh rustling caught the girls' attention, silencing them. Sage wore her disguise in a blink—nothing more than a mortal once more. She stared out at the surrounding forest and Eve peered past her, unable to see whatever caught the faerie's attention.

A beat passed. Then another. Sage walked away from the forest's edge.

Sage spared Eve a warning glance before disappearing as if she was never there. It was only the slight glimpse of shimmering wings taking off that convinced her that Sage had gone.

Eve stared out into the forest for a long moment. Nothing came out, but she could swear she heard the faint croak of a frog.

Composing herself, Eve yanked her dress back on and stepped back onto the dirt road. Their chat took longer than she'd expected; the sun was steadily making its way past the trees, and Nan would be waking up at any moment.

Plucking some wisteria from the arch, Eve stepped through the threshold.

Her heel came down hard on the snow, right where the staircase should have been.

"No."

The word escaped from her lips in a sharp breath. Eve stared through the gaping arch at the trees on the other side. The trees that should have been hidden behind the tunneled staircase. The staircase that Eve had used several times now to travel between her realm and Faerie. The stairs that would take her home.

The stairs that were now missing.

Thirty-Seven

"Hailey, wake up."

Hailey groaned, tossing the thick velvet blanket over her head. Eve shook her friend's shoulder again.

"Hailey, you've got to get up," she whispered urgently. Eve was going to be sick. She couldn't be trapped here. She couldn't be.

The blankets shuffled and Hailey groaned, cocooning herself inside. "Five more minutes."

Eve ripped the blanket from Hailey's grasp, tossing the bulky fabric onto the floor. Hailey hissed as the cold air hit her, and she curled into herself like a pill bug. She scowled up at her intruder, blinking slowly through her disorientation before she realized *who* she was scowling at. "I thought you went home."

"I can't."

Eve explained what she had seen—rather, what she *hadn't* seen—in the forest. Hailey yanked on a jacket and shoes in the meantime, determined to see it for herself.

"You were probably dropped off at the wrong spot," Hailey said optimistically as they trudged down the snowy dirt path. Eve hoped she was right.

They each grabbed a small bundle of wisteria from the arch for good measure. The staircase did not appear.

"We need to talk to Sage," Hailey said, worry seeping into her voice. They grabbed more wisteria, just in case, but the arch remained the same.

I'd rather not, Eve thought, but what choice did they have? They needed to get home.

The estate was quiet upon their return. A few servants wandered through the halls, nodding absently to Eve and Hailey as they passed by. Everyone else had retired for the day, worn out from the party.

"I need to be back by noon," Hailey said as they ascended to the second floor. Eve had opted to leave her heels behind in the foyer, her feet too sore to carry on, and her dress dragged behind her in a heavy lump as she struggled up the stairs. "I have basketball practice, then I'm going out with my dad to get a Christmas tree. Then I'm—oh, crap, I need to take my ADHD meds, too."

The dull pulse in Eve's head that had formed over the course of their walk grew into a full-blown headache as Hailey rattled off her plans for the day. She rubbed her temples in a poor attempt to fight it off.

"I need to check on Nan," Eve murmured, more to herself than to Hailey. She wasn't supposed to be gone this long. She *definitely* wasn't supposed to leave Nan home alone, period. What if something happened? There was no way her parents were going to let her finish out the year if they found out.

"Oh God, that's right—your grandma." Hailey's face paled. "Maybe I can call Michael to check on her." Hailey pulled her phone out of her jacket pocket, but Eve could see over her shoulder that she had no service. Eve checked her own device: nothing.

A door behind them creaked open. Liam glared out into the hallway wearing no more than a thin silk robe, his body slouched from exhaustion—and perhaps a hangover—as he leaned onto the door frame for support.

"Hailey, I swear, if you wake me up one more time with your incessant chattering—" Liam's rant cut off when he spotted Eve. "What are you still doing here?"

Eve crossed her arms. "That's what I want to know."

"Excellent, you're still awake." Evren appeared at the top of the stairs with a brilliant smile, his fungi suit exchanged for a silky pair of pajamas and strange, ribbed robe. He appeared refreshed, but something told Eve that he hadn't slept either. "Come, we've prepared a morning snack."

Hailey perked up. "Actually, Evren, we have a problem—"

"Yes, yes." Evren waved her off with his slender hand, already disappearing down the stairs. "We will discuss it all over food. Liam, do get your siblings, will you?"

Liam grumbled something under his breath but padded out into the hallway to do as he was told. Eve didn't miss the look he gave her and Hailey as he passed, but she couldn't tell what it meant.

Evren's idea of a morning snack was an understatement; a wide assortment of cheeses, meats, berries, jams, and creams awaited the girls on the dining room table as they arrived. Evren was already seated at the head of the table, sipping a glass of peach-colored wine as Eve and Hailey took their seats.

Liam and Sage arrived shortly after, sitting opposite of Eve and Hailey. They were uncomfortable beside each other, their posture tired and stiff as they pulled their chairs further apart.

"What's this about?" Sage asked through a yawn. She plucked one of the cubes of cheese and popped it into her mouth before gesturing for Hailey and Eve to do the same. At least the food was safe to eat. Eve nibbled on a piece of bread and some jam, her appetite lacking.

Evren ignored her, his gaze cast patiently on the empty seat on the other end. After a few minutes, Eve heard a soft *ribbet* from her side. Evren sighed.

"Preece, you know I hate it when you get mucus on the chairs."

Eve peered down at the chair to her right. A small green frog sat on the plush cushion. It hopped up onto the tabletop, its long pink tongue stretching out to grab a cube of cheese half its size. It swallowed the cheese whole.

Preece. The name struck her at once: Liam and Sage's older brother... was a frog. Eve stared at the small creature, too baffled to turn away. It had to be the same frog that gave her ginger during her period, right? And the same one that she'd seen with Liam a few times now? It was too much of a coincidence not to be.

Evren gave the frog a flat look. Clearing his throat, he said, "It's come to my attention that there has been some concern regarding favoritism among my children."

Sage and Liam eyed each other, then the frog at the end of the table.

"While that is true," Evren continued, "I've decided to rectify that. As you all know, in the past, the Bone Court has always been handed down to a chosen heir."

Evren gauged each of his children for a reaction. Liam slapped some jam on a piece of bread and chewed, uninterested in the conversation. Sage's breath caught.

"Have you decided on one?" she asked casually, but Eve could see the tension in her shoulders. Sage didn't touch any of the food on the table, her attention clinging to Evren's every word.

"No." Sage's shoulders sagged in disappointment. "I think the tradition is terribly dull. In the spirit of fun, I thought we would turn this into a game."

This earned a few cautionary glances around the table. Even the frog looked suspicious, its tiny sticky toes tapping impatiently against the table as it watched Evren with slitted eyes.

"A game?" Sage repeated slowly, as if she'd misheard.

"Isn't it brilliant?" Evren beamed with pride. "I've given each of you an outside companion to assist you"—he gestured toward Eve and Hailey—"although yours will need replacing, Preece. I'm afraid the lad couldn't handle some rough-housing last night." Evren chuckled to himself. "Regardless, come the dawn after Yule, whoever proves themselves to be worthy of the position before nightfall on Ostara will inherit the Bone Court."

Silence filled the room. Eve shifted uncomfortably in her seat, exchanging a cautionary glance with Hailey.

"What is Ostara?" Hailey half-whispered.

"The spring equinox," Sage explained absently. Her brows were pinned together in deep concentration as she stared at the wall opposite of her.

"How do you expect us to prove ourselves to you exactly?" Liam scoffed.

Evren shrugged with an impish grin. "That is entirely up to you. I want you to use the tools you have at your disposal." Again, his eyes landed on his mortal guests. Eve pressed her fists onto her lap under the table. "I'm sure you'll figure something out."

"I don't get what this has to do with me," Eve said. Evren turned to her with surprise, as if he hadn't expected her to object. "Hailey and I have responsibilities at home. We have stuff to do, people to take care of. We can't stay here."

Evren cocked his head to the side. "My dear, that is *exactly* what you're supposed to do. Didn't you tell me last night how you wished you wouldn't have to go back?" Eve bit down on her lip. "Think of this as a gift, for both of you—and an opportunity. The fair folk are known to reward young acolytes who go beyond their measure for us."

"And what happens if we succeed? Can Hailey and I go home?" Eve pushed. It was obvious Sage and Hailey would be paired together, so it only made sense she would have to work alongside Liam. She regretted her betrayal even more now.

"The heir's companion will be rewarded accordingly," Evren promised. "For those who fail, I think it's only fitting that the heir chooses what happens to them—and to their companions. That is, of course, if everyone survives to Ostara." Evren chuckled again, but Eve got the sense that this wasn't a joke. "Any more questions? No? Then I'll be taking my leave."

The tall faerie rose from his chair, his robe billowing behind him as he strode out of the hallway. No one spoke for a long time. Hailey trembled at Eve's side, her long hair only partially disguising the silent tears that rolled down her cheeks. Eve couldn't bring herself to cry. She couldn't bring herself to do much of anything. The shock of the past twenty-four hours numbed her inside and out, and Eve was more akin to a hollowed-out husk than a person.

She was in danger. Nan was in danger. If either of her parents found out she'd disappeared out of the blue, they would hunt her down and kill her themselves.

Sage stood up so quickly her chair almost tipped over. She held out her hand across the table. "Come with me."

Hailey shakily took it, and Sage wasted no time ushering her out of the room, already set on a plan.

Eve reluctantly met Liam's gaze. An understanding passed between them, a hesitant truce to their feud. Eve already knew what Sage would do to Liam if she won—maybe even before. Would Eve receive the same treatment? She didn't want to find out.

Liam understood the sentiment. He picked up one of the glasses of wine and clinked it lightly with her empty one. "To not coming in last."

"To staying alive," she said. She'd come too far to let Evren's task unnerve her. She had other priorities, other men to worry about, and she wasn't going to apologize for putting her problems first this time.

Eve had asked for enough forgiveness in her life.

It was their turn to beg for hers.

Epilogue

The forest was a labyrinth. It was as if the wood was a living thing itself, twisting the trees and trails around and around, leading the men in circles both new and unfamiliar.

Time did not exist in the forest—or if it did, it played by its own rules. Sometimes light would peek through the snow-frosted trees, shining the sun's rays down onto the world with just enough warmth to keep the chill away for a few minutes at a time. More often, night would stretch on for hours—maybe even days—in endless darkness. The harsh bite of winter nipped at their ankles and fingertips, but there were worse things in the forest than frostbite.

So many teeth. So many wings.

So. Much. Blood.

They might have given up on escaping a long time ago if not for their missing companion. Nick was always hotheaded, and as time stretched on, their faith in his survival waned. It was already shocking enough that the two of them had lived, but to see Nick in the flesh would be a miracle.

They trudged through another cycle. Another sunset. Another night.

Logan hated the forest. Colton embraced it.

The forest was wild and unpredictable, with inhabitants that were stranger than what his nightmares could come up with. Women with hair made of leaves and teeth sharper than knives. Men with the legs of goats and the horns to match. Children with eyes black as the ocean's depths and voices that only spoke in a harp's notes.

He recognized some of them as memories—dreams, he thought, from not long ago, with midnight-tasting alcohol on his lips and some winged-girl's tongue down his throat. He'd almost forgotten about them, but the forest brought them back, like missing pieces to a puzzle.

So, he knew which ones were easy to fight. Which ones to skin for fur to keep warm, which to take to his makeshift cot at night when his belly was full.

Those years of Boy Scouts weren't for nothing—if it came to survival, Colton could manage. Logan was a leech, sucking off his friend's success, but he was a pleasant one. He made for good company, and Colton loved to be entertained.

There was nothing more entertaining than hunting down the creatures that held him hostage.

Liam. That little faerie shit. It had been jarring enough to be kicked out of his party all those years ago, left with nothing but the knowledge that Colton and his friends had grown too predictable for Liam's tastes. But for Liam to come back out of the blue? To compel him to return to the festivities for one more night, only to stab him in the back?

He supposed it was inevitable that Liam would betray him, but it still came as a shock. Colton thought they were friends once.

How horribly mistaken he was.

"Colt," Logan whispered, grabbing his friend by the dark sleeve of his cloak. They hadn't changed since their escape from the party. Logan was dying to tear the degrading fabric off and replace it with something more valuable, but the robes reminded Colton of his time at the seminary. He was sure the others wondered where he was by now.

He didn't miss it as much as he thought he would.

"What is it?"

Logan said nothing, his face pale under the stark moonlight. The forest had changed again—he could hear the soft splash of water nearby, accompanied by the midnight croaks of a family of frogs. Colton edged forward through the trees.

A large lake stretched out before them, the water untouched by the shade of tree branches or ice. The water should have frozen over by now, and yet it rippled and waved, as free as a summer's breeze. Rocks lay scattered around the edges, and if not for the glimpse of a fin or shining eyes beneath the water, the men wouldn't have given the lake a second glance.

"Do you think we're close?" Colton could hear the desperation in his friend's voice. It took everything in him not to slap Logan. Why would they want to go home to such a boring, structured reality when this world promised so much more excitement? Colton had a purpose here. His time in ministry taught him of the demons in this world, the vices and sins of man and animal alike.

He planned to purge them all.

"Perhaps," Colton mused for the sake of his friend's appeasement. Logan's eyes lit up, but Colton paid him no further mind as he walked toward the edge of the lake. It appeared peaceful and undisturbed until he got closer—fresh marks dug into the ground, mixing the mud with snow and blood. Whatever lived in these waters wanted their prey alive when they pulled them under.

Colton picked up one of the stones and skipped it across the lake. Water rippled as the creatures within moved out of the way. He got a glimpse of yellow eyes glaring in his direction before they disappeared into the inky depths once more.

He found his entertainment for the night.

Colton picked up another stone. Then another. They skipped over the water, and the creatures within had to dash and dive out of the way before the rock came down on their heads. They didn't come to collect their prey, though—either he was too far away, or he hadn't pissed them off enough yet.

"Colt, can we go now?" Logan eyed the lake uncomfortably—he, too, had seen the creatures and was not eager to find out what they would do to them.

"Relax. Just one more," Colton promised. Logan bit back an argument. Colton was his key to surviving, after all; they both knew who had the upper hand.

This time, he did not reach for a small stone—Colton grabbed a rock, hefty and large enough to cause a real headache among the beings. It appeared this was not the rock's first time being used. Its large gray base was covered in dried blood.

The blood was old, browning with age, but the splatters told the story; there was a fight here, and Colton had missed it. He wouldn't have given it another thought if he hadn't seen the clothes stashed underneath, sunken into the ground for the earth to claim: a wife beater and jeans.

Nick hadn't made it, after all.

Colton gestured for Logan to look. His friend blanched.

"Can we *please* get out of here?" Logan pushed. He was getting antsy. But there was nothing he could do on his own.

"In a minute. Don't you think we should bury these?" Colton was never a huge fan of Nick—they were friends, sure, but the man was stubborn and irritable. He never knew when to leave well enough alone. But Colton was also a Catholic man—a priest in training—and he wanted a proper burial for his friend. What was left of him, anyway.

"Sure, whatever, fine. Just hurry up."

Logan paced at his side—keeping a wide berth from the lake—as Colton dug a small hole in the ground. It was not enough for a body, but the clothes would fit. He picked up the bundle. Something small slipped out.

Colton bent over to examine it.

A cross necklace. It was simple and plain, except for the initials carved into the back of the metal. Colton recognized it at once.

Nick didn't own this, but he knew who did.

Now, *this* was interesting.

Colton finished burying the clothes and stuffed the necklace into his pocket. He gave a quick prayer. Perhaps in the afterlife, Nick wouldn't be such a jackass.

"Are you done?" Logan asked impatiently. So much for being a Catholic—Logan hadn't even stopped to mourn his friend. It rubbed Colton the wrong way, but this was something they had plenty of time to discuss. The forest wasn't quite ready to let them go yet, and Colton wasn't ready to leave either.

"I'm done," Colton promised, and launched the rock into the pond.

Acknowledgements

Acknowledgements, to me, are like a speech at the Oscars. Tearful, full of love, and absolute terror for missing someone in an endless list of thank-you's. I have never been great at expressing my own feelings, but I hope I can convey the gratitude I feel towards everyone that encouraged, supported, and shared in my passion for this book.

To my Grandma Linda, Grandma Carol, and my late Great Grandma Hogan, thank you for giving me the words to write and the freedom to imagine life outside of the lines. Your ability to listen to a three-year-old's endless tales of make believe is what instilled in me the love of storytelling I have today. I love you dearly, and you are always in my thoughts.

Thank you to my mother, Michelle, who has always read my work and encouraged my writing, even if it was terrible (and, quite often, it was). Your love is always felt, and I look forward to introducing you to each new story I create. Also, thank you for raising me on a healthy diet of weird, gothic, and horror stories. I may never get the chance to live out my gothic heroine dreams, but at least my characters can!

To my father, thank you for introducing the concept of writing as a career to me at the tender age of 10. I've latched on and never looked back.

To my in-laws and my family, Sandy, Gary, E, Duncan, Aunt Ber, and Grandma Carol: First, thank you, Sandy and Gary, for letting me live in your home while I wrote this during COVID. Pandemics suck, but being able to tough it out with you guys definitely made it a little better. Thank you all for showing so much interest and love and support towards me and my writing. I know a lot of my writing can get pretty dark, but I promise I'm (kind of) normal! Anyway, thanks for accepting me and my weirdness! Love you guys!

Emmy. My writing mentor and, more importantly, one of my best friends for over ten years. I told you when we met that I wanted to be a writer, and I kept my promise. Thank you for the constant writing practices together, the round robins and critiques for each other's work, the inspiration for new stories and building upon old, and for every moment of friendship in between. Here's to the first of many stories to come, and I'm rooting for your work to hit the shelves next!

Abbey, Micah, JC, and Elliot: my friends, my family. We've been together through thick and thin, and when I think of found family tropes, you are the first to come to mind. You have supported my dreams and encouraged me to keep going, even when I want to throw my writing out the window. Thank you for showing interest in my stories, and thank you even more for promising to read them. It's okay if you don't, but the love is always there.

Maddi Leatherman, my editor extraordinaire. This story wouldn't hold a prayer up to the version it is now without your help. Thank you for putting up with all of my misplaced commas, plot holes, and messy scenes. I promise to do better in the next book (hopefully)!

Jessica Sherburn, the book cover illustrator that brought my mental images to life. The cover you made is stunning, and I couldn't have asked for a better artist nor kinder person to work with. I'm deeply appreciative of all the little details and thought you put into this, and I can't wait to see what you create for book 2!

To the incredibly talented writers, designers, and social media gurus of the Eclectic Pages group—Sam, Jorjor, Isa, Ruthie, C. J., Elena, Mimi, Courtney, Ciarra, Em, Miranda, Laura, and the others who helped me learn how to manage an author brand, promote my book, gave me advice, and all the other terrifying marketing stuff that I'm still figuring out—THANK YOU! This group has been so supportive and I am wishing you all massive success in every endeavor!

To my college professors, Steve and Rick, thank you for all of the lessons, critique, and lectures that have stuck with me beyond graduation. All of those hours crafting and revising scripts gave me the patience, organization, and skills I needed to complete this book (and many other pieces of writing!). Thank you, from the bottom of my heart.

Vanilla, who got me through the first draft of this book, and to Maple and Caramel, my dearest kitty children, who got me through the rest (and participated several times by walking on my keyboard). Since you cannot read this, I will ask your father to translate this for you: meow meow meow meow meow meow meow, meow meow meow meow meow meow meow meow. Meow meow, meow meow. Meow. Good luck, Connor.

Finally, the most important of this journey: my husband and my beloved, Connor, I cannot begin to express how grateful I am for your endless love and support for my writing. You've repeatedly given me the push to keep going when I was ready to give up. Thank you for the constant rereads, the brainstorms, the critique, and every moment in between. This book wouldn't be where it is without you, and I would certainly be way more of an anxious mess than I am usually. Thank you, my love.

And to you, my readers, my weirdlings, my supporters through it all. THANK YOU! There is no book, no writing, without someone to read it. I hope that you enjoyed this story and look forward to the next, but even if you didn't, thank you for taking a chance to read it anyway.

I think somewhere in the middle of all of this, the Oscar music started to play, and it's time for me to step off the stage.

About the Author

Paige N. Regan is a Pittsburgh-born author with a penchant for laughter amongst the macabre. In her free time, she can be found spoiling her feline children, Maple and Caramel, and streaming anime with her husband. You can follow more of her writing journey on Instagram and TikTok @pnrwrites, or find more of her work at pnregan.com.

Milton Keynes UK
Ingram Content Group UK Ltd.
UKHW032329221024
449917UK00004B/282